Operation Make Naomi a Boss

MEGAN REINKING

Dedication

This one's for the people-pleasers. The ones who have a hard time saying no. I hope you're able to put aside the endless pressures and guilt trips of life to get lost in Naomi and Robbie's story- and I hope you enjoy every last second of it!

CHAPTER ONE

Naomi

My father often berated me as a child for having my head up in the clouds. It was a well-known fact that my whimsical musings were much too immature for his high-achieving, status-driven life.

I knew this because he was never afraid to say it to my face.

But see, I never saw fault in it. To me, I wasn't just daydreaming. I was allowing myself a safe space to let my imagination run free. It was the only way I was able to experience a life filled with wild possibilities and grandiose adventures, one I've always yearned for more than anything. A life that was liberating and exhilarating all at once. One that I savored—even if I was only ever allowed to experience it in my head.

"Ma'am?" A soft, yet urgent male voice breaks me out of my thoughts.

I blink at the handsome stranger in front of me, suddenly remembering his presence.

That's right. Clear your head, Naomi. This could be it.

Your meet-cute.

Granted, I didn't anticipate I'd meet the love of my life in the middle of the murky car ramp at the Minneapolis-St. Paul Airport, but hey, I've imagined more bizarre things.

The mystery gentleman in front of me has a strong jawline, probing espresso-colored eyes, and a mischievous dare to his smile that only tilts up partway. Not to mention, he's dashingly handsome. The kind of good looks that inherently guarantees he's had a lifetime of women falling at his feet.

And he's here to sweep me off my feet.

That tracks, anyway, with the life I've just created for us in my head.

I'm envisioning us with a lovely two-story colonial along the bank of the Mississippi River, where we spend our weekends chasing after our twin four-year-old girls. Each night, his art supplies can be found strewn about several rooms throughout the house. Toys clutter the floor, and baking flour coats every inch of the kitchen from my thriving at-home bakery business. Most nights, the mess sits abandoned, left to be dealt with after our sunset pontoon ride up the river to the ice cream shop.

Or life option number two has him sweeping me off my feet right here and now, with nothing more than a proposition and a plane ticket. In a fit of spontaneity, we book the next flight out of this airport without a clue where it's taking us.

Maybe we'll end up in Paris, sitting streetside at a little cafe, sipping espressos between bites of the most mouthwatering chocolate soufflés either of us has ever had. All the while, we fall deeply in love on a three-month love affair that we'll tell our children about someday. Or maybe—and this one's my favorite—we end up in Cabo, where we spend four sizzling days on the beach, covered head to toe in sand, sunscreen, and sticky drops of melting piña coladas.

"Do you have change for a twenty?" he repeats firmly. The hint of impatience that comes through in his tone has me sobering up again, clearing my thoughts.

"Oh, um...yes." I start rummaging through my crossbody purse for my wallet, trying to calm the slight tremor of my fingers. For the life of me, I can't seem to taper the nerves—falling in love can be so exciting.

"Just one second..." I'm honestly not sure if I do have cash, but I suppose I owe it to the potential love of my life to at least check, right?

While I rummage, I wonder what his initial pickup line will be, whether he has the fashion sense to compliment me on my comfortable-yet-chic travel outfit or not, or if he'll tease me about how much I overpacked for the two-day baking industry trade show I'm returning from in Cincinnati.

Heck, it's 2025. Maybe I should be the one to make the first move.

"Ah! I found it." I raise my wallet in victory, feeling pride amidst the excitement, oblivious and not at all prepared for the harsh interruption about to shatter my plans.

In a split second, before I can pull the wallet open to grab cash, he reaches out and snatches it directly out of my hand. I've barely had a second to process what's happening when he takes off, bolting in the opposite direction, leaving me frozen in place.

"Thanks!" he shouts wickedly over his shoulder, sprinting in between cars until he vanishes out of sight.

My mouth falls open in shock and a rush of fear snakes up my spine all at once. The reality of what just happened hits me all in full force, sending a heavy pit of dread to the bottom of my stomach. Any trace of merriment from my musings just moments earlier is gone in an instant.

Well, I can confidently say I will not be getting swept off my feet today.

"Are you okay, dear?" A woman approaches with concern from somewhere on my side.

"He just... That man stole my wallet," I stammer, still staring off in the direction of where he disappeared. Shame, embarrassment, and frustration flood my senses, washing over me in waves. I feel sick to my stomach—and incredibly stupid. Here I was, just trying to be nice to a stranger in need and potentially meet the man of my dreams. Instead, I've lost two credit cards, my ID, and an ATM card—not to mention my judge of character.

At least I still have my car keys.

"Let's head inside and talk to security, okay? It's going to be alright. What's your name, sweetie?" the woman croons, running a comforting hand down my arm.

"Naomi Tillman," I murmur grumpily. She gently wraps her arm around my torso, guiding my still-shocked body back toward the airport entrance.

One hour, one police report, and one whopping parking fee later, I'm officially on the road back home. The low hum of my tires against the freeway serves as a futile distraction from the lingering humiliation that simmers just under my skin. I don't even have the desire to turn on my pop dance playlist that I belted out on the drive down to the airport a few days ago.

Instead, I replay the interaction repeatedly, convincing myself it was my fault for being too trusting of a stranger, too willing to help, foolishly jumping at the smallest request, all the while naively believing some grand gesture would alter the course of my life.

With nothing else to distract me, I've soon spiraled into obsessing over all my other shortcomings as well, wallowing in self-pity. Who was I kidding even coming on this conference trip in the first place? It's not like I'm realistically ever going to open my own bakery anyway. That dream seems even further out of reach now than it did this morning. If I learned anything at the conference, it was that business owners require a certain level of grit and tenacity that I'm self-aware enough to know I definitely don't have.

After about thirty minutes into my three-hour drive, my friend Gabby's name flashes on the display screen as an incoming call. I know that talking to her won't be able to pull me out of this self-loathing funk—in fact, it might make it worse—but I answer anyway. I don't have it in me to ignore her.

"Hey, Gabs," I say wearily. "You'll never believe what just happened to me."

"What happened? A flat tire?"

"I was robbed." Saying the words out loud brings a sour taste to my mouth, and I brace myself for what her response will be. She's not exactly my most compassionate friend, so the conversation really could go several different ways.

"Where are you now? Are you okay?" she has the decency to ask, although her tone is slightly bored and uninterested.

"Driving home. He stole my wallet. It happened in the car ramp at the airport, of all places."

"See, that's why I don't like heavily populated areas," she says pointedly, as if I have any control over where the airport is. "But yikes. That must have been scary."

I can hear her rummaging for something in the background, clearly distracted, but to her credit, she does have genuine concern etched in her voice.

"It was," I admit quietly.

"Well, at least you're okay."

I'm not exactly okay, but instead of correcting her, I inhale a calming deep breath and continue to wallow silently.

"Hey, would you be able to do me a huge favor?" Her upbeat question suggests she's already moved on from my situation. "I'm here at your house, doing laundry—thanks, by the way—and seeing your running shoes reminded me to get some for myself. I knew you would be driving through St. Cloud on your way home, so I called in an order at Scheels. Do you think you could swing by and grab them for me on your way home, please?"

"Uh, yeah...sure. No problem." To be honest, making a pit stop is the last thing I want to do right now. I want nothing more than to make it home and disappear under the weight of my comforter as soon as possible. But...I suppose it *is* on my way home. And it's not like we travel this far south that often.

I can do this favor for her.

"Ugh, you're the best. They should be right at the front desk. I already put your name on them. Listen, I've gotta run. Call me when you get home. Love you, bye!" She hangs up before I can get a word in.

With a defeated eye roll, I refocus all my attention on the road and on any damage control from the robbery that I can do hands-free while I drive.

The rest of the drive home to central Minnesota—minus stopping at Scheels to pick up shoes, that is—has me on speaker phone with my bank, canceling cards, and generally wallowing in my misfortunes. Not to mention dreading the condescending lecture that will surely be coming my way when my dad finds out what happened.

It's not until I see the *Welcome to Pine Falls* sign that I'm able to feel my shoulders release a small amount of tension. The stress from driving in the city—let alone navigating the airport and the wallet incident—slowly dissipates with every mile into my quiet, small town. No matter where I go, even with my vast love of adventure, I'm always reminded why I belong here when I come home.

The high-rise buildings that were next to the airport have been gradually replaced with patches of towering oak trees and modest homes that are amply spaced apart underneath them. What used to be highway markers and billboards in the city are now *watch out for wildlife* markers and mayor candidate signs along the side of the road. Dirt driveways with old dilapidated mailboxes are scattered by the road, and I pass a hand-drawn sign advertising the farmers market that runs on the east side of town all summer.

There's a quiet, soothing effect that seems to happen every time I pass through the streets of Pine Falls. I grew up driving on these same roads and know them so intimately that somehow every inch of tar feels like a part of the very fabric of what makes me—me.

When I finally pull onto Pebble Street and then the gravel driveway of my quaint single-story rambler, my eyes inadvertently well with tears. The sight of my cozy front porch and the glistening lake out back serves as the final source of comfort for me, a balm to my soul, allowing it the safe place to finally process everything that happened today.

Chapter Two

Naomi

I barely make it all the way inside to my couch before collapsing onto it in a heaping pile of misery, self-loathing, and pity. So much for returning from the trade show on a high, like I'd hoped I would, enthusiastically ready to move forward with starting my own baking business. I don't see that happening anymore—at least not anytime soon.

My purse that I dropped next to the couch starts ringing with an incoming text message notification. I fish it out and see a message from Robbie, my longtime friend from high school. A message from him can only mean one thing—he must be back in town. That's the only time he ever reaches out, and I already know what it's going to say before I even read it.

Robbie: Swinging through town for a couple days. You up? Can I crash on your couch?

I glance at my watch and shake my head with an amused huff.

Ten o'clock at night.

Like clockwork, he never fails. Every single time he rolls back through town, I always get a last-minute, late-hour message looking for a place to stay.

He's far too nonchalant to ever seem concerned with the fact that I might be busy or could even have company. He's lucky I have a soft spot for him. Although we only talk sporadically these days, our bond from high school—that was strengthened through late-night cliff diving, secret sharing over campfires, and being a source of comfort to each other during breakups—has remained strong. It's not even a question I need to consider—the answer is always yes for him.

Naomi: Door's unlocked.

I toss my phone on the floor and bury my eyes in the crook of my elbow, not bothering to get up to watch for him. The creak of the front door opening less than five minutes later brings the faintest of amused smiles to my lips.

He must have been close by.

I shift up to sit as he comes barreling through the door, his backpack falling loosely off his shoulder as he comes to a stop. As always, he's a disheveled mess with an aura of chaos and whim whirling around him. He comes in as chaotically and as swiftly as I know he'll eventually leave. Robbie has a habit of coming and going with the wind, never staying long enough to do much more than whatever simple task brought him here and to occupy my couch for a night or two.

"Whoa, what's wrong?" He immediately stops in his tracks, zeroing in on what I'm sure is my mess of a face. My brows feel like they may be permanently stuck in a frown from here on out, and my mascara feels sticky at the corners of my eyes. His forehead tightens with concern, the faint line between his green eyes growing deeper. He runs a hand through his thick, unruly brown locks, keeping his worried gaze intently on mine.

"Nothing." I dramatically wrap a knit blanket over my shoulders as he quickly comes to my side of the couch. "And everything. I'm giving myself one solid hour for a pity party. Want to join?"

"Always," he responds instantly. "Mind clueing me in as to why, though?"

He slides onto the couch and rests his fingertips against the outside of my arm, a level of comfort and familiarity settling between us. I'm instantly glad he came home tonight. Robbie is another layer of familiar comfort for me. I might not see—or hear—from him for months at a time between his gigs, but when he does come home, there's never any doubt that we'll fall right back into the easy friendship we've always had. I've always been able to count on that.

Am I a fool for letting him breeze in and out of my life, taking advantage of me and my couch, when he knows I'll rearrange my entire life and plans for him when he decides to drop in? Probably. But I'm loyal to a fault. Truthfully, he could ask for anything, and I'd give it to him. If I'm a fool, at least I'm a hospitable one.

"Are you ready for this story?" I clear my throat as he nods, then I fill him in on everything that happened at the airport.

"That son of a..." His eyes grow dark with rage, his body stiffening in a protective stance. "Did the police catch him? Are you okay?"

"Not that I know of. The officer said he'll call with any updates." I tuck a blonde curl behind my ear to clear it away from my face. "And yes, I'm fine. My spirit is a little bruised, but nothing a little tequila can't fix, right?" I give him a timid smirk.

"Well, that's a winning attitude." He huffs, though his concern lingers.

I push myself off the couch and cross the room to the kitchen. "Do you want a glass?"

"Sure. You got any of that fancy stuff left?"

"Yup." I pull out the bottle of expensive tequila I've been saving to finish with him.

"Sweet. Fill 'em up tall. You'll forget about that loser in no time—I can't believe that happened to you," he laments.

"Want to know what's even worse? Right before he took my wallet...I was hoping he was about to ask me out," I admit, dropping back onto the couch.

He thins his lips and pushes them together, a knowing look on his face. "Mm-hmm. Was he a slow-burn, friends-first kind of situation? Or was he hot and heavy from the get-go?"

I nudge his shoulder with a begrudged laugh. I'm used to his teasing when it comes to my daydreams. He's well aware of my tendencies, as I've processed my thoughts aloud to him many times over the years. In fact, one might say he enjoys feeding into them.

My laughter gradually fades, and his eyes soften while he waits patiently for me to answer.

"He was hot and heavy," I finally admit through a mumble.

"Figures," he says seriously. "I really am sorry. What a bummer of a day."

I shrug sadly. "What can you do? Anyway, enough about me and my pathetic life. Where'd you blow in from this time?"

He takes a sip, then dangles the cup from his hand resting on the back of the couch. "We just finished a gig in Fargo. We were in South Dakota before that for a four-day music festival."

Robbie's been traveling the country playing bass guitar with his band, Copper Snake, for the better part of two years now. He's one of only a few from our graduating high school class that actually left our small town and went on to live a life I only dream about. He's constantly off traipsing from one city to the next, one escapade after another.

"That sounds like fun." I take a sip from my own glass, letting it burn my throat on the way down to distract me from a twinge of jealousy.

"I'm telling you, you gotta come with me one of these times. You'd love it. Besides, nothing attracts the groupies more than having a pretty woman following me around." He wiggles his eyebrows. I laugh at his antics, but the culmination of today's events start to make me feel weary.

"Yeah, someday," I answer softly. My eyes start to feel heavy, from both exhaustion from the day and the warm buzz of tequila.

"Are you sure you're okay?" he asks, the crease deepening again.

"Yeah." I give him the most convincing smile I can muster before climbing off the couch to dispose of our glasses. "I am kind of tired, though. I think I'm going to call it a night."

"Alright." He yawns as if suddenly realizing his own exhaustion too. "I'll be out here if you need me."

"See you in the morning. Goodnight, Robbie," I tell him, grabbing the wool blanket from my basket in the corner of the room and tossing it to him as he stretches his legs out.

"Night, Naomi," he says sleepily, already half-asleep on my couch.

CHAPTER THREE

Naomi

A text message notification brings me slowly out of a deep sleep the next morning. With a groan, I hastily pull my comforter up over my face.

What time is it?

When another message irritatingly dings, I sigh, sneaking my arm out from under the covers to blindly feel around my nightstand. Pulling my phone back into the darkness with me, I reluctantly push one eye open, just enough to see who it's from.

Dad: Accounting department says there was an issue with their printers yesterday.

Dad: I need you in the office in forty minutes.

My stomach sinks. Even his text messages have a way of making me feel about as small as a popcorn kernel. It's not lost on me that there are no '*Hey, how was your trip?*' or '*What time are you coming in today?*' messages coming through from him.

Nope.

All I get is a curt message demanding I come in early. Not that I expected anything different, though. I've spent my entire life trying to live up to my father's high-achieving expectations—most of the time being painfully aware that I'm falling miserably short. My one redeeming quality in his eyes is the IT work I do for his large car dealership—never mind the fact that I have no passion whatsoever for the inner workings of computer systems.

I'm aware of the way he takes advantage of me. And yet, he's always been the hardest to say no to. I've done every single thing he's ever asked—or let's be honest, demanded—of me, which is absolutely and irrefutably pathetic of me...but that doesn't mean I won't give in like I always do—even if it is five-thirty in the morning.

I often dream of a time in my life when I might get the courage to pull the trigger on starting my own baking business, getting out from under his thumb once and for all. I imagine busy days in my kitchen stuffing piping bags with icing, rolling fondant, and decorating commissioned cakes...waiting for dough to rise in a bowl on the counter while my stand mixer hardly ever gets a break...my phone constantly ringing with new orders coming in...the smell of sugar, flour, and dough filling every corner of my house.

I yearn for that life so much I can practically taste the sweetness on my tongue.

Why can't I have that?

His message leaves a bad taste in my mouth, and it mixes with just enough of the lingering shame from yesterday's robbery that it gives me a surge of something unfamiliar—assertion, maybe? A desire for some semblance of control?

I toss the phone on my mattress, letting this new feeling marinate until, finally, I hurl myself out of bed with a newfound and unfamiliar surge of determination.

As I pull a sweatshirt over my head, I head directly to the living room. I step over Robbie's discarded shirt and socks that are laying in the middle of the floor to where he's snoring softly on the couch. There's a pillow over his face to block out the aggressive morning sunlight from my floor-to-ceiling windows the couch is positioned under, and one of his arms hangs off the edge. I gently lower myself to sit on top of his feet at the far end of the couch, perching there like a bird watching its prey.

"Hey," I whisper, pinching his calf with a gentle squeeze that's firm enough to rouse him. I should probably feel bad about waking him up, but I'm too focused on keeping this newfound ambition rolling to be sympathetic right now. He can go back to sleep later.

"Robbie." I pinch him again, this time squeezing harder.

"Argh," he grumbles from under the pillow, starting to stir.

"Are you awake?"

He lifts one corner, revealing his sleep-muddled face. "Are you insane?"

"That's debatable, actually, but I need your help with something."

He drops the pillow back onto his face and tries to shift his body—with no success, obviously, since I'm firmly cementing his feet in place.

"Do you think I let people walk all over me?" I ask.

"What?" his muffled voice says from under the pillow.

"I think being a pushover is starting to affect my happiness," I muse.

"Oh, for Pete's sake." He heaves a large sigh and lets out a grunt as he sits up to face me.

"Come again?" His mouth tilts up in confusion.

I roll my lips to keep from making a teasing remark about his impressively disheveled hair—I'm well aware that now is not the time.

"Do you think I let people walk all over me?" I ask again.

"Um..." He gets lost in thought as he considers my question.

"Here's the thing," I jump in before he can answer. "I'm not good at saying no. I'm terrible at it, actually. With my dad mostly—you know how he is. But also, just in general. In my day-to-day life with my friends, coworkers, and acquaintances. People constantly ask of me, and I say yes, regardless of what it is. It's a big problem I have. Saying no. And I'm officially sick of it."

He blinks at me.

"Being at that conference sparked something in me—an even stronger desire to start my own baking business. I want it so badly, Robbie." My voice comes out desperate before going soft again. "But I don't know if I can do it. How am I supposed to be a respected self-employed business owner if I'm nothing but a giant pushover?"

"Okay." He nods slowly, his brows knitting together. Clearly, his still-sleepy brain is slowing down his processing time.

"I need help getting comfortable setting boundaries," I continue, feeling the determination brewing stronger within me. "Enough is enough, you know?"

He runs a hand through his messy brown hair, bringing it down to scratch the back of his neck. "And how exactly am I supposed to help?"

"You're going to help me practice," I say decisively, feeling confident about what I'm asking of him.

"I am?" He tilts an eyebrow.

"Yes. Starting right now." I clear my throat. "Please ask me if you can sleep on my couch."

He stares at me blankly.

"Just do it," I urge.

"Can I...crash on your couch?" he asks, oblivious as to why he's asking.

"No. Get out," I say as firmly as I can.

Again with a blank stare. To his credit, though, he actually moves half a muscle to get up.

"Stay where you are." I assure him with a wave. "I'm just practicing. Ask again."

"Uh...do you have room on your couch?"

"Nope. I'm busy. Find somewhere else to stay. Okay, this feels really good."

"Glad I can help." he says with a hesitant smirk. "Again?"

I nod eagerly.

"Mind if I stay on your couch?"

"I do mind. Door is locked."

"Not bad." He nods, fully aware and invested now in the purpose of this exercise. "Can I crash with you tonight?"

"Absolutely not."

"Nice," he states his approval. "Why do you let him walk all over you, anyway?"

"That's a loaded question." I huff, looking down at my hands. "He's my dad...and it's complicated."

"So just tell him off. Tell him how you feel." He lifts a shoulder in an encouraging shrug, as if it would be no big deal at all.

"It's easier said than done, Robbie. You know...hence the practicing we're doing."

"Fair enough. Hey, will you make me a bagel?"

"Yeah, are you hungry? I think I have some—"

"Don't you dare get up. That was a test—which you failed miserably. Try again." He leans back against the arm of the couch.

"Oh. Um, yes, I do have bagels. But I need to get ready for the day. Help yourself."

"Nice." He flashes me an approving side grin.

I glance at my watch. "I really do need to get ready. Dad needs me there early."

He raises his eyebrows and pins me with an unimpressed stare, which makes my cheeks flush.

"I know, I know." I raise my hands in defeat. "Baby steps, okay? Maybe we could practice more later? How long are you in town for?" I climb off the end of the couch and head across the living room back to my room.

"Just a couple days. Hey, do you really want me to go? I can find somewhere else to stay if you want?"

"No, you're fine. I like having you around." I twist my neck to look at him before closing the door. "But a little more notice next time would be nice."

"This is Naomi."

"Naomi, it's Austin"—the head of IT, aka my department boss—"I just talked with Fran at reception. She's having trouble connecting to the server. Any chance you can head over and help?"

"On my way."

"You're the best."

I start making my way to the welcome desk at the front of the dealership showroom. The obnoxious four-inch heels my dad insists we wear clank on the tile floor as I adjust the bottom of my skin-tight business suit while I walk—something I find myself doing several times a day. This ridiculously fancy dress code makes me feel like even more of a fraud than I already am when I'm here at work. I dislike wearing this outfit just about as much as I dislike the fact that I know the inner workings of wireless access points and disaster recovery.

"What seems to be the problem, Fran?" I round the large oval-shaped desk to where the reception computer is set up.

"Hi, Naomi. I don't know what I'm doing wrong, but it's telling me there's a server error." She lifts both palms in frustration at her screen.

"Let me take a look."

She scoots her swivel chair back to give me space to investigate.

"Thank you," she says, her voice slightly frazzled at the edges. "This is a terrible time to be without internet. I'm up to my eyeballs getting things ready for the grand opening. Invitations are supposed to go out this week, you know."

Before I sit down, she grabs the fancy pair of work heels from under the desk and quickly switches them with the comfortable walking shoes she has on. As friendly as we are with each other, I am the boss's daughter after all. Not that I care about her discretion one bit—I'm more jealous of her brave attempt to undermine my dad's rules.

"I'll get you up and running in no time," I say, sliding into the chair. She shuffles some paperwork that's scattered loosely around her computer, moving them out of my way. All of them have to do with the grand opening of my dad's second dealership in Brainerd next month. Fran is leading the charge with planning the event that all of Pine Falls has been buzzing about.

I get busy putting my tech skills to work—the skills I reluctantly acquired when I blindly followed my father's career nudging straight out of high school. My own attempt to apply to culinary school was met with laughter and ridicule, as most suggestions I made to him at the time were.

While I test the connectivity between the computer and server, I unintentionally zone out, my mind drifting to imagine what Fran's home life and relationship with her husband is like. I don't know much about him or their life together, and my curiosity gets the best of me. Does he also stash a pair of walking shoes at his work—or perhaps in his car—so they can meet at the nearby hiking trail in the late afternoons? Or perhaps now that they're empty nesters on an adventure-seeking quest to reconnect with each other, they keep a bucket list of national parks they hope to hike someday.

"Just another minute," I tell her with a smile, secretly hoping that my second assumption is correct. I really do try to rein in my wandering mind when I'm at work, but I've admittedly come up with multiple home-life scenarios for each one of my coworkers.

"I've got nowhere else to be." She smiles back. "Hey, did you ever try out that new sushi place you were talking about last week? Over in Crosby?"

"Oh, yeah, I was there on Wednesday. It was delicious." I say.

"Cindy said she liked it too. Maybe we can do an outing for lunch one day," she suggests.

"I'd like that," I reply with a smile. I'm usually up for anything that'll get me out of the office during the day.

After a few more minutes of rebooting the software and checking connections, I finally get her computer running properly.

"There you go, Fran. Good as new." I step around the desk as she takes the seat.

"Thank you so much, my dear." She stops me before I get too far. "Hey, will you do me a favor? Could you bring this folder over to accounting on your way back to your office? That would really help me out."

She smiles sheepishly, as if she doesn't ask me for favors almost daily. And just like it does each time, my stomach does a flip, uneasiness swirling in my gut.

Is running paperwork all over the building part of my IT job description? Nope. Am I going to do it anyway? Probably. What if she's not feeling well and actually needs my help? Or what if I turn her down and she ends up resenting me? I can't bear the thought.

Robbie's face briefly flashes in my head, reminding me that this is precisely what I'm supposed to be saying no to, but I just can't find it in me to turn her down. When I think of saying no to Fran, my throat physically starts to close up, and my chest gets impossibly tight. What happened to all that determination I felt this morning? Because I don't feel an ounce of it now.

"You bet," I agree with a timid nod.

"Oh, thank you!"

I grab the folder and return her wave as I walk in the opposite direction of my office to accounting. The walk there makes me feel more defeated by the second. If I can't even say no to Fran, how in the world am I ever going to be able to stand up to my dad?

When I eventually make it back to my office, I close the door and call Robbie as soon as I sit down. The last thing I want to do is regress back to how I felt yesterday after the robbery, so I'm grasping at straws here to keep some sense of determination.

He picks up after the third ring. "What's up?" he says, his voice low and throaty in my ear. The sound of it alone seems to cut through some of the still-thick haze of insecurity—a familiar solace that I cling to desperately.

"Were you sleeping?"

"No." He clears his throat.

I wait, knowing full well that my silence will get to him eventually.

"Maybe," he finally admits.

"Really?" I snort. "It's the middle of the day."

I can perfectly picture the discarded clothes he has tossed around my living room and the contents of his backpack that are likely dumped out on my coffee table by now. His mess will, of course, be all picked up by the time he blows out of here, but boy does he bring a tornado of disarray with him wherever he goes. The man is nothing if not a quintessential chaotic artist.

"Listen, I've got nowhere to be," he explains nonchalantly.

"So you're going to spend the next two days rotting away on my couch?"

"Living the dream, baby."

"Okay. Ask me to take a file to accounting."

He pauses. "This another one of those practice sessions?"

"Yes."

"Okay, good. I was hoping you were going to ask again. 'Cause I really think I can do better than this morning. You caught me when I was still half-asleep."

"Yeah...I would apologize for waking you up early, but it looks like you've caught back up on your rest."

He ignores my remark as I hear him climb off my couch and slide my deck door open while he clears his throat.

"Alright, ready? Take this file to accounting right now, or you're fired," he demands aggressively.

I stifle a laugh. "Let's try that again, but how about less *deranged boss* and more...*sweet receptionist* vibes."

"Be a peach and take this to accounting?" I ignore his ridiculously high-pitched voice and pretend it's Fran who's asking me. Again, it feels like there's a brick pressing on my chest, and a wave of uneasiness flutters across my skin.

"No?" I manage to squeak out.

"That would not intimidate a mouse."

"Well," I say in an exasperated tone, throwing my hands up, "it's harder than it sounds, okay?"

"Let's try again... Sugar, my knees are sore. Could you take this across the building for me?"

"Now that's actually a valid reason."

"Not the point."

"Okay, okay." I clear my throat. "I can maybe do it later?"

"Meh."

"I'm heading the opposite direction for a meeting, so I won't be going that way."

"Better."

"Sorry, I can't."

"Straight to the point, I like it."

"Thanks." I heave a deep breath in, feeling slightly more at ease. "Okay, I feel a little better about it."

"Glad I could help. Oh, by the way, Mrs. Pelinski cornered me when I was walking out to your dock this morning. She grilled me for twenty minutes straight, demanding to know who I was. She acts like she didn't just see me here last month."

I chuckle. "Ah, yes. You can't escape her. You should know by now that crashing at my place inevitably comes with an interrogation from my sweet neighbor. She's protective of me. And her memory is a little hazy."

"I gathered that."

"Be nice to her." I may be just as protective of her.

"I'm always nice."

"Listen, I've gotta get back to work. I'll see you back at home later. Try not to eat all my brownies, okay?"

"Good luck with the receptionist."

Chapter Four

Robbie

"What's this stuff?" I stick my finger in one of the many bowls that are spread out on Naomi's kitchen counter, unable to resist a taste. She immediately slaps my hand out of the way.

"Get out of there. It's sugar."

"But it's green," I point out, licking my lips.

"It's sanding sugar, genius. Used for decorating."

"Oh." I grab one of the hoodies I left on the stool earlier and toss it on top of my open backpack that's leaning against the wall before sliding into a stool. Naomi's house has always felt like home to me. It's one of the only places in all of Pine Falls where I can actually let my guard down and relax.

"So your day was productive, I see." She tips her head toward the living room as she grabs a carton of eggs out of the fridge. I follow her gaze to where open magazines are scattered across her coffee table, along with two half-empty milk glasses, and the contents of my toiletry bag are spilled out on the end table. I cringe, feeling embarrassed. Admittedly, I've never been a great house guest. Might as well add it to the list of my many downfalls.

"Sorry. I'll be out of your hair in two days max," I assure her.

"Where's your next gig?" She pours another cup of flour into the stand mixer and turns it on.

"That's a great question," I muse. "I can't remember."

I pull out my phone to ask Dane, my bandmate and the only person who gets me from point A to point B. He texts back almost immediately.

"Oh yeah, we're playing a two-night show in Okoboji." I tell her. "There's some big lakeside music festival there this year."

"Ooh. Tell me more about the festival." The gleam in her eye shines bright. She always listens eagerly to the details of my travels with my band—the more random and off-the-beaten-path things we do, the better in her eyes. I do my best to indulge her when I relay the details. I like it when she's happy.

"Oh, you know, the typical things. Corn dogs. Beer by the liter. Funnel cakes. Fan misters that attempt to cool the crowd of sweaty, half-drunk people. I live an extravagant life, you know."

"That sounds amazing," she says earnestly.

"Should be a good time," I agree.

Although, if I'm honest, waiting two days to leave for this festival feels like two too many. There's a constant sense of dread that follows me around whenever I come home, and I'm already over it, to say the least. I've been counting down the minutes until I can get out of this city since I arrived. Not Naomi's place specifically, but Pine Falls. The entire twenty-mile radius surrounding here, really. There's a reason—okay, several reasons—why I never stay home long.

The air here...it's stifling. Much like my memories from my childhood.

If I didn't have an appointment at the bank tomorrow, I wouldn't have even come home.

"How did the rest of the day go with your archnemesis?" I ask, redirecting my thoughts.

"You mean Fran?" She smiles, wiping flour off her forehead with her forearm. A streak of flour sweeps across her blonde curls that she has pulled back into a ponytail. "She's not my enemy."

"She just asks you to run files to accounting more than what would be considered an appropriate number of times?"

"It's not the fact that she asks me for a favor—I'm more than willing to help people out. But it's gotten to the point that I almost wonder if they're starting to take advantage of me. Actually, I don't have to wonder. I know for a fact they are. Because I never say no, which has brought me to my current predicament: needing to practice standing up for myself." She shakes her head. "It's pathetic, really."

"I wouldn't say that," I protest.

"You're just being nice. Anyway, it's not her—or anyone else's—fault that I don't have a backbone."

"You could probably blame your dad a little bit," I point out softly.

"I could," she admits with a somber whisper. I haven't had a lot of interactions with her dad over the years, but I heard enough gossip within our friend group to know he can be a real jerk at times.

"Can I ask you a question?" I ask. "What about your mom? She's always seemed super sweet to me. Did she just stand by and let your dad treat you like this?"

"She is sweet," she agrees. "That's the problem. She's too sweet. She doesn't stand up to him either. I get my people-pleasing ways from her, unfortunately."

"Hmm," I hum in response, not quite knowing what else to say.

"It was easier when I was talking to you, though." She smiles gently as she pours the batter into two cake pans. "It feels different when I say no out loud to you—it helps for some reason."

"I mean, I'm glad...but personally, I don't think there's anything wrong with you," I offer. "I mean, other than your questionable taste in music."

"You don't see half of it, though," she says, ignoring my jab. "No offense, but you're not exactly around much anymore, are you?"

"Touché."

"Today, in the break room, my dad made a comment about my appearance and how juvenile he thought my hot-pink hair clip was—right in front of three sales guys. It was so embarrassing."

"Well, that's rude." Irritation slides through my veins. What a jerk to comment on a woman's appearance—let alone his own daughter's—in public, no less.

"Tell me about it. And all I did was stand there. I couldn't think of anything to say. Pathetic."

I can see a hint of a blush spread across her cheeks, which makes my stomach uneasy. I hate seeing her feel so defeated. I don't like it one bit.

"Do you want me to stop by the dealership tomorrow?" I offer. "I can bring you lunch and be moral support in case you want to practice again before I leave."

I suppose if I'm here, I might as well help her out. It really doesn't sit right with me that she's struggling with this. Naomi has always had the 'Minnesota Nice' kind of amenable attitude, which has always been endearing to me. But the fact that she feels like people walk all over her breaks a piece of my heart. And I feel guilty for playing my part in that.

"You'd do that?" The tender look behind her sapphire eyes solidifies how much this means to her, which further fuels my willingness to help.

"Sure." I shrug. "You've not-so-nicely pointed out that I don't have anything else worthwhile to do while I'm here." What I don't say out loud is that, while I'm all for helping her out, a distraction while I'm home is exactly the kind of thing I need. It's the only way I can tolerate being here.

"I mean, that's true."

"It's no big deal, honestly. I'm not home that often, but when I am, I'm at your service. Whatever you need, I'm happy to help."

She pauses to tilt her head at me with a crooked smile. "Thanks, Robbie. You know, if you'd show this side of yourself to your fans, you'd be batting the ladies off with a stick. Everyone loves a genuinely nice rock star, you know."

I chuckle. "Who says I'm not batting them off already?"

"I mean, I don't doubt it."

"Knock, knock," a voice interrupts us, calling from the front door.

"Hey, Gabby, come on in. We're in here!" Naomi calls.

"Well, well, look who the cat dragged in," Gabby says, patting me on the shoulder as she passes behind to sit next to me. "Love what you've done with the place. Are dirty socks part of the decor on the West Coast or wherever you rolled in from?"

"Gabriela. Nice to see you, as always, and yes, we make a point to be as absolutely disgusting as possible while we're touring. Helps with the image," I say with a sarcastic grin.

"That's gross." Her lip curls up in disgust.

Gabby is the one friend in our group from high school that I consider more of an acquaintance than a friend. I find her to be a bit abrasive for my taste, but she's fine in small doses—as is true with most things here in Pine Falls.

"What are you making?" Gabby asks Naomi, scanning the mess on the counter.

"A vanilla-raspberry cake with buttercream frosting." Naomi stares longingly at the oven.

"Just for fun?" I detect a tiny bit of judgment in Gabby's tone.

"Yes, for fun." I don't miss the slight drop in Naomi's shoulders. "I've told you before that baking relaxes me."

"When did you learn to do all this baking anyway?" I ask, shifting the conversation away from Gabby. "I can't remember when you started. Just that you all of a sudden started bringing baked goods with you everywhere we went. I still think about those truffles you brought when we went tubing down the river."

"Don't you remember? In high school, we had the option to take some classes at the tech college in Leighton. I chose some culinary courses just for fun. You know, some of us actually applied ourselves in school instead of chasing after girls."

I know she means it as a joke, but the sting from the jab cuts deeper than she intended, hitting a little too close to home. I mentally brush it off and smirk at her with a knowing shrug.

"Kidding. Then when I moved in here, Mrs. Pelinski took me under her wing and taught me everything she knows. She's an amazing baker."

"As fascinating as this trip down memory lane is," Gabby cuts in, somewhat rudely, "I want to go to The Squirrely Bear for two-for-one margaritas. You guys want to come?"

"Oh, I don't know," Naomi says, looking around her kitchen at the clear amount of baking she still had planned to do.

"Come on. Beats hanging in your kitchen all night, doesn't it?" Gabby pleads.

I bite back a retort fueled by annoyance and wait patiently to see what Naomi will say.

"Oh, uh...I was going to do a quick batch of cupcakes too...but I guess I can save that for tomorrow," she says with a nod of her head, as if she's trying to convince herself as well.

"Great! You in, Leery?" Gabby uses my last name as she slides off the stool.

"Whatever you guys want to do." I don't mind going there if Naomi is really okay with it. It's one of the few places in town I know I won't run into a member of my family, whom I avoid at all costs. The Squirrely Bear is far too unsophisticated for them.

I make eye contact with Naomi, and she smiles softly, reassuring me.

"I'll do these dishes later," she says, stacking the bowls in the sink. "Just let me change quickly."

"Hey, you know, my mom was just telling me about a bridal shower she's hosting," Gabby says as we walk out of the kitchen. "She probably needs a dessert. Maybe you could make it, Naomi?"

Naomi's entire face lights up instantly. Her excitement is cute but perhaps a little too eager given everything I now know.

I clear my throat loudly to get her attention then raise my eyebrows when our eyes connect, silently reminding her to speak up.

"Um, yeah..." Naomi says. "As long as she's willing to pay for my services, I would be happy to do that for her."

"Okay." Gabby shrugs. "I'll let her know."

"Great!" Naomi disappears into her room while I grab my wallet from the coffee table. I shoot our friend Charlie a quick text to see if he wants to join.

"Don't you ever get sick of sleeping on her couch?" Gabby asks me from the doorway.

"Well, everyone else is coupled up or doesn't have room. What else am I supposed to do?"

"Maybe rent your own apartment?"

"You know I'm not home enough for that to be worth it," I say firmly. Unlike Naomi, I have no problem putting Gabby in her place.

"Ah, that's right. You despise it here. You're too good for all of us small-town peasants."

"I've never said that."

"Maybe not with words." She smirks.

Naomi saves me from this conversation by emerging from her room. I effectively skirt right over Gabby's comment by opening the door.

"After you, ladies."

The whole ride there, I attempt to stay out of their conversation and prepare myself for everything an evening at The Squirrely Bear entails—drinking, dancing, and talking about the good ol' days back in high school.

As much as I enjoy seeing my friends, I already know the one thing on the forefront of my mind tonight will be the same thing I've been doing all day—counting down the seconds until my flight out of here.

CHAPTER FIVE

Naomi

Robbie's hand comes to rest on the swell of my hip, his eyes smoldering intensely into mine. We're vacationing in Italy for a few days—the Amalfi Coast, to be exact. With only a few days in between his international tour dates, we couldn't resist the enticing pull of the Tyrrhenian Sea that laps onto the beach behind him. The warm air adds an extra layer of heat to the sizzling chemistry sparking between us. His other hand comes up to cradle my head as he tilts his own, bringing his mouth closer—

"Are you having a stroke or something?" Robbie's real-life voice breaks me out of my daydream. My brain takes a minute to catch up as I blink rapidly at him. I'm pretty sure there's a sheen of sweat on my skin, and I can practically feel where his hand was just burning warmth into my hip. Where in the world did that come from?

"Huh?" I manage to squeak out a bit shakily.

"You're looking at me weird." He runs a hand across the line of his jaw. "Do I have something on my face?"

"Sorry. No, you're fine." I take my sub sandwich from his hand and walk briskly back into my office before anyone else witnesses the flush on my cheeks.

That was incredibly weird.

He's obviously spending way too much time in my house. Why else would I be having daydreams of him? Of Robbie—my scattered, commitment-phobic, drifter, not to mention very platonic, friend?

"Are you sure? 'Cause a little notice before you hurl would be nice." He follows closely behind, shutting my office door behind him.

"Don't worry, I'll be sure to aim for your lap." I flash him my best cheeky smile as he sits in the chair opposite my desk.

"How's the morning been?" he asks, taking a bite of his sandwich. "Anyone I need to intimidate?"

"It's been pretty quiet, actually. I've spent most of the morning here in my office. Oh, my new credit cards finally came, though. I guess that's good."

"Any leads on identifying the robber?"

"Nope. From what I gather, I'm just one case out of many, so I probably won't ever get closure. Which is a bummer, but what do you do? Anyway, I don't want to focus on it anymore. How was your meeting at the bank?"

He shrugs. "Fine. I just needed to confirm my proof of residence in order to keep my account open."

"You mean the residence you haven't lived at for over a year?" I suck in a slow inhale before taking a bite of my sandwich, still trying to clear the mental effects of our fictional moment in Italy.

"Hey, it's not my fault Toby moved Rachel in and didn't want me crashing there anymore. I, for one, think I would have been a great third-wheel roommate. I'm not there enough to have an opinion about anything."

"Yeah, but you leave your crap everywhere," I point out.

"Ouch." He feigns being insulted, clutching his chest.

"Isn't this what I'm supposed to be doing? Being more forthcoming with my opinions?" I'm only half-joking.

His face falls. "Does that really bother you?"

I don't have a chance to say no with my mouth full of food.

"It does, doesn't it? Man, this trip home has been eye-opening to me. Your random self-help journey is shedding light on all my flaws. I don't like what I'm seeing in myself," he mutters.

I shrug, snickering to myself. "I accepted the way you are a long time ago, my friend. Stinky socks and all."

He scowls, rolling his eyes playfully.

"Did I tell you Gabby's mom called me this morning? I'm officially doing the cupcakes for her shower," I tell him excitedly.

"Really? That's awesome. Tell me you brought up payment."

"She asked my price before I even thought to mention it." I beam. I may not have been the enforcer on that part of the conversation, but I'm counting it as a win anyway.

Anticipation prickles across my skin at the thought of actually having a baking client.

"Amazing. And I've had your cupcakes—I bet you'll get even more orders after everyone at the shower tastes them."

"Gosh, wouldn't that be great? Maybe everything will snowball, and I'll start a chain of bakeries all across Minnesota. Or maybe Netflix will seek me out to be on one of their top-rated baking competition shows. OH! Or maybe I'll be recruited as the official pastry chef for The White House after the president tastes my lemon tart while here on the campaign trail for re-election."

He shakes his head in amusement. "Your brain is a scary place."

"Tell me about it." I pop the last bite of the sandwich in my mouth. "Okay, I have to get back to work."

"Alright, I'll take the hint," he says, gathering our trash while he stands.

I follow him toward the door. "I'll walk you out."

"After you." Robbie holds it open for me, but I immediately stop in my tracks to avoid a near-collision.

"Dad," I sputter.

"Naomi." My dad is standing just outside my office, and the sound of his cold voice alone makes my shoulders slump. "I thought I'd stop by to check on that project I asked you to complete."

He's referencing the thirty-page report that is due tomorrow—that he just gave to me this morning.

"Uh, I'm still working on it," I tell him as confidently as I can, but I'm afraid it doesn't come out as strong as I'd hoped. Robbie steps forward, closer to my side. I appreciate his presence, even without saying a word.

"I'll need it by the end of the day today, even if you have to stay late to finish it, okay?" Dad demands, not even acknowledging the person by my side.

I can feel Robbie's eyes burning into me, silently challenging me to push back, but I ignore him and nod in agreement anyway. "Dad, you remember Robbie?"

My dad lifts his chin in a show of authority and then slowly scans Robbie from head to toe. The unnerving look on his face makes my stomach turn. My dad prides himself on being intimidating—and I hate that he can do it to me so easily.

"Robbie," he muses. "Hey, I remember you. Didn't you take my daughter to a dance back in high school?"

"Sadie Hawkins," Robbie replies confidently. I'm jealous of his strong voice and solid stance. How can he do that so effortlessly? I feel an urge to draw closer to him, as if I might be able to absorb some of his confidence if I get close enough. Or maybe it's to seek his comfort, I'm not quite sure.

"That's right. That's the one where she asked you, right?" My dad smirks.

Robbie nods, acknowledging the time we went to the senior dance as friends.

"But you never became an item, right?" My cheeks heat with a blush as my dad's tone turns to one of amusement and ridicule. "Isn't that the whole point? To ask the person you're interested in?"

"No, we weren't an item," I say quietly, wondering how quickly I can get this conversation to end. Out of the corner of my eye, I see my coworkers' heads turning our way. I despise when he comments on my personal life, especially in front of my colleagues. It makes me feel like I'm nothing more than his child here.

"I can't say I'm surprised," my dad mutters not at all quietly, and this time I can feel Robbie's arm brush mine as he protectively inches a little bit closer to me. Shame floods my entire body, embarrassed that I can't stand up for myself in front of him.

"That never was one of your strengths, was it? Catching or keeping a guy?" My dad sneers.

Kill me now.

"No, we weren't an item back then," Robbie cuts in, further deepening my embarrassment. "But we are now."

Wait, what?

My head whips to Robbie in the same amount of time it takes for my dad's jaw to drop open an inch.

"I was an idiot back then," Robbie continues confidently. "Couldn't see what an absolutely phenomenal woman I had right in front of me. Thankfully, I smartened up and finally came to my senses."

What is happening?

"Is that so?" My dad's eyes narrow, flitting between us.

"Absolutely. And while it's still relatively new, I already know that she's the best thing that's ever happened to me." Robbie slips his arm around my shoulder, squeezing the top of my arm. His warmth radiates against my side. Am I daydreaming again? I really need to cut back on caffeine—these visions are getting way too real.

"Oh, well, uh…" I don't think I've ever seen my dad caught off guard like this. Obviously, this was the last thing he expected to hear—which makes two of us. I pinch the skin of my forearm to make sure this is actually happening in the present moment, and then, to my relief, a coworker motions to speak to my dad.

"Well, your mother and I will have to host you two for dinner sometime soon, then. You know she'd love to meet whoever you're dating." My dad dips his head and looks between us once more, clearly still processing this new information.

I can't say I blame him since I'm doing the same.

As soon as he turns the opposite direction, I push Robbie's arm off me and pull him by his shirt back into my office.

"Uh, what was that?" I shut the door and bring both hands to my head.

"What?" He has the nerve to look innocent.

"Um, I'm sorry, but I'm going to need you to explain what you just said to my father." I point aggressively at the door.

"That we're dating," he says nonchalantly, as if those aren't the most ridiculous words I've ever heard come out of his mouth.

"Still not following… Why would you do that?"

"He was being a jerk," he says pointedly, his brows creasing with disgust.

"He's always a jerk," I point out. "And now you want to just pretend that we're dating…so that he's not a jerk?"

"Sure." He shrugs, emphatically nodding his head, a bit of anger now fueling him along. "I know you're aware of the way he speaks to you. It's ridiculous, Naomi. You don't deserve that."

"Well, I know, but…" My voice trails off, any attempt to refute him falling flat.

"Think about it. You're clearly on a quest to feel more confident setting boundaries, right?"

I nod, no actual words coming to my brain as he stares at me intently.

"And for whatever reason, I help you do that. You said so yourself. Well, how serious are you about it? Think of all the practice we could get in if we pretended to date—especially with your dad. I don't mind being your support person when it comes to him. In fact, I would love to put him in his place."

I put my hands on my hips, processing his proposition and everything that would come along with it.

"What if I don't want to pretend to date you?"

"Come on, you would turn this down?" He waves a hand down the length of his body, a smirk lightening his mood.

"Easily. I have a reputation. And standards," I retort with a mumble.

"Ouch." He snickers. "Look, I couldn't help but jump in when he was saying that crap to you. But if you're not comfortable, we definitely don't have to do this. No big deal either way."

I sink into my desk chair and pinch the bridge of my nose while I contemplate. It really would be nice to have him around as my backup. His presence is soothing to me—that has already been made very clear.

"You realize this is never going to work, right? This whole tiny town knows that we've been friends forever. Not to mention that you're rarely ever here. He's never going to buy it," I point out.

"I'll come back after the Okoboji gig," he offers.

"And then what?"

"We'll parade around town together. I'll go with you to dinner at your parents' house if they want. I'll make sure you're standing up for yourself while you struggle to keep your hands off me."

I roll my eyes and shake my head in amusement. "You're really serious about this, aren't you?"

Another shrug. "Let's do it."

The implications of what exactly this whole thing means run through my mind—the lengths we'd have to go to pull it off. I might be just as crazy as he is, because it isn't entirely unappealing.

"I mean, I guess it wouldn't hurt to try?" I say slowly.

He beams at me, making his way to the door. "Great. We'll figure it all out later. I've gotta run. I'll see you back at home..."—just before he closes the door, he sticks his head back in—"sweetie."

CHAPTER SIX

Naomi

Pulling my grocery cart to a stop, I fish my phone out of my purse and check the incoming message.

Mom: Your father mentioned you have a boyfriend? That's lovely, dear! Let's get a date on the calendar for dinner soon!

I've been waiting to hear from her. I push my lips together, fighting the urge to spill the beans and confide in her the truth behind the dating announcement.

We don't have a bad relationship, my mother and I, but we're definitely not as close as we could be. What—or rather, who—holds me back from delving into a deeper connection is the person she's married to. My father. She's comfortable living under his rule—a place I've been desperate to flee for some time now.

Naomi: Sounds good to me!

Hopefully, that can keep her at bay for a little while. I'm not exactly chomping at the bit to schedule a dinner with my parents, let alone face the reality of this ridiculous fake-dating scenario I've found myself in. I huff under my breath at the reminder, but once again, I push the notion out of my head to process later. I've had far too much going on this week to appropriately address Robbie's idea yet. I slide the phone back in my purse and continue down the aisle in search of flour.

It's the second time this week that I've been back to the store to stock up on baking supplies. Robbie was right—I've had three people reach out about baking orders since Gabby's mom's shower. I've been up to my eyeballs in flour and eggs for the past few days, much to my slightly overwhelmed delight. A few of them have even already inquired about recurrent weekly donut orders.

It's happening. What I've dreamed about for so long It feels exciting yet cautiously scary. Like I'm caught in a whirlwind, not entirely sure how to grasp onto the reality of it all or how I'm supposed to handle it. I should probably get an official booking calendar to start.

"Naomi, honey," a voice calls out from behind me.

I turn to see my fourth-grade teacher pulling her shopping cart to a stop next to mine. In a town as tiny as ours it's a regular occurrence to have small talk in everyday places such as the baking aisle.

"Mrs. Fitzpatrick. Hello. How are you?"

"Well, I'm certainly glad I ran into you, I'll tell you that much! Listen, I was at Ana's house the other day for a bridal shower…"

My smile falters, my confidence slipping because I know exactly where this is going. Immediately my mind races, questioning how many more orders can I squeeze in and still stay sane.

"…and those cupcakes you made were just heavenly. That whipped caramel frosting? Absolutely to die for! Any chance you'd be interested in baking the cake for my Susie's wedding next weekend?"

"A wedding cake? Next weekend? Oh, um…" I visualize my schedule in my head, knowing that it's already filling up. At the same time, the last thing I want to do is complain, given this is my actual dream scenario come true. I might need to work until the wee hours of the night to get it done, but there's no way I could turn down an order right now even if I wanted to.

"I know it's super last minute, but you know how that bakery closed down off Main Street. You heard about that, right? That gal from Minneapolis was running it—super cute place. We had her booked for making the cake, but she just up and closed her doors without a word and without giving our deposit back. Terrible, right? Now we're out a cake, and the wedding is almost here! Poor Susie is in shambles."

"That's horrible." Of course I've heard about the bakery closing. Things like that don't happen in this town without every last resident knowing about it. In fact, I'm sure that's part of the reason why I've had so many inquiries.

Obviously, I've already had an obnoxious amount of fantasies about taking it over and running it myself, kickstarting a wonderfully successful baking career. But alas, I've crunched the numbers and don't have quite enough money for the rent they're asking for. Nor am I ready to take the leap to launch a full-fledged business quite yet, if I'm honest. I may be a dreamer, but I'm not a careless one.

Maybe someday.

"It really is. So, what do you say? Are you able to make one? Susie wanted a simple chocolate cake with a raspberry tart filling and fondant icing. Just a few burgundy roses cascading down the side, so it shouldn't be too much trouble. What do you think?" She looks at me expectantly with hopeful eyes.

"Um, sure, I can make that work," I tell her with a reluctant smile. I can't *not* help them out. What else would they do? Surely most other bakeries in neighboring cities would be unable to commit on such short notice. I can't let a bride be cake-less on her big day. I can squeeze that in somehow—I'll have to. I'll do whatever it takes.

This is my dream, after all.

"Are you sure?" she asks cautiously.

"Absolutely. Why don't you have Susie call me tomorrow morning, and we can work out the details."

"You are the absolute best, Naomi. Heaven sent, I tell you. Oh, I can't wait to tell her!" Mrs. Fitzpatrick scurries away with a final wave, already pulling her phone out to deliver the message.

Feeling increasingly overwhelmed with the amount of work in my future, I quickly gather the rest of my ingredients—granulated sugar and two more cartons of eggs—before rushing home.

When I pull into my driveway, I notice Mrs. Pelinski lifting a watering can over her head, straining to reach a pot of hanging geraniums that adorn her front stoop.

"Hi, Mrs. P!" I call out while opening the trunk of my car. She turns her head in my direction and smiles.

"Do you need help with that?" I ask, pointing to the flowers.

"Oh, that would be great, actually." She lowers the watering can and steps aside in obvious relief while I cross the grass in her direction. "Thank you, Naomi."

The way she says my name always brings a warmth to my heart. I never mind all the times I find myself over here helping her with tasks, as I genuinely enjoy her company. But today, I'm finding myself feeling a bit anxious to get back to baking given the work I keep adding.

"No problem." I smile at her while I water the pots. "I can't stay and chat tonight, though. I've been busy with baking orders. Did I tell you that?"

"Orders from your convention?"

"No, that was just for me, to learn about the business and get a feel for the industry. These are all actual orders that people are paying me for."

"Oh, that's wonderful." She beams, settling onto one of her wicker chairs. "Just like I always told you—you're a natural."

"Oh, stop." I wave a hand, blushing.

"I'm serious. There's a certain amount of instinct that goes into baking that can't be learned, dear. A touch of magic. You have that."

"Well, I owe a lot of it to you, honestly." I have a seat on the opposite chair, wanting to soak in her company for a little while longer.

"You were always my best student."

I can't even count how many evenings we've spent together in either her kitchen or mine since I moved in. I caught a lot of heat from Gabby when I bailed on plans to hang out with my elderly neighbor, but every single second of it was worth it. I'm proud to call her my friend.

"I just hope I'm living up to everyone's standards. What if somebody doesn't like something I made?" I allow the insecurity to come through as I look down at my fingers. I can feel the weight of her stare as she peers over at me.

"My dear," she says softly. "You can't please everyone in this world."

I simply nod, letting her words sink in.

"But if they don't like your creations, then they must be stupid—or have no taste buds," she says bluntly.

I snort. "I suppose you're right. I can't make everyone happy."

Her smile is reassuring as she nods patiently at me.

"Thank you. Listen, I'd better get back to work."

"Remember to enjoy the process, dear," she calls as I descend her porch stairs and walk across the grass back to my car.

"I'll try," I say with a wave.

I grab my grocery bags and head in through the garage door. As I did this morning, I once again observe how clean and orderly everything in my house is. There are no stray clothes on the floor, the blankets are neatly folded on the standing ladder next to the fireplace and hanging over the basket on the floor, and the furniture is exactly where it's supposed to be. Not a thing is out of place now that Robbie is gone. He left last week—along with his ridiculous notion to pretend that we're a couple.

I get to putting the groceries away and take the quiet moment to finally ruminate on his absurd idea—the one that came out of nowhere. I may have randomly imagined us frolicking down the Amalfi Coast together, but him—or anyone for that matter—standing up to my dad like that for me has never been part of any vision I've ever had. I guess it's something that has been out of the realm of possibilities, even in my daydreams.

Not to say I don't appreciate it. I know he has my best interest at heart. But I'm not convinced that he fully understands what he just signed up for. You can't just decide to put on a facade like this in a town where everybody knows your business. There's no room for error here.

Although, I'm not sure why I'm even worried about it. If I know Robbie, I'm guessing he'll probably forget about this whole idea before he ends up rolling back into town. He said he'll be back in a few days, but I'll believe that when I see it. I've never known him to be one to stick to a schedule.

My eye catches on a bird as it flutters outside my window to land on the big oak tree in the middle of my backyard. With a smile, I'm reminded yet again of why this kitchen is one of my favorite spots in my whole house. From where I stand, I have a perfect view of both my firepit and the long dock that stretches out into the glistening lake. While it doesn't have a boat in the lift—maybe someday it will—it does have a quaint wooden bench at the very end of it where I spend most of my evenings.

My favorite part of the view is the way that most of the houses on the other side of the lake are hidden behind rows of large trees, with random docks jutting out into the water serving as the only signs of life. I know who lives in each one, of course, but there's enough of a veil of mystery about each property to keep me hooked. Give me a glass of wine and a picturesque sunset, and my daydreams know no limits.

That's not happening tonight, however. There's no rest for this burgeoning small business owner. With a contented sigh, I tear my gaze from the backyard, refocus my energy, and get started making frosting.

Chapter Seven

Robbie

I'm regretting my decision to help Naomi more and more with each passing second in this car. The Uber driver is going entirely too fast for what's supposed to be a routine, leisurely route taking me into Pine Falls. Admittedly, I don't think he's gone one mile over the speed limit, but still. To me, it feels like he's racing at top speed, and I can hardly catch my breath as I watch the line of roadside trees rush past in a green blur.

It's only been a little over a week since I left Naomi's house.

This might be the soonest I've ever come home after leaving. And for good reason, apparently—my mood is souring by the minute. I'm starting to think this whole thing was one giant mistake. Why in the world did I offer to come back when I didn't absolutely need to? Naomi can manage on her own, right?

My phone dings from my pocket with a text message notification.

Dane: Make it back?

If my calculations are right, he should be just getting to LA right about now to spend a few days by the beach in between gigs, and boy, was I tempted to go with him. Lazy days in the scorching sun with a cool, refreshing drink in my hand. Enticing distractions lurking at every corner. Those are my favorite kinds of days off.

But I'm a man of my word. To be honest, I'm not entirely sure why I spoke up the other day with Naomi's dad. Aside from simply wanting to quiet a man who was being an absolute jerk, of course, I'm thinking maybe part of it was my guilt talking for taking advantage of her comfortable couch one too many times.

Robbie: Unfortunately, yes.

Dane: You're missing out on this!

His next message is a selfie of him on the beach with the ocean in the background and a brunette woman under his arm. With a shake of my head, I smirk and type back.

> **Robbie:** Don't fall too hard for her. I can't play without a drummer if you decide to settle down.

> **Dane:** Can't make any promises. Just wanted to rub it in. Have fun in Minnesota!

I decide not to appease him with a response. Instead, the crunching gravel of Naomi's driveway pulls my attention out the window.

"Thank you," I say to the driver before grabbing my bags from the backseat. While I walk to her front door, I shoot off a text message at the same time.

> **Robbie:** Your favorite imaginary boyfriend has arrived.

After a full minute with no response from Naomi, I knock loudly on the door and slowly push it open.

"Naomi?" Loud clanking coming from the kitchen drowns out my voice. What in the world is she doing? I drop my bags in a pile on the floor and round the corner slowly so as not to spook her. She has a stony face and a slight crouch to her knees, as if she's on the offensive, readying herself for whatever sort of battle she's entangled in. I watch as she frantically whisks batter with one hand while simultaneously using her other to stack dirty bowls next to the sink.

"Hey," I say again a little louder, to which she jumps, inadvertently tossing a puff of flour into the air.

"Oh my gosh, Robbie! You surprised me." Her blonde hair sits atop her head in a messy bun with strands falling along each side of her face. Her wild eyes hold just a hint of crazy in them—the look of a person on a mission.

"I sent you a message." I inch closer, assessing the chaotic state of the kitchen. I'm not used to seeing this place in any state but spotless—aside from my own mess I typically make, that is.

"You did?" She glances at her Apple Watch. "Oh, yeah. What are you doing here?"

"I told you I'd come back after my show," I say simply.

"Oh...I wasn't sure if you were serious." She blows a wisp of hair off her face with the corner of her mouth and resumes whisking frantically.

"Didn't you say baking relaxed you? I gotta be honest—you don't look even a little bit relaxed."

"I don't?" She cringes.

"Nope. You have more of an unhinged-lunatic vibe happening...although, even that, you wear well."

"I've been busy." She shrugs me off.

"What are you making, anyway?"

"Raspberry-amaretto cupcakes. Let's just say things have snowballed after the bridal shower, and I have not one, two, or three, but four personal cupcake orders I'm working on. Plus, an actual wedding cake! Isn't that great, Robbie?" She doesn't stop moving, but she manages to beam at me with a hesitant sort of pride.

"Is it?" I ask cautiously. "Judging by the anxious energy that's radiating from you, I might have to beg to differ."

"It *is* great. It's finally happening, Robbie. I'm getting orders. This could be the start of all my dreams coming true."

"I don't want to be a Negative Nancy here, but is it feasible to take on that many orders at a time? When do they all need to be done by?"

"The cupcakes are all due on the same day, and the cake is due a few days after that. Look, I know what you're going to say, but I feel like I can't say no at this point—I've barely begun operating. These are my first few orders. I don't want to mess anything up or burn any bridges, okay?"

"Alright, alright." I watch as she continues bouncing around the kitchen like a ping pong ball.

"Hey, I have an idea," I say as she slides two trays into the oven. "Is that your last batch?"

"For tonight, yeah." She places her hands on her hips, finally able to take a breather, although some of the panic remains in her eyes.

"Why don't you go get changed while these are baking? I'll clean up your mess, and then while the cupcakes cool, we can go out."

"Go out?" She narrows her eyes at me.

"Yeah," I say pointedly. "It looks like you could use a break. Plus, it's good for our image, right? We can pretend it's a date—put ourselves out there while we discuss what our whole plan is here."

"Our plan?" Her brows furrow further.

"You know...the dating scenario."

"Dating scenario..." she says slowly.

"Are you just going to repeat everything I'm saying back as a question?"

"Maybe?" A tiny smile cracks on her face. "No, um...that sounds good, actually. We definitely need to discuss this crazy idea of yours. Are you sure you want to clean? I made a huge mess."

"Absolutely nothing would bring me more joy," I deadpan.

"I know that's sarcasm, but I'm going to pretend it's genuine so I don't feel guilty," she says, already on the way to her room. "Give me twenty minutes!"

The task admittedly does look ominous, with thick batter stuck to the mixing bowls stacked in the sink and utensils scattered across the island, but I jump right in, intent on getting it done. While I scrub dishes, it's not lost on me that I already feel less anxious about being home. Or maybe it's just nice to have something else to focus on. Perhaps having a purpose while I'm here will make it more tolerable.

"Okay, I'm ready," she announces a few minutes later, strolling into the kitchen, bringing a wave of perfume with her. She has on a black sleeveless romper with strappy nude heels. Her long blonde curls are loose and framing her face, and the subtle blush on her cheeks already makes her look more awake than a few short minutes ago. She looks beautiful—like she always does.

"Perfect timing. I'm done here too," I say, drying my hands on a towel.

She grabs an oven mitt to take the cupcakes out of the oven. "Do you mean to tell me that you've been this good at cleaning the whole time you've been posing as a slob?"

"Don't get used to it."

"Are you going to change?" she asks, pointing to my clothes.

I look down at my loose-fitting tee and grungy jeans. "You don't like the starving-musician look?"

"I like the put-together, edgy musician look, not the grungy-looking one." She smiles innocently.

"Ouch. I'm definitely not changing now." There's not one person in this city I'm worried about impressing. I grab her car keys while she places the cupcakes on the cooling rack.

"What are you doing with those?" she asks, pointing at the keys.

"I'm going to drive," I state the obvious.

"It's my car."

"And?"

"It's my car," she repeats, following me out the front door toward her car.

"Do you really think I'm going to show up on a date with the woman driving me around? This might be fake, but I'd like it to look real. I don't want to look like a fool. There's some chivalry buried deep in here somewhere." I ignore her snort and hold the passenger side door open for her to climb in. Before she can sit, a voice from next door calls out.

"Naomi, are you okay? Do you know this gentleman? Are you being taken against your will?"

We both turn toward Mrs. Pelinski, who's sitting on her front porch.

"Hi, Mrs. P. Yes, this is Robbie. You've met him many times," Naomi calls.

"I have?"

I elbow Naomi and clear my throat, calling attention to the perfect opportunity that just presented itself.

"Uh, right," she murmurs under her breath. "Yes, you have," she calls out. "He's been my friend for many years...and he's actually my boyfriend now."

I notice how she has to force the words out, slightly grimacing as if it's painful. I'm well aware that I should probably feel offended, but instead, I feel the need to hold in a laugh.

"Oh, well, nice job, dear. He's very handsome."

"Thank you." I wave, accepting the compliment as Naomi climbs in the car.

"That was weird," she says with a cringe as I start up the car.

"That looked hard for you," I comment nonchalantly.

"Where are we going, anyway?"

"I was thinking The Italian Place. Fancy enough for a date, don't you think?"

"That sounds amazing, actually. I didn't realize how hungry I am. Their ravioli sounds so good right now."

"Only the best for my pookie." I tug at the bottom of her ear, relishing her recoil and look of disgust. This might be more fun than I thought.

After a quick ten-minute drive through the back country roads, we reach Main Street. It runs right through the center of downtown Pine Falls, past the grocery store, bank, a coffee shop, and a few restaurants. Add to that a gas station on the far end of the block and a flower shop on the other and you've got Pine Falls in a nutshell.

I pull into the alley between the bank and gas station and veer right into the parking lot. Tucked back in the corner off Main Street, The Italian Place is a hidden gem known mostly by locals—one of the well-known secrets we keep from the out-of-towners who migrate north all summer long on the weekends.

I hold the front door open, savoring the blend of basil, sage, and rosemary that wafts out of it.

"After you, my precious, the queen of my heart and sole reason for my being," I croon.

"Yeah, yeah. Tone it down there, Casanova." I don't miss her eye roll and huff of a smirk.

"Two, please," I tell the hostess, discreetly doing a quick perimeter check to make sure nobody in my family is here. "And we wouldn't object to a cozy, dimly lit corner booth."

"Right this way."

As I follow closely behind Naomi, a myriad of questions hit me at once. Should I hold her hand? Slide my arm around her shoulders? I feel like maybe I should, to really solidify our image. However, given the half-annoyed look on her face, she could very well straight up punch me if I tried that right now.

I opt for keeping my hands in my pockets until we arrive at a booth that's nestled along the back wall of the restaurant. She slides two menus in front of us and gives us the name of our server before turning to leave. I wait politely for her to be out of earshot before broaching the subject right away.

"Alright, let's get into it." I slide my palms together.

"Already? Jeez, you don't want to wine and dine me first? Loosen me up to see what I agree to?" she teases.

"Nah. You're too much of a lightweight anyway. Okay, first things first." I tap both palms atop the table and lean in slightly. "We should probably talk about ground rules for this whole relationship thing—so it looks smooth and effortless, right? We need to be on the same page as far as expectations go, otherwise it won't be believable. These people already know us too well to begin with, so we need a solid plan."

"That's probably a good idea. This was your brilliant idea...you start."

"That's fair. So, we probably need to, say, hold hands occasionally." I smirk at the look on her face. "Without looking like it physically pains you to do so."

"Sorry." She shakes her head as if to clear her mind. "This is just weird."

"Which part of it?"

"All of it." She points a finger at me. "I mean, you're Robbie. One of my best friends."

"So?" I shrug.

"I mean, this is kind of ridiculous, don't you think? Why do we need to pretend to be in a relationship in order to do this?"

"Well, I hate to remind you, but your dad already thinks we're dating—my bad on that one. You can blame my big mouth."

"You know, maybe I'm fine staying a people pleaser. I've survived this long as one. There are worse things to be, right?"

"Oh, no, no. You should have thought of that before you jumped on the couch to wake me up that morning. You asked for my help, and now I'm committed. I thought about this the whole flight home." Brainstorming on the plane was surprisingly enjoyable. It served to be a good distraction from the negative cloud that always hovers when I'm on my way home.

"Oh my gosh. What are our friends going to say?" She gasps in horror as if it's the first time she's thought about it. Her hands fly to cover her mouth, and her eyes go wide.

"They'll be fine. I'll just tell them I've had a crush on you since high school." To be honest, I haven't given much thought to our friends either. I'm hoping they'll just be stoked that I'm home more often as a result of this whole thing and not read too much into it. They're the very least of my worries at the moment.

"Hello. What can I get you two to drink?" our waitress asks with a smile.

"I'll have a glass of red wine, please," Naomi says.

"And I'll have a scotch on the rocks." Again, I wait for her to leave before turning my attention back to Naomi.

"Alright, what else? I should probably plan to come into your office frequently so we can get some good interactions with your dad. Obviously, we can go to your parents' dinner if and when that becomes a real thing. And we should definitely go on a few dates like this to really solidify the look for everyone else.

"Okay." She nods slowly, taking it all in.

"Oh, and don't think I didn't come up with some practice sessions for us to do together to build up your confidence level. I'm fully committed to this."

"You've got this all figured out, don't you?"

I nod. "Yup. So, we said yes to occasional hand holding. I'm assuming that also includes some light touching of the back, especially as we walk—arms-around-the-shoulders kind of thing. What about kissing?"

She blanches. "Absolutely not. I don't see how that would be necessary."

I can't help but snort. "I mean, that would leave no doubt in everyone's mind if we kissed in public—even just a peck on the lips?"

"Nope."

"You look like you're about to throw up," I point out.

"I might," she retorts back. "How about we just play that one by ear?"

"Fine." Not that I've ever given much thought to kissing Naomi, but I'm realizing that I don't entirely hate the idea of kissing her. Imagining it is definitely less repulsive then, say, kissing any of my other friends. "Now, I wanted to ask you about me staying on your couch. I realize the whole point of this charade is to get you comfortable saying no to the leeches in your life. I'm a leech to you, aren't I?"

She relaxes back into the booth and smirks. "Like I said before, I really don't mind you staying with me. How about you do your best to contain your mess this time?"

"Done," I promise. "See? Boundaries. This is good. What else?"

"Hmm. No coming in at crazy hours?"

"Absolutely. Besides, I'm in a blissful relationship. I shouldn't be out on the town at all hours of the night anyway."

"Maybe you could keep your stuff in my office so it's not out in the open?"

"I can do that."

"Perfect. Then I'm good with you staying. Truly."

"Sounds good." I take a sip of my scotch and hit her with another look. "Now let's discuss your personal goals for *Operation Make Naomi a Boss.*"

CHAPTER EIGHT

Naomi

"You have a name for this?" I stare at him blankly.

"Obviously. Catchy, isn't it?" He beams with pride across the table.

"Operation Make Naomi a Boss," I repeat it slowly.

"I told you...I had a lot of time on the plane." He swirls spaghetti onto his fork. "So, what's your endgame here?"

I take another sip of my wine, enjoying the contented feeling that's come over me. Baking is my passion, and I won't apologize for working on orders. But I was starting to get a little—okay, a lot—stressed out about it. He was right. This break was much needed. Even if he's subjecting me to talking about our whole fake-dating scenario that I still have mixed feelings about.

"What do you mean, exactly?" I take a bite of my piping-hot ravioli.

"What do you want to accomplish at the end of this whole facade with me? Being able to say no when necessary, obviously, but what else? Telling your dad off? Quitting the dealership and starting a full-fledged bakery? What's your plan? I need to know how I should tailor my efforts."

I swallow hard. Everything he just listed causes a pit of nerves to drop in my stomach and a flush of anxious heat to cross my face. "Truthfully? I don't know exactly what I want. I know that I don't want to work in IT forever, and I would love to bake full time, but I don't have the details all ironed out. I can't envision just one scenario. I can see several life paths that I would enjoy, honestly. That's the problem with my brain."

It's the truth. I've daydreamed about each end of the spectrum—from staying exactly where I am, all the way to leaving town and starting an entirely new exciting life. All I know is the idea of me staying at the dealership and under my dad's thumb has gotten so depressing that I'm desperate enough to entertain this ridiculous idea with Robbie.

"So maybe we should start with baby steps? Help you gain some confidence first and go from there? And maybe narrow down what you're looking for, what you really want out of life. You—not anybody else," he offers.

I push my lips together in a small smile, finding that some of the nerves have dissipated. I'm also feeling a twinge of hope in my chest. If feeling validated and acknowledged out loud by him feels this good, maybe there is a chance of drastic results once we put some actual work in. I really do trust him with my life. As silly as this whole thing is, I'm starting to wonder if it just might work.

"Why are you doing this for me?" I ask softly, meeting his gaze from across the table. Holding his stare, I ponder what I did to deserve a friend who'd be willing to go to such lengths for me. To spend more time here than I know he really wants to. To parade around town and put on a show. To ruin his reputation when we inevitably break up and the town is forced to pick sides. What for?

"I saw a friend in need and jumped in to help," he says, flitting his eyes down to his plate, a sudden show of vulnerability. "And for lack of a better explanation, this gives me something meaningful to do between gigs. I don't have a lot of direction in my life at the moment, if you can't tell."

"I thought you loved being in the band?" I inquire.

"I do. And I get a rush from performing. I love it, don't get me wrong...but outside of that I've kind of just been...wandering. There hasn't been much substance to my life outside of shows." He shrugs. "Not that it's a bad thing, necessarily. But this will be a good change of pace. It's nice to have a purpose."

He smiles, lifting the corner of his mouth into a boyish smirk.

"Maybe since you'll be spending more time here, you'll start liking it again?"

"No. Not a chance," he replies emphatically. "Pine Falls isn't for me. I may not know a lot of things, but I'm one thousand percent sure of that. I'm only here until you don't need me anymore, then it's back to my regular schedule of visits. I can guarantee you that."

I nod, completely respecting his stance. He hasn't ever divulged a whole lot about his relationship with his family, even back in high school, but I know enough to know that they're a big reason for it.

"Back to you...I have a question. What would happen if you told your dad you quit? What's the worst thing that could happen?"

"Well, that's where it gets complicated. I can't just up and leave without having a backup plan. He's my boss. He also owns my car—he gave it to me as a hiring bonus. And he co-signed for my house. So, really, he could take it all away at any given time. Not to mention, I don't have enough money to rent a storefront for my bakery yet. I have a nice little cushion saved up, but I'm definitely not where I'd need to be in order to do that. I have to be financially secure before I do anything. I don't want to be impulsive, you know?"

He nods, opening his mouth to reply, but he doesn't get the chance.

"Well, I'll be..." We're interrupted by Iris and Opal, two local elderly women—or the 'town gossips,' as Mrs. Pelinski unaffectionately labeled them. "Opal, look who it is."

"Hello, ladies," Robbie says with a respectful dip of his head, sneaking a glance at me.

"Hi, Iris. Hi, Opal." I smile at them.

"Naomi, sweetheart, you look just stunning as usual. Robbie, I haven't seen you in ages. Your mother didn't tell us you were in town," Opal says.

I notice the way Robbie's expression darkens at the mention of his mom.

"Yeah, she doesn't know." He swallows his words with a sip of scotch.

"Well, she'll be thrilled to know that you're here, I'm sure."

Something else on his face tells me he doesn't quite believe that.

"How long are you in town for?" Iris asks him.

"Just a few days between gigs. I had to come home to see my beautiful girlfriend here." He winks at me, and my stomach immediately clenches, not expecting him to make that specific declaration. I hold my breath, waiting uncomfortably for their reaction. Sweet Opal almost falls right over.

"Oh, heavens. I didn't know you two were an item! Iris, did you know?" I'm surprised my dad hasn't spread the news to the whole town yet.

"Surely no! But it's not surprising—two handsome young kids like yourselves...what a stunning couple." She fans her face as if our news is overwhelming to her even in a physical way.

"Thank you," I say sweetly, forcing the words out. "We're very happy."

"I thought you two were just friends?" Opal asks.

"Things changed," Robbie says simply.

"Oh, I cannot wait until the whole town hears about this," Iris says giddily, not even attempting to hide her tendency to chatter.

"Well, we'll leave you two lovebirds alone. See you soon!"

I hold my breath as they walk back to where their husbands are sitting a few tables over.

"I sure hope you're not having doubts about this, 'cause the whole town is about to know about us within the hour," Robbie says, resuming his meal as if that interaction didn't bother him in the slightest.

"Might as well rip the Band-Aid off, I guess." Unlike Robbie's nonchalance, uneasiness lingers with me.

"By the way, we definitely could have kissed there," he points out. "I think Opal would have flat-out fainted."

I snort out a laugh.

"Maybe next time." He winks. I shake my head, going back to the last few bites of my ravioli. While I chew, my mind keeps going back to what Opal said about his mom.

"So, you really don't tell your family when you're in town?" I ask gently. I know it's a sensitive topic for him, and I don't want to pry.

"Nope," is all he says, his attention drawn down to his plate.

"What are they going to think of us dating? They're probably going to find out."

"They won't care." He gives a firm head shake.

"I know it's none of my business—and please, tell me if I'm prying, because I'll stop—but I'm just curious, as a supportive friend. When was the last time you talked to any of them?" I'm fully prepared for him to shut down the conversation at any minute, and I wouldn't push it, of course, but I can't help but wonder if maybe he might be in the mood to be vulnerable with me.

His jaw ticks as he sets his napkin on top of his plate. "The day we graduated."

"Graduated...high school?" I ask in shock. "That was seven years ago."

"I'm aware."

I watch him, unable to think of the right words to say. That's such a long time to not be in touch with your family, even if you don't have the best relationship.

"I had no idea," I finally say softly. Our eyes connect as he leans back in his seat. For the first time in a long time, I hold his eyes to study them. Wondering what complexities must be hidden behind them and what else he keeps tucked inside. He pushes his lips together in a tight smile.

"I don't like talking about it," he says with a shrug.

I wait patiently to see if he'll give me anything else.

"Come on," he says, scooting out of the booth.

Alright, I guess we're done.

"Let's head back. You need to get some rest, and I plan on spending the whole day tomorrow planning out which exercises we're going to do first."

"Why does that make me nervous?" I follow his gesture for me to lead him out of the restaurant. He follows close, his presence like a comforting, firm wall at my back.

His head dips low, close to my ear as he mutters, "I won't lie—it probably should."

CHAPTER NINE

Robbie

"Alright. Now that the wedding cake has officially been delivered, are you going to tell me what you have planned for the afternoon?" Naomi asks as we head down the steps of Pine Fall's one and only banquet hall.

"Nope," I reply.

"Why not?"

"Just trust me."

"What does trust have to do with telling me where we're going?"

"It's part of the process. Now get in the car."

"You're kind of annoying when you're bossy. Do you know that about yourself?"

My mouth curves into a smile. "I do, actually. Dane tells me all the time."

We head out of the parking lot once in her car, turning right to take us down Main Street. Pine Falls is bustling on this sunny Saturday, and I fight the nausea rising in my throat as I drive through. The pedestrian-clogged sidewalk mimics how congested my chest feels, like there's a weight pressing against it with no sign of reprieve.

As nice as it has been hanging out with Naomi, I'm dying to get out of here. I don't typically hang around long enough to know if I have a limit, but apparently, I'm about to reach it.

Thankfully, I'm leaving tomorrow.

"Ooh, are we going shopping in Nisswa?" She claps her hands together in excitement.

"Negative."

She clicks her tongue. "Boo."

Her phone buzzes from her lap, and I don't even have to look to know who it is. Her phone has been ringing nonstop all day, and it's been the same person nearly every single time.

"Are you going to answer her this time or leave Gabby desperate for answers?"

"I don't know what to say!" She throws up her arms in frustration. "Judging by her eight-minute-long voicemail this morning, she has a lot of questions about you and me and our relationship—as I'm sure all of our friends do. I'm just going to let them marinate with the news for a little while. I feel like if they interrogate me, I'm going to crack under the pressure. You know I'm not a good liar."

"Don't think of it as lying. Think of it as...a game. A game we're playing for the greater good. It's harmless, really."

"Yeah," she agrees, but still looks unconvinced.

"Let me handle it," I offer. "I'll do a group video chat with our friends tomorrow on my drive down to the airport. They can interrogate me all they want—I'm a vault."

I get grilled by them often enough about my lack of communication when I'm on the road, so I already know I can take their heat. I have no problem absorbing this for her.

"Thank you," she says genuinely, squeezing my forearm that's resting on the center console.

After hooking a left at the stoplight, I veer down a county road that takes us heading west out of town. We drive past farmland and long stretches of deserted fields before I slow the car.

"Why are we at Toby's family farm?" Naomi asks, confused, as I turn onto the familiar driveway. This farm was a prime location for many field parties back in the day. We've driven onto this property more times than we can count.

"You'll see," is all I say, bringing the car to a stop underneath a willow tree.

"I'm so confused. How, exactly, is being here necessary?" she asks warily, climbing out. "What in the world do you have planned, Robbie Leery?"

"I wanted a location with no distractions or outside influence," I explain as we walk, our shoes crunching over gravel. "Somewhere quiet. And seeing as how Toby basically kicked me out of our apartment, he owes me one. He said his family is cool with us using the north field between the two cornfields for an hour or so today."

"Now I'm definitely nervous." She grimaces. "You do realize that keeping me in the dark only makes my imagination go wild, right?"

We continue our trek past two towering grain bins, past a large shed, and out onto the field.

"I'm aware. And it's part of my entertainment—watching you squirm." I throw a wink at her.

"That's nice." Sarcasm drips heavily from her voice. I signal her to stop when we reach the perfect spot for what I have planned.

"This is the spot," I announce. "Are you ready?"

"No," she says emphatically.

"That's the spirit. Okay, I'm going to tell you a rule that I just made up," I say, turning to face her.

I almost feel guilty at the look of nervous trepidation on her face, but she nods anyway, going along with it.

"Okay. Before we start each practice session, I need you to think really hard—dig down deep—and tell me one thing that you know for sure you want out of life."

"You mean besides not doing these practice sessions?" She tucks her hair behind her ear.

"Besides that." I watch in amusement as she rolls her eyes. "I'm serious."

"Alright, alright." She takes a deep breath. "Let's see. One thing I want out of life... Okay, I know. I want a family—of my own. I want to get married and have babies someday. There."

"Good." I hold my hand up for a high five. "Now was that so hard?"

I smile when she sticks her tongue out at me.

"Tough. Let's get started." I interlock my fingers, pushing them outward to crack my knuckles. "Today's lesson is all about learning to trust your gut. You need to be solid knowing the difference between excitement and dread. When you can clearly decipher between the two, then it'll be easier to determine what things to say yes to and what you should consider saying no to. Does that make sense?"

"How did you come up with this?" She squints an eye at me.

"I did some research on learning to set personal boundaries," I admit.

"You did?" Her eyes soften, and her endearing smile warms my chest, reminding me of why I'm helping her in the first place.

"I absolutely did. Okay, let's go ahead and warm up to get the blood flowing to your brain. Give me five jumping jacks," I demand.

"Excuse me?"

"Come on," I chuckle. "I'll do them with you."

She reluctantly follows my lead, and we both do five jumping jacks in the middle of the field.

"Now shake it out." I roll my shoulders, shaking my arms and twisting my neck from side to side. To her credit, she follows my lead again and flails her arms above her head. I'm fully aware of how ridiculous we look right now—hence the quiet, private location for today's lesson.

"That's it. Now get those hips moving too." I sway my hips back and forth, biting back a laugh at the sight of Naomi.

"Now add a lip buzz." I vibrate my lips together while I continue wiggling my body. Naomi buzzes her lips together and almost immediately busts out laughing. I can't hold back a laugh myself as we slowly still our bodies.

"I feel good. Do you feel good?" I ask her.

"I'm not sure exactly how I'm supposed to be feeling, but I do feel loose," she says with a smile, still catching her breath.

"Perfect." I rest my hands on my hips. "Alright, we're going to do a rapid-fire round of things and situations. I'll say a single word, and you tell me immediately if it makes you feel excitement or dread, okay? Don't think too hard. Just respond right away with the first feeling that comes to you."

A look of determination crosses her face as she nods. "Got it."

"Okay, here we go." I look her square in the eyes. "Rainstorms."

"Excitement," she answers relatively quickly.

"Sauerkraut."

"Dread."

"Shopping."

"Excitement."

"Vacations."

"Excitement."

"Jalapenos."

"Dread."

"Nail polish."

"Excitement."

"Obtaining a baking order."

"Excitement."

"Good. Do you notice the difference between when you feel excitement about something versus dread?"

"I think so."

"That's what you should focus on when someone asks you to do something. Are you excited about it, or are you dreading it?"

"Makes sense." She nods in agreement.

"Let's do some more. Pickles."

"Excitement."

"High heels."

"Dread."

"Pirate ships."

She blinks. "Uh...excitement."

"Winter."

"Dread."

"Airplanes."

"Excitement."

"Good. We'll come back to that exercise another time. Let's move on to the next part of today's agenda."

"Okay." She nods eagerly.

"We're going to practice saying no. No matter what I ask you, I want you to shout no as loudly as you can. Now, obviously, you're not going to shout when you respond to people in your everyday life, but we're just getting you comfortable with saying it in general here. Do we need to do some more lip buzzes?"

"No." She smirks. "I'm sufficiently loose."

"Okay. Will you pick up that rock over there for me, please?"

"No," she yells, the attempt feeble and weak.

"Louder," I demand.

"NO!"

"Attagirl. Can you take this file to accounting?"

"NO!"

"Can you give me a foot massage?"

"Ew. NO!"

"Can you give me a ride to my buddy's house?" I fire the questions off as soon as they come to my mind, only briefly wondering if Toby's family can hear and might be getting concerned about the defiant yelling. I make a mental note to check in with him later.

"NO!"

"Can you make me two dozen cupcakes by tomorrow morning?"

"NO!"

"Can we go home now?"

"NO!"

I shrug. "Alright, I was going to end there for the day, but if you insist." Then I dodge her fist when she swats at my arm.

"Will you write this report for me?"

"NO!"

"Do you have any spare gas money?"

"NO!"

"Can you do my laundry before I leave?"

"NO!"

"Nice! How do you feel?"

"Great, actually." There's excitement and a dash of invigoration behind her eyes, as if a fire has been lit within.

"Good. My research said the more we do things like this, the easier you'll build confidence."

"Okay. Let's do some more, then."

We spend the next twenty minutes alternating between shouting no and rapid-fire word associations until the sky starts to darken.

"It's starting to get late. Should we head back?" I ask.

"Yes, sir." She salutes me and then falls into step next to me.

"Hey, thanks for today." She loops her arm through mine. "I feel like that really helped."

"You bet. Being shouted at is my exact idea of fun." I mean it as sarcasm, but the truth is, I did have fun—not to mention this feeling of accomplishment our time in the field gave me. I'm not sure if it's from helping someone in general, or if it's from helping her specifically. Either way, it's a welcome change from the heaviness I typically feel just from being home, and it served as a nice distraction while we were out here.

"Do you want to pick up something for dinner on the way home?" she asks.

"Do *you* want to?" I ask her, although my grumbling stomach probably gives away what my vote is.

"Yes," she says confidently. "Chinese food sounds good to me."

"Let's do it," I say as we get back in her car.

"Now, I leave in two days. What are we going to work on while I'm gone?" I ask, shifting into gear.

"Trusting my gut and trying to feel more comfortable saying no."

"That's right. I'll only be gone for five days, so we'll do another practice round when I get back. You can go ahead and get excited about it now."

"Can't wait," she says sarcastically.

"Ah, come on, it wasn't that bad, was it?"

"No," she concedes. In the dimming evening light, the slightest twinge of a spark pangs in my stomach when I catch a glimpse of a smile and her quiet voice when she says, "It really wasn't."

CHAPTER TEN

Naomi

"You didn't have to come with me, you know," I tell Robbie, who scans the parking lot just as he's done every single time we've come in or out of a store today. I know it's because he's been searching for any familiar faces to avoid, which makes me feel immensely guilty and convinced that he's likely regretting joining me today.

"What? And leave you to reach the high shelf for the stand mixer all on your own? A fake boyfriend would never..."

"They do keep them awfully high," I comment as I unlock my car.

We drove to a neighboring city this morning—the only one within thirty miles that has a store with the baking tools I need—to stock up on some supplies to make my home bakery more efficient. Many of my tools are hand-me-downs from Mrs. Pelinski, and this influx of baking orders has opened my eyes to how dated they are. It's time to invest some money into my fledgling business so I can keep it running smoothly.

"No, I'm fine," he insists, but I don't miss how rigid his muscles are, the same way they always are when we're anywhere outside of the comfort of my house.

"I have one more stop if you don't mind." I cringe hesitantly, setting my purchases in the backseat before turning to him.

I watch his expression carefully as I explain, "I was hoping to swing through the superstore while we're here. They have a specialty brand of flour I like to use. Is that alright with you? I can come back another time if it's not?"

"Listen, I appreciate the courtesy of asking, but remember, you're supposed to be working on standing up for what you want." He crosses his arms, leaning against the hood of my car with a pointed look. "If you need to run there, then end of story. Tell me to sit my butt in the car for all you care."

"Well, I'm not going to do that."

He waits patiently, rolling his lips.

I sigh, mustering strength from somewhere deep inside. "Okay, I need to stop in the superstore next door really fast. Would you like to come with me or wait in the car?"

"After you," he complies quickly, stretching an arm out, motioning for me to lead the way. I give myself a silent mission to go as quickly as I can to spare him the turmoil being out and about brings.

"How was my delivery there?" I ask as we cross the parking lot.

He slings an arm around my shoulders in a show of friendly support. "It could use some extra force, but we'll work on that."

"Well, look who it is," a voice comes from the left.

We crane our necks at the same time to spot Iris approaching the superstore entrance.

"Iris, hi," I say with a friendly wave. I push my lips together in amusement when Robbie's shift into fake-boyfriend mode is immediately apparent. He takes the hand that's hanging off my shoulder and quickly places it on my back, drawing circles with a touch that's more in line with what a romantic partner would do. Iris hardly tries to hide her gaze as she zeroes in on Robbie's hand. No doubt she'll be relaying every single second of this interaction to Opal, regardless of how innocent and mundane running errands together actually is.

"Beautiful weather today, huh?" She falls into step next to us as we reach the shopping carts lined up outside the building. "I'm sure you must be doing something romantic. Two young lovers gallivanting around."

"I don't know if you know this or not, Iris, but romantic is my middle name," Robbie says with a smile, leaning in closer to her before saying in a hushed whisper, "but I don't give away my secrets."

I bite my lip to avoid laughing at the way a blush creeps across her face. Then pure delight shines in her eyes when she tips her gaze to where Robbie just interlocked his hand with mine.

I'm now fully convinced that Robbie and I could do something as simple as walk down Main Street, and Iris—along with more than a few other Pine Falls residents—would eat it up like candy.

"Well, you two enjoy," she giggles, waving before pushing her cart toward the fruit section. I lead Robbie to the baking aisle, dropping his hand as soon as Iris is out of sight.

"Did you see how giddy she was when I grabbed your hand?" Robbie chuckles.

"I sure did," I comment flatly.

"I'm telling you, if you let me start throwing some kisses in there, these ladies will tip right over."

"Gross," I mumble, leaning down to examine where the bags of flour are displayed on the bottom shelf.

"Your loss." He shrugs, taking the flour bag from my hand to place it in the cart.

"Okay, while we're here, we might as well get—aha, sprinkles!" I say, selecting the largest container they have.

"Check. What else?" He pushes the cart to follow me down the aisle. We turn left and come to a stop in front of the egg section.

Out of the corner of my eye, I see Iris come into view at almost the same exact time Robbie moves to my back. I reflexively jump when he wraps two arms around me, his head ducking into the nook between my neck and shoulder.

"What in the world are you doing?" I hastily demand in a whisper, completely caught off guard at his sudden closeness.

"Nuzzling your neck," he says simply, his voice innocent and matter-of-fact.

"Because that's what people do in the dairy aisle?"

"I just wanted to see what she'd do." He keeps his head pushed firmly against mine, but he angles it just enough to look in her direction.

"And?" I can't help but wonder too.

"Mm-hmm, just as I thought. She's hiding behind the cereal endcap, spying on us." His voice is tinged with exhilaration, clearly enjoying this.

"What did I sign up for..." I sigh, murmuring to myself. I manage to grab a carton of eggs with Robbie still glued to my back, but I shrug him off as soon as Iris is officially out of sight.

"That's all I need. Are you ready?" I ask him, finally ready to get out of here and head back home.

"After you, peaches."

"What's with the nicknames?" I smirk. I can't help but be impressed with how much effort he's putting into this role.

"Just doing what I would do if this were real," he says. "Believe it or not, but I'm a fabulous boyfriend—real or pretend."

"You know, you don't really talk about your past relationships much," I point out, heading for the checkout lanes. "In fact, the last one I'm aware of was Nikki. That was our senior year, right?"

"Oh, there've been a few since then," he chuckles with widening eyes, as if they conjure up memories he doesn't care to explain. "None worth settling down for, though."

"I suppose the amount of traveling you do makes it hard for anything to last," I comment.

"For sure. What about you? Any dates since you went out with that scrawny little guy...what was his name? Colton?" he asks, opening the mini fridge in lane five to grab two bottles of water.

I snort at the mention of my college boyfriend. "Scrawny little guy?"

"Yup," he says firmly.

"You're just saying that because he cheated on me."

He shrugs, not exactly denying it. The corner of my mouth sweeps up in a smile as I start placing items on the belt.

"No, there have been a few Hinge dates since then, but nothing serious."

He nods as we both fall silent when the checkout clerk turns her attention to our items. The creak of a nearby cart brings my attention to the lane next to us where Iris waves with a bashful smile—one that almost displays her guilt for spying on us, but not quite.

I shoot Robbie a warning glance when he dares to move a muscle toward me. The last thing I need is to be smothered in this tiny aisle. A flash of disappointment shows on his face, so I offer a compromise by running my hand down the inside of his forearm, lazily running my fingertip across his skin A tiny show of affection to hopefully appease both of them.

I pay for my things, miraculously avoiding doing so with a human koala bear on my back, and we give Iris a final wave before heading back to my car.

"This is going to be exhausting, isn't it?" I ask, realizing that every interaction we have in public will likely be similar. He only grins, a smug satisfaction playing on his face. I'm beginning to think he takes far too much enjoyment in our fake dating.

"I'll put the cart back," he offers, turning it toward the cart corral while I put the last bag in my car and get in.

"Do you have anywhere else you need to go?" he asks when he gets in the driver's seat, shifting into gear and back onto the road.

"I do not. Thanks again for coming with me."

"My pleasure."

We settle into a comfortable silence as we drive.

"Are you ready to leave for your next gig tomorrow?" I ask.

"I am," he says a little too quickly. "Can't wait, actually—no offense."

"Well, I always like it when you're home," I say, giving him a soft smile.

"Whoa," he mutters under his breath when we see my dad's second dealership that's currently under construction along the side of the main road. "Look at that beast."

"Yeah..." I cringe, getting mixed feelings about seeing the building. "It's almost double the size of the original dealership."

A few service trucks line the outside of the building, and they have yet to put the dealership sign with my last name up, but the walls of the massive structure are in place. Just a few more weeks until it'll be ready for the grand opening. Yet another excuse for my dad to be the center of attention and boast about his accomplishments. I'm already dreading it.

"Will this one have the same selection of cars?" he asks.

"I believe there'll be more to choose from here," I say flatly.

"You sound so enthused."

"Believe it or not, cars aren't exactly my dream."

"Why did you go down that path, then?" He twists his head to get one last glimpse at the sight of it before we pass. "Let me guess, dear old dad?"

"I felt like I didn't have much of a choice." I leave it at that, not feeling like expanding on the topic. Instead, as Robbie takes the next exit to head back toward Pine Falls, I allow myself to zone out and let my mind wander, daydreaming of a life where I'm not in any way tied down to the dealership.

CHAPTER ELEVEN

Naomi

"You're all set. Everything should be in working order," I tell Carl from sales as I slide his desk chair back for him.

"Thanks, Naomi," he says gratefully. "You'd think I'd be able to figure out the error message at this point—I've only had it pop up about a hundred times."

"It's not the easiest system to work with." I smile sympathetically. "Besides, that's what I'm here for, right?"

"I suppose," he says. His gaze shifts behind me, and instead of sliding back down into his chair, he follows me briskly out of his office. "Ah, there's a potential customer. I've gotta be quick on my feet before Sharon grabs him. She's charmed her way into nabbing the last several walk-in sales. There's no way I'm letting her get this one too."

"Good luck." I laugh, waving him off while I catch sight of the gentleman who just walked through the door. I can't help but notice two things. One, how handsome he is. And two, that he's all by himself. A brief vision of a whirlwind romance flashes through my mind, perhaps one where this gentleman is a famous movie star seeking refuge from the hardships of fame in our quiet central-Minnesotan town.

We could fall madly in love and find the perfect balance between home life and the bright lights of Hollywood. Our weekends are spent under flashing lights on the red carpet, meeting adoring fans and eating Michelin-star meals, all to be back to our quaint cabin in the woods by Monday morning. It's a great life and an exhilarating image, but the next one that pops into my mind is what happened at the airport—the last time I let myself daydream about a stranger.

Pre-robbery me would have taken the long route back to my office passing right next to said gentleman, in hopes that he would say something to kick start our passionate love story. But post-robbery, defeated-spirit me decides to skip it altogether and venture in the opposite direction back to my office.

"Good morning, Naomi," Fran calls from the welcome desk as I pass by.

"Morning, Fran. Is the printer still working alright?" I stop to lean an elbow over the desk.

"It is! Hey, listen, I'm working on the guest list for the grand opening. I'm assuming you're coming, right?"

"I wouldn't miss it." I would actually love to miss it, but I know without asking, that's not an option.

"Should I put you down for one ticket or will you be bringing a guest?"

"Hm, good question." I'm sure Robbie would insist on coming along, but I'm not sure if he'll be in town or not. I suppose I'll need to ask him about that later. "Better put me down for two, please. Just to be safe."

"Robbie is his name, right?" The twinkle in her eye gleams. "I had cards last night with Iris and Opal. They filled me in on your budding romance—very exciting."

"Oh, yeah." I smile, for once not really minding the attention on Robbie and me. There are worse things than being paired up with him. Although, how the town will react when we inevitably break up still makes me nervous.

"He's a handsome fella."

"I think so too." Worried my facial expression doesn't exactly convey a romantic vibe and might give me away, I step back from the desk. "Alright, we'll chat later."

"Oh!" She stops me. "Dear, could you drop this folder onto Roger's desk for me please?"

It takes substantial effort to stop my hand from automatically reaching out to grab it. Nerves start bubbling in my stomach, and my heart rate ticks up. This is it. The perfect opportunity to test what we've been working on.

I take a second to assess how I'm feeling. Excitement or dread? I definitely wouldn't say I'm excited about doing this favor, especially since it's on the other side of the building. Could I? Absolutely. But *should* I, is the real question.

"Oh, um." The words feel thick in my throat, but I force them out. "Actually, I'm not going that way. I have a conference call in ten minutes, so I really need to get back to my office."

She blanches, clearly not expecting me to say no. Guilt starts squeezing my chest, and I hesitate. Maybe I should just do it. It really is no problem—I made the meeting up as an excuse. I'm mere seconds away from ceasing when she finally jumps in.

"Okay, no problem." She blinks.

"I'm sorry," I say with a cringe.

She shakes her head emphatically. "No, don't worry about it. I'll take care of it. We'll talk later."

Her genuine smile starts to put me at ease. "Alright. See you later."

I walk back to my office, feeling a growing sense of pride blossoming in my core. That felt really good—better than I anticipated it would.

When I get to my office desk, I'm still riding the high when I see a missed call from Robbie. I immediately call him back, still sporting a grin as I sink into my chair.

"How's my favorite girlfriend?" he answers, his voice low in my ear. The hum of a motor is faint in the background.

"Your favorite girlfriend just stood up to Fran," I say proudly. "I did it, Robbie. I told her no."

"No way!" His enthusiasm further fuels my excitement. "Do you feel like a badass?"

"I actually do." I wonder if he can hear my smile through my voice.

"Attagirl. And only one practice session under our belts too." The pride is obvious in his voice.

"I guess I did need this, huh?"

"Like I said, there's nothing wrong with you. We're just...fine-tuning some things."

I smile lazily, once again appreciating all he's done for me so far.

"Anyway, what are you up to? I think this is the first time you've ever called me from the road," I point out. Normally when he's gone, he's unreachable. I don't hear from him until he rolls back into town, so this is a first for us.

"We just hopped on the tour bus and have a bit of a drive to our next stop. I was thinking about you, so I figured I'd check in." The rustling of a plastic bag crinkles in the background.

"What's that noise?"

"Oh, just clearing some candy wrappers off my bed so I can lie down."

I chuckle, wondering what his space looks like on the bus. If my house gets chaotic and messy when he's here, I can't imagine the bus is any different.

"How was your show last night?"

"Electric." His voice beams with an adrenaline that spikes jealousy in my gut. What I wouldn't give to do the things he does, to see the things he sees out on the road.

"Where are you heading next?"

"Austin, Texas, I'm told. My favorite city to play in."

"Well, it's a good time for you to not be here. I've barely had any spare time outside of work and baking for anything else. I'm slammed with orders. Did I tell you I'm making a custom birthday cake for Millie's kid this week? She requested a double-layer cake in the shape of the number six with a full-on race car track on top of it."

"Right on." He chuckles low. "That sounds like my kind of cake."

"It will be cool. Time consuming, but cool."

"You're saying no to any orders you can't realistically do, right?"

"Yes," I say, hoping the confidence in my tone will cover up any uneasiness from the lie that so easily rolled off my tongue. I've been doing my best, but truthfully, I haven't been great at turning orders away this week. My eagerness to give this business a successful start has admittedly overridden the few logistical conflicts that have come up.

"Perfect." He yawns through the phone. "I think I might take a nap."

"Dude. It's midday."

"And?"

"No comment." I laugh again. "I should probably get back to work anyway."

"Alright. See you soon."

When we hang up, I dive back into my workday, the hours passing relatively quickly. As I'm wrapping things up for the day, anxious to get home to do my evening baking, my cell phone rings with an incoming call from an unknown number.

"This is Naomi," I answer.

"Hi, Naomi. My name is Cheryl," says the voice on the other end. "I live in Crosslake and got your name from Opal. We're in the same book club, and she was telling me about your new baking business. I was hoping you might be able to help me out with an order?"

My stomach drops, a rush of anxiety hitting me. I try to hold onto the confidence I had earlier with Fran and from talking with Robbie. "Hi, Cheryl. What do you need?"

"Well, you see, I'm hosting a very last-minute bridal shower at my house this weekend, and I'm afraid the bride is being a bit of a bridezilla. She's expecting vanilla buttercream cupcakes in the shape of a ring plus a three-tiered German chocolate cake as well."

In my head, I run through the amount of time and ingredients it would take to fulfill the order. Excitement or dread? Excitement or dread? I repeat the question in my mind.

"I've been calling around, and nobody seems to have the availability for such an order on short notice. Opal thought that maybe you might be able to squeeze me in. She just raves about your orange sherbet cupcakes, by the way."

"That's so sweet of her, and thank you for reaching out. When would you need them done by?" Excitement or dread? If I'm honest, the feelings are fairly mixed at this point.

"Two days?"

Definitely dread.

But...branching out of Pine Falls is an absolute dream. This order could get the ball rolling with expanding outside of the city. More orders means more income, which means I'm one step closer to a full-fledged business.

"Let me double-check my calendar quickly." I scan my phone, knowing full well the number of orders I'm already slammed with. Then my mind starts to wander. What if I tell her no, and she tells everyone she knows that I'm rude or hard to work with? What if nobody outside of Pine Falls ever calls me again? What if my dream is over before it ever really begins?

"I think I can make that work," I say quietly, any confidence I had completely disintegrating.

"Really? Oh my gosh, you're an angel. Are you sure?"

Nope.

"Yes." I muster up as much conviction as I can, although the anxiety that buzzes under the surface of my skin continues to get worse. "I'll email you an official order form. The sooner you fill that out, the better, so I can get started as soon as possible."

"Perfect. Thanks again."

When we disconnect, I toss my belongings in my purse and frantically rush out the door. I try to push down the almost overwhelming panic. Maybe I haven't made as much progress as I thought.

Chapter Twelve

Robbie

"Honey, I'm home!" I call out as I open Naomi's front door. Just like the last time I came back, I'm met with no response and a lingering smell of lemon zest and sweet berries.

"Hello?" I say again, shutting the door behind me and dropping my things in a pile by the door. "I brought you something—Naomi?"

A full-body panic hits me like a brick wall when I finally catch sight of her in the kitchen. She's leaning over the top of the island with her head resting on her folded hands in the middle of a small mound of flour. Her eyes are closed, strands of her hair are lying haphazardly across her face, and her mouth is slightly parted. The way her body is positioned makes it look like she just ran out of energy and slumped over right on the spot.

"Hey," I say urgently, rushing to jostle her shoulders in an attempt to wake her. Her skin feels hot and clammy under my fingers, and upon closer inspection, her cheeks are flushed a crimson red. She's burning up and completely lifeless. I jostle her again, a frantic dread surging inside my chest.

"Hmm?" she murmurs. A wave of relief extinguishes a bit of my panic when her eyes slowly open, but not enough to quell the way my mouth has gone completely dry, or the way my heart is racing a million miles per minute. What the heck happened here?

"What's going on?" I demand. "Why are you passed out in the middle of the kitchen?"

"I'm baking..." She attempts to stand upright but, instead, doubles over, collapsing her body weight against me.

"Are you sick?" I hook my arm under her rib cage and grip tightly to steady her.

"I mean, I wouldn't say I feel great," she slurs her words before taking a deep breath, widening her eyes. "I can't stop." She attempts to push against me. "This order needs to be delivered tomorrow morning."

"I don't think so, sweetheart. The only place you're going is straight to bed," I tell her.

"Mm-hmm." Her attempt to disagree with me is nothing but a weak hum and a minuscule shake of the head.

"Let's go. I'll help you to your room." I tighten my grip and start leading her across the living room, one unsteady step at a time.

"But...there are cupcakes that need to be frosted," she murmurs, barely lifting a finger to point to the kitchen.

"Yeah, no offense…but I think we're just going to throw this batch away," I say under my breath.

She leans her full body weight against me, unable to hold herself up any longer. We make it halfway across the living room when her head slumps lower, going completely limp as she faints into my arms. Seeing her unconscious sparks a fire of panic in my stomach.

"No, no, no," I grunt, using my other arm to hoist her up at the knees, holding her horizontally against my chest as a desperate worry sends me racing to the garage.

"Come on, Naomi. Wake up," I plead. Once I have her carefully buckled into the car, I dash inside to grab the keys. Terror floods through me as the panic deepens with each passing second—I feel like I'm walking through quicksand with each step, not able to go nearly as fast as I need to. I manage to grab what I need and race out of the driveway, her body still slumped against the passenger door nearly lifeless.

The entire drive to the hospital is a panicked blur—one filled with desperation and me constantly reaching over to check her pulse. She manages to come to eventually, but she's too weak to give me any kind of verbal confirmation that she's okay.

I screech the car to a stop in front of the emergency entrance and sprint to her side of the car. As I hoist her into my arms, she curls her head under my neck, the entirety of her weight falling against me. This entire situation is saturated with fear and desperation, but the weight of her body against me provides some small amount of comfort. As long as she's in my arms, I can carry her to get help.

It's not until a nurse waves me over to a triage bay and I lay her down on an exam table that I feel like I can take a full breath—only for it to be immediately taken away a moment later. As a group of medical professionals rushes to surround Naomi, I step out of the way and come face to face with a person I didn't even think to brace myself for potentially running into here.

My brother, Steven.

I freeze, completely immobile as he darts past me to assess Naomi. My eyes follow Steven's movement, but all I can do is stand frozen in place. At some point within the chaos of beeping machines and medical lingo, someone ushers me away to the waiting room down the hall.

I slump into the nearest chair, letting my head drop into my hands, reeling from not only what's happening with Naomi but also from seeing my brother. I was not at all prepared for this amount of emotional onslaught today.

This right here—this entire situation—is exactly why I don't like coming home. The chance of running into one of my family members lurks at every corner—a jarring encounter I've dreaded but managed to avoid for years now.

As upsetting as it is in itself, all the pain I'm feeling is secondary in this moment. I push aside thoughts of my brother and focus on the most important thing right now.

Naomi.

For thirty minutes, I pace the floor, trying to quell the fear that's gnawing away at my stomach. What could possibly be wrong? Why did she lose consciousness? What if something is seriously wrong with her? I won't know what to do with myself if she's gravely ill. I refuse to let my thoughts stay there, but my body doesn't get the same message. I'm a completely sweaty, panicked ball of nerves as I wait for any updates.

After what feels like forever, my pacing is interrupted by the swing of the door opening. Steven makes direct eye contact with me immediately as he steps inside the room.

"Is she okay?" I blurt out, rushing to him.

"She's fine," he says, holding his palms up to reassure me. "And she's coherent enough to give me permission to update you. I knew how worried you were."

"What's wrong with her?" I demand.

"Our tests show she has Influenza B. It's a particularly nasty strain that's going around," he explains.

"But it's summer. We're nowhere near flu season," I blurt out, confused.

"It can spread at any time," he explains. "From what I gather, she's been under a considerable amount of stress, which I'm sure played a part in how hard it hit her."

"Jeez." I run my fingers through my hair, a mix of relief and concern swirling through my body.

"She's resting. We're giving her fluids and monitoring her for a while, but then she'll be discharged to rest at home."

The words 'thank you' sit at the tip of my tongue, but my stubborn mouth can't commit to saying them. Instead, I give him a quick nod. Now that the intense worry for Naomi has loosened its grip, the fog clears enough to remind myself who is in front of me.

"Listen, Robbie—" he starts.

"If this isn't about Naomi, I don't want to hear it," I cut him off. I have no interest in discussing anything else with him, especially right now.

"Come on, I just—" he tries again.

"I mean it," I say firmly.

My expression must match my stern tone, because he backs away, silently retreating out of the room with a look on his face that I'm too distracted at the moment to analyze.

Once he's gone, I sink into a chair, dropping my head into my hands with pure relief. A few deep breaths help to calm my heart rate—at least enough so I can think straight. Then I can't help but start analyzing my emotions. Why did I get so worked up like that? Concern for a friend, yes, but it feels like there was something more there that I can't put my finger on. Seeing her in that state gave me such a visceral reaction I clearly had no control over.

But why? It's not like she's the first person in the world to get the flu.

A small, nagging thought creeps up in the back of my mind. A reason, an explanation, that would also rationalize why I felt the urge to call her from the road. Why she hasn't strayed far from my mind. And why I'm even here in the first place.

Nah.

I shake the implication from my head. I was simply worried for somebody who means a lot to me—in a completely platonic way.

Yes. That's all there is to it.

Shoving the thoughts out of my head, I leave the waiting room to go sit by Naomi's bedside.

CHAPTER THIRTEEN

Naomi

So much for hoping that exhaustion might quell some lingering humiliation. An overwhelming sense of shame tugs on my chest, swirling with still-present nausea and a dull headache at the base of my neck that hasn't completely gone away. Through weary eyes, I watch Robbie move around the kitchen as I sink deeper into the couch. The kitchen shines from here. There isn't a speck of flour on the countertop, and all the dishes have been cleaned and put away. The appliances even seem to be sparkling.

"Honey or no honey?" The break in his voice is miniscule, but I pick up on it all the same. Another twinge of guilt washes over me. I absolutely hate that he has to see me in this pitiful state—and how embarrassing it is that he had to worry about me in the first place.

"Yes. Honey, please." My head suddenly feels like it weighs a thousand pounds as the pressure of my headache surges. I settle farther against the couch, resting my temple against the leather cushion, letting my heavy eyes drift closed.

"Your echinacea tea." Robbie's voice brings my eyes open as he hands me the mug. "With a side of 'Thank you, Robbie' and 'I've learned my lesson, Robbie.'"

I clear the congestion from my throat as I take the first sip, savoring the warmth that travels all the way down to my stomach, soothing me from the inside out.

"Listen, I agree that I'm a pathetic mess right now, but you're going to have to help me out here—what lesson is that?" I say wearily, watching him put the honey right back where it belongs. Despite my current state, I'm coherent enough to notice and appreciate him cleaning up after me.

"Well, I'm going to take a wild guess here, but I'm betting that maybe you took on too much? They said stress most likely played a role in how aggressively the flu affected you. Did you overbook yourself?"

I wince, scrunching my nose. "There might be some truth to that statement..."

"So you took on too much and ran yourself ragged," he says pointedly as he returns to the couch, sinking right next to me. His gaze snags intensely on mine, holding a mix of compassion, worry, and a shred of indignation. A shiver runs through me at the depth of his stare—or maybe it's from the virus. I'm not entirely sure anymore.

"You probably don't want to sit too close to me," I croak out, effectively ignoring his accusation.

"I'm not worried about it." I swear he inches even closer. "Besides, that caution went out the window when you were drooling on my chest on the way into the hospital."

I roll my eyes, too physically spent to think of a comeback. He reaches to tuck the blanket around me with gentle precision before again roaming his gaze over my face. He leans forward to slowly tuck a strand of sweat-dampened hair behind my ear. Embarrassment flushes through me once again, but it quickly vanishes when I watch the emotion in his eyes deepen. And as his finger moves behind my ear, I can't help but notice there's a certain charge to the way it feels. Almost as if he's leaving a trace of a spark along my skin as he moves.

It's something he's done countless times before, touching me this way, but for whatever reason, this movement feels different. It comes with a layer of vulnerability and rawness that hasn't ever been there before.

Maybe it's the shadow of concern that still burns hot in his eyes. Or maybe it's the way he's been doting on me with a fervor that's rare for him. Either way, I'm all of a sudden hyperaware of how he's looking at me—and of how close he is to me. Have my daydreaming tendencies short-circuited from illness, and now I'm imagining things? Or is whatever this tension is that's ruminating between us actually real?

"Honestly...what happened?" he asks softly, resting his head against his knuckles, perching an elbow on the couch ledge. Even with the intensity of his stare, I feel vulnerable in the same comfortable kind of way I always do with him.

"I don't know," I admit quietly, looking down at the tea, blinking back a sudden surge of unexpected tears. "It's just hard."

When I bring my gaze back up to sheepishly meet his, I notice the way his jaw clenches before he rolls his lips.

"What's hard?" he gently prods. I inhale a deep breath, feeling my emotions rise even closer to the surface. Exhaustion lays heavy on my entire body, making it too hard to attempt to hold anything back.

"Standing up for myself," I whisper, feeling a wet tear slide down my face. The air in my chest gets caught in my throat when he brings his finger up to swipe it away. I force myself to look away from his stare, unable to face the weight of his attention any longer.

"I don't know why it's so hard," I say softly.

"Your dad?" he asks. There isn't a harsh opinion or malice in his tone. He simply waits patiently for me to continue.

"Yeah...I'm sure that's where it all stems from," I continue slowly, speaking the truth I know deep in my soul. "The way he's always made me feel. Being an only child, the attention on me was stifling—and his expectations were astronomical."

I sniffle, feeling the weight of insecurity and shame pressing on me, just as heavy as the exhaustion. "Nothing I did was ever good enough. And you know him... He's never afraid to express his disappointment."

His wordless nod serves as encouragement to continue.

"So, I've spent my entire life trying to do more. More of everything. More of my time and my energy. More effort. Although, even my max efforts still always fell short in his eyes. I guess, at some point, that mentality bled over into every other aspect of my life, and here we are... I'm a twenty-five-year-old woman who pathetically searches for Daddy's approval, can't say no to save her life, and constantly dreams of a life she's not brave enough to make reality."

Robbie swallows hard, eyes still pinned on me. Then he gives a slight shake of his head. "You know what I see?"

I shrug, feeling completely defeated and worn down.

"I see a kind-hearted woman." Again, his voice cracks. "One who's willing to help at the drop of a hat. One who sees the beauty in the world and isn't afraid to dream of its endless possibilities. That's inspiring, Naomi."

I offer a half-smile and am about to protest when he cuts me off.

"I also see a woman whose true beauty—in every sense of the word—hasn't been appreciated in the way that it should have been—by myself included. And I'm sorry for my part in that."

His words make my mouth clamp shut, too stunned to respond. I blink a few times before managing to squeak out, "You didn't do anything wrong."

"Maybe not, but I'm still a fool for not seeing you fully before all this."

I pause, wondering what context sits behind his words and why they suddenly make me feel like I can't breathe again. The fact that he's looking at me in a way he hasn't before makes me wonder if he's also talking about something that he hasn't yet voiced.

The thought alone makes my stomach twist with a swoop. Not feeling even remotely steady enough for any direction this conversation may potentially take, I avoid his gaze by taking a steadying sip of tea.

"Are we going to talk about your brother?" I ask, redirecting the topic. "I might have been mostly out of it, but I would recognize a Leery hairline anywhere."

His face hardens as his jaw clamps shut again.

"We don't have to talk about it," I blurt out, regretting asking.

"No, it's okay." He gives me a small smile, but I can see the pain behind it clear as day. He clears his throat, adjusting his position on the couch. The struggle to find the right words is written all over his face.

"I wasn't expecting to run into him," he finally admits softly.

"Was that the first time you've seen him? Since graduation?"

He nods solemnly.

I wait for him to say anything else, but it doesn't come.

"Is that why you don't like being here? Because you don't like seeing your family?"

"Pretty much," he says slowly.

"Did something happen?" I know I'm pushing my luck, and fully expect to be shut down at any moment, but I can't help wanting to know more.

"More or less."

Again, I wait for anything else he'll give me, but it doesn't come. I swallow against my scratchy throat. The thoughts start to feel fuzzy in my head as exhaustion grips me once more with a vengeance. I drop my head against the couch, feeling the heavy pull of sleep.

Robbie's smile hangs crooked as his eyes slowly roam every inch of me. A shiver runs down my spine, and again, I'm unclear whether it's from the flu or from the weight of his stare.

"Are you tired?" he asks gruffly.

All I can do is nod in response, too tired to form words at this point. My eyes drift closed when I can no longer hold them open.

"Go ahead and sleep." I feel him grab the teacup from my hands before the blanket is tucked tightly over my shoulders. The last words I hear before drifting off to sleep are whispered softly from somewhere close.

"I'm not going anywhere."

Chapter Fourteen

Naomi

"Are you sure you're up for this?" Robbie asks from behind me, his hand gently gripping my shoulder. With his other hand, he slides a glass of strawberry lemonade onto the patio table. I've been told my backyard deck is the ideal location for whatever he has in store for this second practice session of ours. I'm assuming it's because of the view and the ample fresh air out here by the lake, which he's been adamant about me getting for days now.

His touch feels gentle yet firm, a heightened protectiveness to it that further confirms a truth I've been ruminating over the past few days—that something in our friendship has shifted. I'm not sure what it is, exactly, but the air between us feels...charged somehow. Call it the effects of sharing a vulnerable moment on the couch, or maybe it's just his lingering worry from me being sick, but either way, there's undoubtedly an unfamiliar tension between us now.

I'm not quite sure what to do with this awareness other than to silently acknowledge it...and wait to see what might come of it.

"As I keep telling you, I've been fully recovered for several days now." My playful eye roll does nothing to crack his serious facade.

Luckily, while the illness did hit with a vengeance, it only lasted forty-eight hours. However, it did cost me several re-funded baking orders, which I'm still trying to appease the guilt from. I've had to actively talk myself down from spiraling over potentially destroying my business as a result of all this.

"You were also moving around here at a snail's pace for quite some time, so don't look at me like that," he says pointedly.

"Hello, Naomi," Mrs. Pelinski calls as she steps out onto her own deck next door, squinting in our direction.

"Hi!" I wave, offering her a smile.

"Who's that you're with, dear?" she asks, pointing at Robbie. I stifle a laugh at her continued questioning of him.

"Still Robbie, Mrs. P. My boyfriend, remember?" The words feel different this time when I say them out loud...a little smoother, perhaps.

Robbie twists in his seat to wave to her across the yard.

"Oh, that's right. Beautiful day, isn't it?" She points out to the lake, where the sunlight glistens across the top. The calmness of the water as it softly ripples has the same soothing effect on me it always does, and my shoulders loosen, relaxing me in a way only this view can.

"Gorgeous. Do you need help with that watering can?" I ask.

She places it under the hose that sticks out of the side of her house and turns the faucet on. I know her daily routine well enough to know she's preparing to make the trek around the perimeter of her house to hit the many flower pots she has hanging. I attempt to stand to help her out.

"I'll get it," Robbie offers, jumping out of his seat to bound down the deck stairs. A smile tugs at my mouth as I watch him trail behind Mrs. P., following her instructions as he waters wherever she points. The juxtaposition of a sweet elderly lady and a strong young man working together is incredibly endearing, and I rest my chin on my palm as I soak it in. When they disappear around the side of her house, I swat a mosquito out of my face and twist in my chair to soak up more of the calming view.

Robbie eventually comes back, settling into the chair across from me once again.

"She asked me to remind you to stop by to relax and chat on the porch with her later," he says, "which I, for one, think is a fabulous idea."

I huff a smile. "Noted."

"Alright, let's begin our second lesson of Operation Make Naomi a Boss, shall we?" He gives me a crooked smile, a boyish one that I've seen many times over the years but seem to get snagged on now for some reason. "As with every session, tell me one thing you for sure want out of your life."

I twist my mouth to the side, thinking hard. What do I want? "Hmm. Okay, I've got one. I definitely want to travel."

"Alright. Good one." He nods in approval. "Okay, today is all about life rules for you to live by, also known as life standards. I was planning to do a different exercise, but given recent events, this was an emergency change."

I cringe, pushing my lips into a sheepish smile.

"Look, I'm all about you growing your baking business, and I really do hope you keep getting flooded with orders, but I, under no circumstances, want you ending up back in the ER," he says pointedly.

I listen patiently with a complacent nod. This last week has taught me that arguing with him about the subject of my well-being is futile. He took a no-nonsense approach to caring for me while I was sick, despite my attempts to convince him I was fine. I found it to be both annoying and heartwarming at the same time.

"So, we're going to make a list of general rules." He taps his stack of papers on the glass table, looking at me expectantly. I hardly try to hide the lack of enthusiasm on my face.

"Go ahead. Tell me what you're feeling. Excitement or dread?" He chides with another grin.

"Dread," I answer flatly less than a second later, to which he chuckles.

"Too bad. It's for the greater good. Now let's get started. Number one." He writes the number at the top of the page under the title *Naomi's Life Rules* and begins scribbling words as he recites them out loud.

After an hour or so, we've successfully downed an entire pitcher of lemonade and filled both sides of the paper with the ideas that we've come up with.

"This is a pretty good list if I do say so myself." Robbie peruses it. "Should we do a recap?"

"I have a feeling you're going to do one whether I want to or not." I settle back against the seat.

"Number one." he announces, brushing right past my comment. "Set baking hours. You will reserve any baking to be done during these set baking hours: five p.m. to eight-thirty p.m. on weeknights and nine a.m. to three p.m. on the weekends, at least until you are able to transition to full-time hours. In that case, we will reevaluate."

"Yup." I nod in agreement.

"Two. You will not bake past the allotted times except to take your delicious baked goods out of the oven to cool. Three. You will not schedule more orders than what you can easily complete during said baking hours, even if it means turning customers away."

Another nod.

"Four. You will go to bed no later than ten-thirty p.m. on weeknights. Adequate rest needs to be a priority. Five. You will take a five-minute break every forty-five minutes of baking. And to piggyback off that... Number six. You will immediately take a break if you start feeling overwhelmed, stressed, or frazzled. Fresh air and a margarita outdoors will do wonders. Lastly, number seven. You will say no to any order that you do not have the capacity for in any form—logistically as well as mentally."

"Works for me," I agree. As uncomfortable and embarrassed as I am to need to do these little practice sessions in the first place, I'm beginning to see the value in them. I'm determined to make these positive changes to improve my life if it means I'll be taking steps toward fulfilling my dreams. These rules are an important step. I already know that.

"Great. I'll laminate it and stick it to the fridge."

I huff a laugh, not doubting him for a single second. "Wonderful. So, are we done here?"

"Oh, that was just phase one of our session today." The way his mouth curls up into a sly smile immediately makes my stomach uneasy.

"I'm scared to ask what phase two is."

"Phase two is..." He drums his hands on the table. "Bar Bingo at The Squirrely Bear."

"No," I protest, shaking my head vehemently.

"Oh, yes." He nods with a grin.

"But it's Saturday night," I argue. "Everyone will be there."

"That's the point, genius. You'll be my arm candy while the locals whisper about us, and I'll be here for moral support if any of our friends are rude, which some of them most likely will be. We can't ignore them forever. It's time to show up."

"Ugh." I dramatically roll my head to hang all the way off the back of my chair.

"It's one thing to practice confidence with just me, but you also need real-life experience out in the wild."

I stick my tongue out the side of my mouth in disgust.

"Don't look so enthused," he chides. "Your eye roll is slightly insulting. You were fine when we went to dinner, remember?"

"Yes, but our entire group of friends from high school wasn't there to overanalyze our relationship. Not to mention most of the town. If our friends call us out and throw us under the bus, do you know how humiliating that would be? In front of everybody? What if they find out this is all a facade and see it for what it is—a stupid arrangement all because I have no backbone?"

"Well, then we just have to do a good job of convincing them, don't we?" He scoots his chair back. "Come on, go get ready."

"Fine," I grumble, reluctantly taking his hand. "But no karaoke after bingo, okay?"

"Suit yourself." He grins, following behind me into the house. "Meet you back out here in twenty."

CHAPTER FIFTEEN

Naomi

Robbie's hand radiates warmth as he presses it against my lower back, gently leading me to where our friends are taking up the corner table in the back of the dimly lit bar.

"Are you ready?" He winks at me, removing his hand from my back only to interlace his fingers immediately with mine, as if he somehow knows that physical touch is as much a necessity for my nerves as it is for show.

I nod back, gripping tightly.

"Well, well," Toby shouts over his beer when he spots us coming, "if it isn't the lovebirds! You're just in time."

I can feel the warmth of a blush as it spreads across my cheeks, feeling uncomfortable with the attention. I mentally brace myself for the interrogation we're about to get.

"Hey, guys." I wave timidly, trying my best to act casually.

"Thanks for finally making an appearance. Are you done ditching us now? 'Cause I'm not going to lie—it's rude," Charlie says as I slide into a chair across from him. Robbie eases into the one on my left while Gabby, Rachel, Owen, and Luke take up the rest of the table.

"Don't mind him," Luke says, passing us two bingo cards and daubers. "He's just upset that we had to hear about you two from Opal and not directly from your mouths."

"What gives? I thought we were besties?" Charlie chimes in, pouting.

"Yeah, sorry about that," Robbie says calmly. "Like I told you over FaceTime, it happened so gradually that we wanted to wait to say something until we knew for sure what this was before announcing it to the group."

He says it so nonchalantly. I marvel at how easy this facade is for him. Meanwhile, I'm sweating bullets over here.

"And what is it exactly?" Rachel asks, a quizzical look in her eyes.

Robbie and I lock eyes, and I can't help but mirror the smile he flashes. "We're official. She's my girlfriend."

He emphasizes the moment by bringing his hand to my thigh, resting it a little higher than a friend would. If my cheeks weren't blushing before, they certainly are now. The heat of his hand burns through my jeans, sending a warmth straight up my spine.

"Right on," says Luke with a mischievous smile, clearly nothing but happy for us. Gabby, on the other hand, practically drills holes into me, so I dip my head, actively avoiding her stare.

"Good evening, ladies and gentlemen. Welcome to Bar Bingo," Trey, the announcer, says into the microphone from where his table is set up next to the stage. I find my next breath to be easier to take, relieved that the attention can finally shift off Robbie and me. Maybe it's naive of me to hope that'll be enough to appease our friends.

"I'm not buying it," Gabby cuts in sharply, and my gaze snaps back up to meet hers. Her eyes flit between Robbie and me, intensely scrutinizing the both of us while Trey drones on in the background. "You two have been friends forever. You can't tell me it just all of a sudden turned into something more."

Robbie shifts his body ever-so-slightly toward me, his presence feeling solid, giving me a strength that I only feel when he's nearby. I capitalize on that strength to force an assertive tone for once. "Why not?"

"It just...doesn't usually happen like that," she retorts.

"Are you trying to say that friends don't ever turn into lovers?" Charlie asks with a laugh. "Especially in a town as small as ours? Isn't that what all those romance novels you love are filled with?"

He turns to us. "I think it's sweet. I'm happy for you guys."

"Thank you, Charlie." I appreciate his support and silently hope it's enough to quiet Gabby.

"Nope. I'm not buying it." Her sharp words make my stomach twist. *Ugh.* What else could she possibly be looking for?

"The first number is…C23," Trey calls from behind me.

"What do you mean?" I attempt a lighthearted giggle, avoiding Gabby's scrutinizing stare by scanning my bingo card.

"I need proof of relationship," she demands in her signature biting tone that has just enough sweetness to it that no one ever calls her out for it.

"What exactly does 'proof of relationship' mean?" Uneasiness swirls through me. The man's hand is on my thigh. What more could she want?

"A kiss." The dare is clear in her mischievous stare. A challenge. "Plant one on him, and I'll leave it alone."

"Come on, Gabby." I roll my eyes, smirking to cover up the rush of anxiety that just hit. There's no way that's happening right now. I look at Robbie, expecting to find him ready to divert and laugh it off with me, but instead, I find him stoic and void of any humor.

He swallows slowly as his eyes smolder intensely into mine. I freeze in place, momentarily forgetting how to breathe. What in the world is going through his mind? And why isn't he jumping to help me deflect?

"Aw, do it! Kiss. Kiss. Kiss. Kiss."

To my horror, Toby starts chanting, drawing the attention of half the bar to our table. The hairs on my arms rise with a wave of goosebumps and the nerves in my stomach kick in tenfold. I was hoping a potential kissing scenario wouldn't come up until much later on, if at all...and I certainly didn't expect it to come completely out of nowhere like this.

I bite my lip, keeping my focus on Robbie, who doesn't seem at all concerned about anyone else. Only me. My stomach starts to do this weird flippy thing when he tilts forward, inching ever so slowly toward me. He's not really going to kiss me, is he? My eyes stay glued to his, waiting with bated breath to see how on earth he's going to get us out of this one.

"Excitement or dread?" he murmurs, just loud enough for me alone to hear. His question sends a light wave of chills down my arms. I take a deep, steadying breath and focus enough to assess my emotions. If I'm completely honest with myself, the idea of kissing Robbie isn't entirely unappealing. In fact, maybe I am a little curious about what it would be like. With this newfound tension between us...I can't say I'm not somewhat intrigued.

I summon any morsel of bravery I can muster and give him the tiniest dip of my head as permission. Then I hold my breath shakily in my chest as he moves even closer. The warmth of his hand touches me first as it comes to cradle the back of my neck just moments before he presses his lips to mine. Our mouths fit together with an easiness, as if this is something we've been doing our entire lives. Nothing holds me back as my entire body relaxes and I press against him.

Instantly, I'm transported to another world. One where Robbie isn't Robbie, but my doting fiancé. We're on a cross-country pre-wedding road trip, making a point to stop at a different dive bar every night to test out their version of steak nachos and whatever local beer they have on tap. He's passionately kissing me after one of his many declarations of love and promises of a lifetime of adventure together.

Robbie pulls away first, ripping me abruptly from my daydream. As my eyes flutter back open, the heat I find in his eyes causes a rush to swoop low in my belly. He backs away ever so slowly, running his hand lightly down my arm as he does. I'm faintly aware of some whistles coming from the nearby tables, but they're blurry and out of focus.

My body takes longer to catch up than my brain does as I blink wordlessly at him. I feel a little like a giddy schoolgirl as my heart races wildly. Surely from the daydream. That has to be it. With a clearing of my throat, I turn back to our friends, who are all staring at us. My cheeks heat when I notice Gabby has a dumbstruck look on her face, her mouth slightly ajar.

"Okay," she finally says with a nod, shrugging in acceptance. "My bad."

"Are we good?" Robbie asks the table, somehow seeming completely unfazed while I'm still struggling to breathe normally over here. "Can we move on now?"

"Get the next round of beers, and I'll never bring it up again." Toby points at him jovially.

Robbie throws a peanut shell at him. "Don't act like you ever gave a rip."

"G-23," Trey calls out.

I press my dauber in the square, feeling much lighter now that the attention can move away from us. What doesn't go away is how hyperaware I am of his proximity in the chair next to mine and the replay of our kiss that's cycling through my mind on a recurring loop.

As if he's thinking the same, he flicks his eyes to me, a gentle probing in them. His brow quirks up, a way of silently asking if I'm okay. I push my lips together in a simple smile for a response, then focus down on my bingo card while he brings his hand back to my thigh. I don't mind the touch one bit. In fact, it further fuels the anticipation that lingers from his kiss, and I admit that I might be relishing the way it makes me feel.

"B-19," Trey calls.

I can feel Gabby's eyes on Robbie and me for the entire round, a hint of suspicion still left in her stare, until finally Bar Bingo ends, and the group starts lazily chatting while the music resumes from the speakers.

"When did this start again?" Gabby asks, shouting over the table.

"Let it go, Gabby," Robbie retorts. I act on a sudden surge of confidence, wanting nothing more than to stop Gabby in her tracks, by wrapping my arm around his forearm and leaning into his ear.

"Come sing with me." I jump up, pulling him out of his chair to drag him to the karaoke stage.

He doesn't skip a beat, willingly matching my energy with a slick smile as we make our song selection and climb onstage. Being in front of the whole bar is truly the last thing I wanted out of tonight, especially to sing, but I'm finding I don't mind as much in this moment. As always, I'm comfortable as long as Robbie is with me.

As we sing, sharing a microphone and dancing in step with each other, my mind keeps slipping back to the feeling of his lips as they were pressed against mine. Not to mention the flash of a burning heat in his gaze that followed. One that was bold and piercing. And maybe my mind is wandering a bit too much...but I'm left wondering why the whole thing felt monumental in a way. Why it felt like some sort of branding on my soul.

CHAPTER SIXTEEN

Robbie

"Yo, Earth to Robbie."

A wadded-up piece of a cocktail napkin hits me in the center of my forehead, breaking me out of my trance.

"What was that for?" I toss it back to Dane, who's lounging comfortably across from me with an arm thrown over the back of the booth. Soft music thumps around us in the dimly lit hotel bar in Reno. Rylie, our lead singer, is bellied up at the bar while the rest of our bandmates are scattered across the dance floor.

"You're in another world. Either that or you're ignoring me. Both options are rude." He points at me with his beer and then takes a long swig of it.

He's not wrong. I'm nowhere near the present mentally. I've been living right back at The Squirrely Bear with my lips locked on Naomi's. I can't seem to shake it from my mind. That kiss—and the way it affected me—has been consuming every spare second I have. It's entirely too distracting for a kiss that wasn't supposed to be real in the first place. I wonder if this is how Naomi feels when she's daydreaming—completely absorbed and unable to decipher what emotions might be real or not.

As much as I tried to shrug it off initially, I felt something when I was kissing her. Something small, granted, but it was definitely there—something a guy should not be feeling toward his best friend. Add that to the irrational way I reacted when she was sick, and I can confidently say I'm edging toward deep water here.

"How do you think the show went?" Dane asks. "That was our biggest venue yet."

"Best crowd too," I agree with him. The condensation on the whiskey glass makes my fingers slip as I leisurely rotate it in my hand. "It took a second to get used to the acoustics, but overall, that was a banger of a show. We nailed it."

Our manager, Aiden, slides into the booth next to Dane. The two of them start up a conversation—something about the bus schedule—and my mind zones out again, going directly back to Naomi. It's not lost on me that this is, without a doubt, the first time I've ever felt any hint of a longing to be back in Minnesota—solely because that's where Naomi is.

My phone buzzes in my pocket, and I pull it out immediately, pathetically eager to see if it's a text from her. Instead, I see the next best thing: a group message that she's included in.

Charlie: Anyone down for a boat day to-morrow? The weather looks nice!

Toby: I'll bring a cooler.

Naomi: Sure!

I respond immediately after seeing her message come through.

Robbie: I'm in!

If Naomi is going, I'm going.

I pull up my flight information to book the red eye tonight back to Minnesota. While doing so, another text comes through. This time it's from Naomi in our private text thread.

Naomi: I thought you weren't coming home until next week? At least that's when you scheduled our next prac-tice session for on my office calendar. Thanks for using a hot-pink marker, by the way. It totally throws off my whole aesthetic."

> **Robbie:** Change of plans. And you're welcome. What are you doing?

> **Naomi:** Cleaning up the kitchen while waiting for my scones to finish baking.

My thumbs are poised to reply, but her next message beats me to it.

> **Naomi:** Don't worry, my timer's set to go off in four minutes, and then I'm forcing myself to go sit on the dock with a glass of wine.

> **Robbie:** Excellent.

Again, a deep tug inside of me wishes I was right there with her. I do my best to force the urge—and the memory of the kiss—out of my mind as best I can. Regardless of these newfound feelings and my desire to be near her, a sobering reminder pops into my head that convinces me there's no reality where I can let anything come of it. Even on the off chance she did like me back in that way, she lives in the one city I despise the most in this entire country. I can't live there—that won't change. The best I can do is visit for a few days at a time, like I have been, but what kind of relationship would that be?

As long as my family is there, I won't be.

Besides, it's not like I have a stable life settled somewhere else to ask her to join me. I don't see any easy way a real relationship between us would work, and I can't ruin our friendship or risk hurting her in the process of...what? Selfishly acting on my feelings? Nope, this fake relationship will have to be as close as we're going to get.

However, that doesn't mean I can't enjoy every second of pretending while this whole fake-dating situation lasts—as I fully intend to do.

> **Robbie:** Are you okay if I fly home tonight? If so, will you leave the door unlocked for me?

> **Naomi:** Sure. Thanks for asking. See you soon.

I close out my messaging app just as another wadded-up napkin hits me in the face.

"He's been doing this all night," Dane tells Aiden.

"Sorry. I just had to change my flight home. I'm leaving tonight," I tell them.

Dane narrows his eyes at me. "You are aware that we have a gig in three days, right? Why don't you just stay on the bus? You've got to be spending a fortune flying back and forth."

He's not wrong, but that's beside the point. "I've been helping a friend with something," I say simply.

"Well, I don't care what you do as long as you're back and mic'd up by showtime," Aiden says. "I need to ask you guys about booking the Starfield Festival in October. It's a five-day commitment, so I want you to consider carefully before agreeing. They're expecting record crowds, and you'll play on a different stage each night. Are we in?"

I raise my brows at Dane, looking at him to make these kinds of decisions, like I usually do, while I casually sip my whiskey. I'm usually just happy to go wherever they tell me to.

"Heck yeah." He nods enthusiastically with a grin. "We're absolutely in."

"I'm there," I agree. "Sounds like a blast."

"Great. I'll check with the rest of the guys, but in the meantime, I'll put it on the schedule."

They start talking logistics and travel itineraries, which leads my thoughts straight back to kissing Naomi. I sink into the small swarm of butterflies that flutter in my stomach, letting myself enjoy them while I can. Then I throw a twenty down on the table and slide out of the booth.

"I'm off to pack. Stay outta trouble." I give both of them a handshake, and then head off to my room to get ready to fly home to Naomi—for the sake of our fake relationship.

Nothing more.

"Jeez, how much did you put in this thing?" Toby grunts as I help him haul the heavy cooler into the boat from the dock.

"The precise amount to ensure we stay well-hydrated and the vibes stay strong," Charlie replies nonchalantly from the captain's seat, where he's messing with the radio.

Owen helps guide the cooler into the boat and I catch sight of the girls sprawled out on the front platform of Charlie's wakeboarding boat, already soaking up the sun. My chest squeezes in an almost painful way as I zero in on Naomi, the sight of her sucking the breath right out of me.

Toby drops his handle on the cooler, jerking on my arm as it lands with a thud. Toby gives me a long side glance with a knowing smirk, following the direction of my gaze with his own eyes.

Sure, he thinks he knows what he's seeing. But what he doesn't realize is that I'm not a man staring longingly at his girlfriend, as it looks on the surface. Instead, I'm a distracted man trying with all his might to turn off developing feelings for a platonic friend—one who he happens to be inconveniently fake dating.

It's complicated.

"And we're off." Charlie gives me a nod as I give us a strong push off the dock post at the public landing, taking us out onto the water of Gull Lake.

As the boat works its way smoothly over a few waves, I sink into the vinyl seat next to Luke in the back. I twist my baseball cap backward to avoid it flying off as Charlie shifts into gear, turning the radio up at the same time.

The sun is hot as it beams down on us, already causing a sheen of sweat to surface across my skin. The girls in the front of the boat sit up to better brace themselves against the waves as we start a cruise around the perimeter of the lake.

Gull Lake is located in a neighboring city to Pine Falls It's one that we've come to countless times—although not for a few years for me—and the route he takes on our cruise is a familiar one. Not much seems to have changed, from the wide array of cabins and resorts tucked between long stretches of lush trees, to the restaurants scattered between the shoreline and sandy beaches. All of it holds a rustic beauty I don't often see in my travels out of state.

I admit, this is nice.

My attention immediately goes to Naomi at the first minuscule movement she makes, watching from behind my sunglasses, my heart pounding, as she climbs toward the back of the boat to grab a water bottle from the cooler.

"Naomi, can you grab me a seltzer?" Gabby practically shouts at her. I don't like her tone, but I keep my mouth shut.

It's not the fact that she asked for a drink, but more the way she said it—she's too bossy for her own good sometimes.

Naomi, being the nice—yet sometimes too accommodating—friend that she is, complies, digging all the way to the bottom of the cooler. After she passes it up to Gabby, she grabs the container of cookies she made this morning.

"Cookie?" She passes them around to our enthusiastic friends, myself included, before putting them away and coming toward the back of the boat. I practically shove Luke and Toby over with my elbows, patting the seat next to me. The skim of her arm against mine as she settles sends a rush of something exhilarating straight through my veins—a spark of sorts.

With a smile, I eagerly curl my arm around her, fully relishing the freedom of how I'm able to act with her in front of an audience. There's no overthinking, no worrying about my inconvenient feelings and what I should or should not be doing with those said feelings. Today I'm free to fully enjoy a taste of what it would be like to be with her for real. And I plan to take full advantage of that.

To my absolute delight, she nestles comfortably into my side, our bare skin rubbing against each other, tinging it with a heat I'm positive isn't from the sun.

I force my gaze on the homes nestled along the shore, concentrating on admiring the landscape instead of the way her bare shoulder feels under my fingertips, which threatens to become all-consuming. The urge to be even closer than we already are is almost overwhelming—a force I have to taper back.

While our friends sing along and enjoy the music, I zone out, allowing myself a brief moment to admire the strong column of her neck and the way a blonde wisp of hair that fell out of her ponytail swirls in the wind, crashing repeatedly against her skin.

When the hair sticks to the place just under her ear, I dare to slowly move it out of the way with my fingertips. She stiffens slightly under my touch, but once the moment of surprise passes, I swear she almost leans into me. Before I know it, I'm suddenly leaning in to place a chaste kiss right in the same spot. For show, right? This is what an adoring boyfriend would do—and one thousand percent what I would do if this were real.

I zero in on her reaction again. I'm familiar with her enough to know that she isn't tense or wanting to move away at my closeness. There's no sign of her being uncomfortable and I can even feel the slightest shiver against my lips.

"Gross," Gabby shouts over the music.

"What's her problem?" I mutter against Naomi's skin before pulling back.

I may not be able to see behind her sunglasses to gauge the look in her eyes, but what I can see is the small way her mouth twists up in a whisper of a smile, the way she hides it by rolling her lips.

She's not bothered.

And I thoroughly enjoy that fact.

"Get a room," Charlie chides. I chuckle at the blush that creeps across Naomi's cheek and squeeze her shoulder playfully.

"Sand volleyball, anyone?" he asks, steering us toward the northeastern side of the lake toward one of our favorite hangouts in high school—Sunny's on the Lake.

"Oh, it's on." Luke rubs his hands together.

"Do you still leave the court with your swim trunks full of sand?" I tease. "Or has your agility improved in the last couple years?"

"Ha-ha." He shoves my arm. "Keep running your mouth. While you've been gallivanting around, being some kind of rock star, I've been practicing my volleyball skills. I've got moves now you wouldn't believe."

"It's true." Toby laughs. "He's actually pretty good."

"I'll believe it when I see it," I say, getting up to help grab the dock posts as we ease next to it. The girls grab their beach bags while the guys tie the boat securely. Then one by one, everyone else climbs out of the boat.

I hold out a hand for Naomi, who's the last to step onto the dock. I motion for her to wait so we can fall back from the rest of the group.

"I hope that was alright...the kiss," I whisper quietly, feeling nerves rise in my stomach that I don't typically feel around women but that I'm finding are creeping up more and more when I'm near her.

She shrugs with a cheeky smile. "I suppose it's necessary to do unappealing things like that."

"Glowing review. Thank you."

"Try harder next time." She beams, a hint of a dare flashing along with her smile.

I reach for her hand, relishing how her fingers feel wrapped between mine, and we head off the dock to join our friends

CHAPTER SEVENTEEN

Naomi

I let Robbie lead me across the sandy court to the outdoor patio of Sunny's. Just past the group of umbrella-clad tables and under the neon-yellow sign is a door that leads to the inside dining area and bar. Sunny's on the Lake is widely known as the best place for tacos within the tri-city area—something we've taken advantage of more times than I can count.

As we climb the creaky wooden stairs toward the table our friends have already claimed, I tighten my grip on Robbie's hand and let my mind drift. What if we actually gave in to this newfound chemistry between us, and this whole thing wasn't fake? What if he wasn't just holding my hand to prove a point but instead because he wanted to? What if we really were two friends who happened to fall in love?

My mind slips easily into a daydream, imagining that, in another universe, we were dragged here by our friends for a surprise engagement party inside the bar, where everyone we know is hiding in the corners to jump out and congratulate us. They will, of course, gush over the sweet and intimate proposal that Robbie executed, complete with a heart-shaped flower display in the middle of the bridge overlooking the river. We told everyone of the engagement immediately—all the details except for our secret plan to run away and elope in Vegas before spending a solid three weeks on a houseboat on Lake Tahoe for a honeymoon.

"First round is on me," Toby announces. His voice brings me back to reality, where I'm, in fact, not engaged to the love of my life, but am, instead, pathetically pretending to be attached to my friend. Clearly, I'm allowing this facade to mess with me as the lines between reality and pretenc are getting much too blurry.

The tension that had been slowly building after my illness seems to have only been further cemented after our kiss at The Squirrely Bear. I've been living in this continuous limbo state, not knowing what any of it means or what he's thinking. My mind has been absolutely swirling with possibilities, and if I'm honest, it's getting a bit exhausting.

"Thank you," I say to Toby as I grab a spicy margarita from the tray he sets on the table.

Wasting no time, Charlie bounds down the stairs heading toward one of the sand courts near the lake. "Boys vs. girls. Who's ready to get demolished?"

Luke hops over the side railing, falling to the sand while the rest of us file down the stairs.

"Good luck." Robbie winks at me before jogging to the opposite side of the court.

"For what it's worth"—Rachel nudges my arm with her elbow—"I think you guys are adorable together."

"Thanks, Rach." A slow smile tugs at my lips as I watch the guys perform a ridiculous team handshake to pump themselves up. "It definitely wasn't expected."

"Sometimes the best things aren't," she says before taking her place at center court. For the next half-hour, we play a rowdy game of volleyball, getting sufficiently coated with sand. It ends with the girls beating the boys by one point, much to my delight.

"I still think you cheated," Charlie accuses as we head back to our table, each one of us sufficiently out of breath and sticky hot from playing in this heat.

"Because that's the only way girls can beat you?" Rachel challenges.

"He's just a sore loser. You are absolutely the alpha sex," Owen says through staggered breaths.

"Especially after a few too many drinks," Toby says, patting his stomach.

"I need to use the ladies' room. I'll be right back," I say to the group as I pass by our table. I've only made it about two steps when Gabby interrupts me.

"Hey, on your way back, can you grab me another margarita?"

I slow, stopping in my tracks completely. The old me would have said yes immediately, but I feel a small wave of resistance to giving in. Still, my throat feels stuck, and I can't quite force the words out. I glance over at Robbie for moral support.

His eyes are already on mine, and he eagerly gives a tiny nod of encouragement. Apparently that's all it takes to stand a little straighter and look Gabby dead in the eyes, the resolve within me growing stronger.

"Why don't you come with me?" I suggest, my voice calm and direct. "We can get the next round together."

I don't miss the flash of surprise in her eyes, but it's quickly covered by an obnoxious eye roll as she reluctantly stands to follow me.

"Whatever," she grumbles under her breath.

A surge of pride rushes through me as we walk inside. I know, without even looking, that Robbie is also watching me with the same look of pride. Once inside, Gabby heads straight for the bar without so much as a word in my direction.

I meet her there after freshening up in the restroom, passing by the dart board and pinball machine on the way.

"Got 'em ordered?" I ask, leaning over the bar top next to her. I make a point to have a friendly tone. Just because I'm learning to set boundaries doesn't mean I need to lose my ability to be nice. I can be a respectful person who also has limits.

"Yup." The annoyance in her tone isn't lost on me. "You can carry it out."

She's almost all the way to the door before I have a chance to respond. So much for being friendly. I watch the bartenders as they work, feeling more defeated by the second. This is exactly why I don't want to ruffle any feathers and why I always say yes to people.

I hate seeing anyone upset—especially at me.

With a sigh, I grab the tray of margaritas and head back outside, pushing the door open with my hip.

"Round two, anyone? I need to redeem myself," Charlie calls, already bolting to the courts. I slide the tray carefully onto the table while smirking at him.

"I'm out this round." I wave them off, watching the rest of the group follow behind him. Robbie's the only one who stays in one place, leaving us alone again.

"This seat's open," he says, patting the top of his knee. I suppose we are within eyesight of the group. I assume that's the sole motivation for the invitation, but it doesn't stop my stomach from swooping all the same.

I slide sideways onto his lap, zeroing in on his hand that immediately wraps around my waist. I'm slightly embarrassed to admit that my first thought is wondering what I can do to convince him to kiss that spot under my ear again. The sheer memory of it sends a shiver straight down my spine.

"Nice job standing up to Gabby," he murmurs quietly.

"Yeah...except now she's mad at me," I grumble.

"Let her be." He shrugs, tightening his grip. "You're not responsible for her emotions."

I sit with his words, allowing them to comfort me the same way his touch does as his hand slides across my hip. Before I can get too distracted by his touch, my phone trills with a message notification from inside my boat bag.

"It's from my mom," I tell Robbie as I skim the message. "She invited us to dinner tomorrow night. We don't have to—"

"Let's go," he says instantly.

"Really?"

"Absolutely. My flight out is the morning after tomorrow, so that's perfect timing."

"You know my dad will be insufferable," I point out, hoping I can somehow get him to be on the same page as me and we can avoid going at all.

"We can handle him...together," he says close to my ear. The confidence in his voice sends a surge of something exciting to my core. Whether it's a rush of courage or something more like attraction, I'm not so sure anymore. I'm finding at this point, I don't really care. Either way, it's something I'm enjoying.

"Alright," I say hesitantly, still not convinced he understands what a dinner with my dad entails. "If you're sure?"

"I'm sure," he says firmly.

"The girls beat us again," Owen announces, bounding back up the stairs.

"That's because we suck," Robbie says, handing him a margarita.

"I don't know about you guys, but I worked up a sweat," Charlie says when everyone is back at the table. "Let's go anchor at the sand bar and swim for a bit. What do you guys think?"

"Yes!" Rachel agrees enthusiastically.

Robbie's hand grips my hip to guide me reluctantly off his lap, and I immediately feel the absence of his touch when we part. Greedily, I put on my best doting-girlfriend act and grab his arm by the elbow, attaching myself securely to him as we walk through the sand back to the boat.

Pushing the looming thoughts of dinner with my parents out of my head, I decide to make the most out of today, soaking up as much of the sunshine and these stolen moments with Robbie while I can.

CHAPTER EIGHTEEN

Robbie

"Do you think they'll notice if I steal one of these muffins?" I carefully set the last freshly baked banana nut muffin inside the pastel-pink bakery box that has the *Naomi's Nummy Bakery* logo printed on the top right portion, right above the window. The rest of the boxes she ordered last week are stacked neatly on the corner of her countertop with an extra shipment of them tucked away in her office.

"Uh, yeah," she retorts with a chuckle from the sink. "Seeing as they ordered eight of them, I would imagine they won't be happy if I deliver the box with only seven."

"Rats." I pause before trying another angle. "You know what I was thinking? I don't know why I didn't negotiate this into our plan details, but I think I deserve payment for being your fake boyfriend. These long, tedious hours of acting are starting to get to me."

"Is that so?" Her tone is unbothered as she scrubs dishes.

"It's just so physically and emotionally taxing—"

"I saved you an extra muffin," she cuts in, pointing to a lone one tucked behind her recipe book next to the refrigerator.

"Oh, sweet. Never mind, I'm good." I grab and bite into the still-warm muffin. I let out a hum of approval as I manually key in the customer order on the spreadsheet from her computer. "So should we do some practicing before we head to your parents'?"

She lets out a long dramatic sigh while drying her hands on a towel.

"I'm going to assume that displeasure is in reference to dinner tonight and not my practice sessions."

"As much as I truly love your ideas, we're running out of time. I still need to change," she says as she checks her watch.

"No worries. I'll just shout to you from out here," I offer, following her out of the kitchen.

"Is that really necessary?"

"Yes. I want you to feel confident going into tonight. Go ahead, get ready." I shoo her into the bedroom while I head for my backpack that I've been storing in her office. I pull out my black button-up shirt—the fanciest option I have—before taking the T-shirt off my back to stuff inside.

"Are we going to be strong and assertive tonight?" I call out, loud enough so she can hear me from the other side of the house.

"Yes." Her muffled voice is weak behind the cracked open door of her bedroom.

"Are we going to let your dad walk all over us?"

"No."

"Louder." I cross the room to the couch to sit, pulling some socks on.

"NO!" The rise in her aggression could either be toward the exercise or directed at me. I'm honestly okay with either in this situation.

"Are we going to speak up if we're not shown the bare minimum amount of respect?"

"Yes."

She comes out just as I'm stuffing a stray sweatshirt I found along the back of the couch into my backpack.

"I saw that," she laughs, just as I toss the bag back into the office. Then she gestures at the living room while I struggle to maintain focus on anything other than the way she locks. "For real, though, it looks nice in here, Robbie. Thanks for keeping your mess somewhat contained."

I open my mouth to reply with a witty remark, but I'm too distracted by the sudden effect she had on me when she came into view. The way she looks in that sapphire-blue babycoll sundress and the way her wavy blonde hair cascades over her shoulders makes it suddenly hard to think straight. Man, I must have been blind to have never truly appreciated how stunning she is before. I am a very stupid man.

Blind and stupid.

"It's one of my attributes—I'm fully trainable," I mumble quietly as my mouth goes drier with each slow step she takes toward me.

"You look nice," I tell her, raking my gaze over every inch of her.

"So do you," she says when she comes to a stop mere inches from me. Her voice is just above a whisper, and the breathiness of it sends a shiver across my skin. I didn't realize I'd gotten to a point where her voice alone has this effect on me, but here we are.

Her hand reaches out to smooth a wrinkle on the bottom of my shirt, and I'm suddenly desperately wishing some-one—anyone—were here so I would have an excuse to lean in and kiss her. Or hug her. Or, heck, I'd settle for a squeeze of her hand.

I roll my lips together as her eyes rise to meet mine, and I zero in on the way her own breath seems to catch. Is she affected by our closeness too? Is she having as much trouble breathing as I am? The thought alone makes my heartbeat go wild.

The moment her eyes meet mine she clears her throat, zapping us both out of the moment.

"Are you ready?" she asks, backing away slowly.

"After you," I reply, eager to get to the fake-dating portion of the night so I can finally touch her skin like I'm desperate to do. I don't even mind that we'll be around her insufferable dad if it means I'll get to feel her under my fingertips.

"Oh, hold on. I forgot one thing." She rushes back into her room and emerges a few seconds later with a bright-yellow headband atop her head. I wink my approval and follow her outside.

The drive to her parents' house is spent in complete silence. While I assume she might be mentally preparing herself for the upcoming interaction with her dad, I'm focusing every last bit of my own energy on not opening my mouth. Because I know if I do, all my thoughts and feelings that are sitting right on the surface could come spilling out, and I won't be able to take them back—which could alter our friendship forever.

I can't risk that.

"How are you feeling?" I finally say once we come to a stop in front of her parents' house and pause for a moment on the sidewalk.

"Resigned," she admits with a small smile. "And a little guilty for bringing you into this."

"Don't worry about me," I assure her, taking a step closer.

"I know, but I do." Her head tilts shyly and the tip of her shoulder lifts in a shrug. "My dad can be a lot."

"Nothing we can't handle, remember?"

"I know, but this is it, Robbie. This dinner." Her eyes grow serious, a subtle panic starting to simmer behind them. "This is why we're doing this whole thing in the first place, right? So I can stand up to him. That's a lot of pressure."

"Hey, don't stress." I run my hand down the side of her arm. "It's still early in our process, okay? Think of this as a stepping stone."

She gives an unconvincing nod.

"Do you want to knock out some jumping jacks to get the nerves out?" I offer.

A laugh flies out of her mouth. "Not in this dress."

"Fair enough." I reach out my hand, holding her stare. "Shall we?"

She slips her hand into mine, and immediately it feels like a small piece of my world has shifted into place. A correction on some level. I can't explain it...but it feels right.

Pushing aside the implications of what that means, I squeeze her hand and follow her inside the house.

"Knock, knock," Naomi calls just as her mom rounds the corner to greet us.

"Hello, sweetheart," she says lovingly, wrapping Naomi in a hug.

"Mrs. Tillman." I hold my hand out, which she shakes enthusiastically.

"Robbie." She opens her mouth to say more, but Naomi's dad strolls in. Her mom instinctively shrinks against the wall, her head dipping ever-so-slightly to her chin. I imagine that's what Naomi is used to doing too. Admittedly, the air does get sucked out of the room with his boasting presence taking up all the space. I almost succumb to it myself.

"Robert." He holds out a hand in greeting.

"Actually, it's Robbie," I correct politely.

A smirk pulls at his face, and I can feel every inch of his gaze as it scans the length of my body. Noting the absence of an Armani suit, I'm sure. As intimidating as he was in the dealership, he's even more intense here now that we're on his own turf. I force down a shiver, refusing to be affected by him. I have a job to do tonight—and that is to be strong for Naomi.

"Marion, get Robert a glass of wine, please," he says. It's only then that he releases my hand.

She doesn't hesitate, scurrying off into the kitchen as I place a hand on Naomi's lower back, staying close behind as she leads us into the formal dining room.

"Thank you," I tell Marion as she hands both Naomi and me a glass of red wine. She only smiles, giving a dip of her head before retreating quietly to the chair next to her husband. A wave of pity runs through me as I slide into the seat next to Naomi.

"It smells delicious in here," Naomi says, filling the awkward silence with something other than tension.

"Your mother made chicken parmesan with roasted garlic potatoes and spicy green beans."

I'm guessing speaking for other people is standard for him too.

"Thanks for cooking, Mom." Naomi directs her words to Marion, her voice strong and assertive. I know that takes effort, so I slide an arm around the back of her chair, a silent show of support.

Marion beams, smiling to herself as she starts passing platters of food.

"So, Robert, your brother is a doctor, correct?" His question hangs heavy in the air.

I immediately freeze in place, my stomach dropping with the weight of sudden tension. Here it comes: the inevitable comparison that always happens. Heat inundates my core, spreading out in every direction, despite how much I try to repress it. I didn't prepare myself for this particular topic tonight—not even a little bit. I naively assumed we would be focusing mostly on Naomi while we are here.

"He is," I answer curtly, abruptly bringing my arm off her chair and back to my lap. From here I can roll my hands into balls to focus my energy somewhere tangible to release some tension.

Feeling caught off guard, I fight the urge to go cold, but I'm afraid I don't do a very good job. My muscles feel rigid, cementing me to my chair.

"Your parents must be proud."

It's either a wildly ironic choice of words, or he somehow knows exactly how to push my most sensitive button. My jaw tenses, and I look down, unable to focus on anything except the restless energy threatening to explode within my chest.

"Oh, Dad, I forgot to tell you," Naomi cuts in, changing the subject. "When I saw Linda at the grocery store the other day, she absolutely raved about her new Jeep. You can add another happy customer for Tillman Motors to your list."

Her soft voice brings me out of the haze I'm in, just enough to notice her hand when it comes across to rest on my knee.

Her thumb slides across the fabric of my jeans, a soft motion that I zero in on.

"I can't say I'm surprised," he boasts, effectively following Naomi's redirection. "No dealership within a fifty-mile radius offers the selection we do."

"That's right." Marion encourages him with a light tap on his forearm.

While he rambles on and on about how amazing his dealership is, I tune him out, focusing intently on the way her hand feels on my leg. Not to mention the way my discomfort dissipates with every soft stroke of her thumb.

Chapter Nineteen

Naomi

"So, Robert, should we expect to see you at the second dealership grand opening?" Dad asks before taking a bite of his food.

"His name is Robbie, Dad." It's only after the words leave my mouth that I clamp it shut, realizing how forward it was of me to say them. An anxious heat blooms in my chest while I look down at my plate, feeling uncomfortable with my show of authority.

Yet, even through the sudden shame, I keep my hand placed firmly on Robbie's knee. I cemented it there when I noticed him starting to struggle under Dad's pressure, feeling an overwhelming need to make sure he was okay. I haven't brought myself to let go yet.

Out of the corner of my eye, I can feel my dad's stern glare fixed on me, assessing my boldness, before he redirects it to Robbie.

"If it's all the same to you, I prefer Robert," Dad says flatly. "It's more sophisticated."

"That's fine," Robbie cuts in, his voice steadier and more familiar than a few moments ago. "And yes, I wouldn't miss it. It sounds like quite the event."

"Mom, did I tell you about the side business I've started?" I ask, making a point to include her in the conversation. I always feel bad for the way he talks over her—the same way he's always done to me.

"No, you didn't. But that's wonderful, dear. Tell us more about that. What are you doing?" she asks with an eager gaze.

"It's a baking business. People are actually paying me to bake for them." The look of pride that blooms on her face makes a rush of soothing warmth run through me.

"This hobby of yours..." my dad cuts in. "Are you keeping track of your expenses?"

His tone clearly displays his lack of confidence in my business sense, but at least he's not admonishing me for doing something outside of the dealership.

"Of course."

"And you're allocating for taxes?"

"Yes." Again, his stare feels heavy, and I almost crack under the pressure, feeling my resolve wobbling at the edges.

"She makes the best apple cinnamon muffins I've ever tasted," Robbie boasts.

"That's lovely, Naomi," Mom says. "We're so proud of you, honey."

The look on my dad's face makes that remark questionable, but I do my best to focus on the praise coming from mom instead.

"Can we do anything to help clean up?" I ask once I know they would consider it to be an appropriate time to excuse ourselves.

"Absolutely not," Mom says, dismissing me as we all stand. "It'll give me something to do tonight."

"I'm sure I'll see you around, Robert," my dad says in a cutting tone when we reach the front door, offering what anyone would deem a little too much strength for a farewell handshake.

"I'm looking forward to it." I can see that Robbie matches his energy from the corner of my eye while I give Mom a hug.

"We'll talk soon," I say to her with a smile.

As we head down the sidewalk, my parents' stares practically burning holes in our backs, Robbie offers me the crook of his arm in a show of support. I slide my hand down the length of his inner forearm slowly, savoring the steady comfort it brings—and the quiet hum it sends down my core.

As my fingertips graze the softness of his skin, I wonder what it would be like if this were real life. If I weren't walking away from my parents' house with a friend-slash-fake-boyfriend but, instead, hand in hand with someone who adores me as much as I do him. Someone who sees me on every level, cherishing me in a way that no one has before.

Except, this time...the image isn't far-fetched and make-believe.

I can actually see it.

A life with him.

A life where he's actually falling for me the same way I admittedly am for him. Robbie and me. The timid, small-town girl and the confident, unrestrained musician she has always trusted more than anyone else.

I can see a reality where it makes sense.

And that realization makes my mouth go impossibly dry. As soon as we're out of my parents' line of sight, I let go of his arm, suddenly unsure of what lines aren't supposed to be crossed and when. We're out of eyesight, so technically I'm not supposed to be touching him anymore, but my body tells me that I most definitely want to.

Is he feeling this too? I have no idea where his head is at, if it's as much a jumbled mess as mine is.

"That wasn't so bad, huh?" he asks once we start the drive home. I roll down my window and stick my arm out, letting it lazily cut through the humid air while I let the wind ground me all the way back to reality.

"It was just another day for me." I rest my head against the headrest. "You tell me how it went for you. I'm sorry he brought up your family."

He gives me a sidelong glance. "Yeah, he definitely isn't going to win my *favorite person of the year award,* but it was good to see what a normal family dinner is like for you."

We let the quiet settle between us as we drive slowly through town.

"Out of curiosity, who won your *favorite person of the year award* last year?" I tip my head toward him, keeping my back pressed against the seat.

"Harrison Ford," he answers immediately.

I let out a laugh. "I wasn't expecting that. Can I ask why?"

"*Indiana Jones*, duh."

"Those movies were from, like, a million years ago."

"Badassery doesn't age, Naomi."

"Okay," I chuckle as we turn into my driveway.

"Don't get out. I'll get your door." He's rounding the front of my car before I've even unbuckled my seatbelt.

"Thank you," I say sweetly, grabbing his outstretched hand to climb out. His hand brushes the lower curve of my spine, and for a moment, I involuntarily gravitate closer to him as I slowly brush past. In the next moment, I notice Mrs. Pelinski sitting on her front porch, and a surge of disappointment hits me.

So that explains why he opened my door and offered his hand.

"Hi, Mrs. P.," I call across the yard. With a crossword puzzle in hand, she barely looks up but gives a distracted wave anyway.

"Do you want to sit out on the dock with me?" Robbie asks from somewhere close behind my shoulder as we walk inside the house—as if my answer would be anything other than yes. The idea of spending a quiet night on my dock with him sends a soothing wave over me, tinged with a flurry of excitement.

"Sure. I'll get the tequila," I offer.

We part ways in my kitchen as I grab two glasses and a bottle while he unlocks the deck door. When I meet him there, he takes the glasses from my hands, and we venture down the grassy slope of my backyard to the long dock. I follow him onto it, the wooden boards creaking under our steps. The sky above the line of trees across the lake is painted by the sunset. Splatters of bubble gum-pink and fire orange swirl together, making the colors dance in the sky.

"Which side of the bench has the best view?" Robbie asks when we reach the last section of the dock.

I snort. "They literally have the same view. But maybe this left side? You can't see the obnoxious inflatable gymnasium in front of Sneed's dock in your peripheral vision from here."

He looks over at the inflatable in question while dropping onto the right side of the bench, of course leaving me the side with the best view. "Serve me enough of this tequila and I might go jump on that thing."

I bite a giggle back while he pours us both a small glass, handing one of them to me.

"Cheers," he says quietly, growing serious. He holds my gaze for a few charged beats, and I momentarily get lost in his eyes, feeling glued to them, unable to look away.

"Cheers," I whisper before taking a small sip, the liquid burning my throat. I break our stare and wonder where his mind is at right this very minute. What he's thinking about as he sits here on the dock with me, and wishing desperately I could read his mind.

"Isn't it beautiful out here?" I sigh, relaxing against the back of the bench. Its sharp edges cut into my shoulder blades a little too roughly, but I don't mind. There's nowhere else I'd rather be right now.

"Stunning," he agrees, setting the bottle of tequila on the wooden boards by our feet. I don't miss how, when he straightens, he slides a breath closer to me, enough so that our arms lightly brush against each other.

"Does stuff like this ever make you want to stay in Pine Falls?" I ask quietly, nerves twisting my stomach as I wait for what his response will be. "Nights like this?"

"Not the scenery, necessarily...but being with you does." He doesn't put any emphasis or emotion behind his words. Nor does he elaborate. It's simply a statement that leaves my mind whirling in a million different directions.

"Yeah?" I murmur, daring a tilt of my head to meet his stare. There's a simmering edge to his green eyes as he rolls his lips, pushing them together with force.

He gives a timid nod before cutting the moment with a sip of his drink. I clear my throat and look back out at a loon that just dipped below the water. Its movement causes a ripple of waves to disperse around him, the reflection of the sunset moving along with it. I focus on the lake instead of Robbie, not quite sure what to make of this energy between us and certainly not confident enough to sway the trajectory of our conversation.

"Do you ever use that swing back there?" he asks out of nowhere.

I arch my neck to peer back toward my house. There's a tree swing that consists of an old wooden slab that has two long ropes attached to the towering oak tree on the right side of my property. It sways quietly with the wind, as if a reply of its own to his question.

"That old thing?" My mouth tips up with a smile. "No. That was there when I moved in. It's probably not sturdy enough to hold anybody."

When I twist back, he's already standing with an outstretched hand. "Come on. I'll push you."

His stare holds the same amount of smolder as earlier, but now it also holds the weight of a quiet dare. Somehow, it feels like more than just a dare to test the swing.

Either way, nothing holds me back from slipping my hand immediately in his. He holds my hand low behind his back while he leads me off the dock slowly. All the while, I bite the corner of my lip to keep from letting my smile grow too big. I don't dare let my mind wander into a daydream. This moment with him requires as much clarity as I can muster.

"Are you going to test it for me?" I ask.

"Oh, that definitely won't hold me." He pushes down to test the swing then holds the two ropes steady. "But you'll be fine. I'll catch you if you fall."

The night sky is fully dark now, hopefully concealing the blush on my cheeks as I lower onto the board. I let out a whisper of a squeal when he gently pulls back on the ropes and guides them forward, sending me swaying under the tree branch. The wind brushes against my cheeks as I soar in the night sky, the lake barely visible in front of me. Robbie's steady hands meet me at every downswing, gently pushing me forward again.

Swinging back and forth like this, I feel carefree and exhilarated. A rush of adrenaline surges through me, making even my fingertips feel electric. I haven't had this much fun in my own backyard in...I don't even know how long.

He eventually slows the swing to a stop, but when it stills, he doesn't back away. His steady frame stands firm against my back like a concrete wall, and I swallow hard as I attempt to compose myself. Blood pumps through my veins from still-surging adrenaline, and then a shiver runs down my spine at the feel of his breath on the back of my shoulder.

Words sit at the tip of my tongue...so many questions that need to be asked. Feelings that need to be clarified. But I'm also hyperaware that there's an anticipation in this moment that feels delicate. Fleeting. Like it could all be blown away with the wind at the sound of either of our voices. Instead, I hold my breath, not feeling brave enough to turn around and face him.

The water softly lapping onto shore is the only sound other than the crickets chirping somewhere in front of me. My grip on the ropes tightens when I feel his hand slowly touch my chin. He gently hooks his finger and tilts my face backward in his direction.

The pounding of my heart only intensifies when I follow his guiding hand and meet his stare, which smolders intensely into mine. A million thoughts run through my head as he ever so slowly moves forward.

Is he going to kiss me? He feels this too, right? Is this only for pretend? For show?

His mouth is barely an inch from mine when suddenly I'm desperate to know the truth.

"Is this for Mrs. P.?" I whisper against his lips, asking the question that holds so much weight. "Is she watching?"

His eyes flick to mine with intensity, as if he's silently probing for an answer—perhaps to the same question I asked him. His brows crease, as if he's debating the right move, the path he wants to take in this moment.

"No," he says gruffly with a slight shake of his head. I ponder his answer while he hovers, his proximity making me feel lightheaded and exhilarated in the most overwhelming way.

"What do you want, Naomi?" he whispers quietly. His question brings a smile to my lips, despite the intensity of the moment. Because for once, I know exactly what I want.

"You," I simply say, a mere millisecond before he crashes his mouth to mine. I squeeze the ropes as he slides his hand to cradle my jaw. Just like our brief kiss in the bar, my heart flutters, and my stomach swoons as I mold my lips to his. Except, this time, there's an honesty in the way he kisses me, a gentleness that nearly brings tears to my eyes. I can taste the faintest hint of tequila as he deepens the kiss, and when he curls his fingertips along my jaw, it sends a shiver across my already hypersensitive skin.

When he pulls away, my next breath is bated, as if I've forgotten how to breathe. I blink a few times, taking it all in.

"What was that for?" I ask carefully, my voice weak as I lean against one of the ropes, keeping my eyes on him as he hovers close.

"Honestly?" He rolls his lips. "I've been obsessing over kissing you since that pathetic attempt at The Squirrely Bear."

There goes my breath again.

"For real?" I manage to squeak out.

"For real, for real," he says calmly with a smirk.

"What does that mean, exactly?" My heart pounds wildly in my chest.

"That it's starting to feel like the only pretending I'm doing is being your friend," he whispers.

His words warm a place in my chest, sending a rush of butterflies swarming low in my belly.

"For me too." I nod, unable to stop a bashful smirk from pulling at the corner of my mouth.

"I do have that effect," he says with a wink. Then he blanches when my fist connects with his stomach.

With a laugh, I straighten on the swing as Robbie pulls it back, holding it steady before letting go. I fly through the night air, pumping my legs slowly. As I listen to the crickets chirping, I can't help but let my mind wonder what our shared confession means now that we've spoken it out loud. And what it all means for us going forward.

Chapter Twenty

Robbie

"Tell me one thing you want out of life," I say as we come to a stop at the corner of Main Street and Bingham Lane. Once again, it hasn't even been a full day since my last gig, and here I am, already back in Pine Falls. This evolving connection with Naomi has been a powerful force that pulls on me as soon as I leave. A gnawing in my gut that doesn't go away until I'm able to see her again. A force that's almost starting to rival my aversion to this place.

Almost.

"Um." She pushes her lips together while she thinks, tapping her finger on her chin. I savor the opportunity to unabashedly roam my eyes over every last inch of her, starting with her hair that's adorably pulled back into two low pigtail twists. Then I note small details, like her square-shaped sunglasses that sit on the bridge of her nose, the sparkling star earrings that dangle from her ears, and the tan crossbody purse she has draped over a pair of jean short overalls.

But what keeps snagging my attention is the way her lips have a slight sheen from the Chapstick she applied on the drive over here, which inevitably brings me right back to the other night in her backyard. I can't stop thinking about how compulsive it felt to lean in and kiss her—like it was inevitable and absolutely necessary in that moment. A need that was as vital as my next breath.

"I want to have a good work-life balance," she states proudly, pulling my attention back up. "I want to always make sure I can carve out time for hobbies and adventure while still running a successful business."

"I like it. Okay, let's begin our next lesson for Operation Make Naomi a Boss."

I continue on, smiling when she rolls her eyes at the name. "Today is all about building confidence in marketing your business."

"Alright. Give it to me." She rubs her palms together, readying herself.

I pull the stack of freshly printed business cards out of my pocket.

"Oh." Her brows lift in surprise when she spots them. "I was planning on putting those in the delivery boxes."

"You have to be proactive with your marketing if you want to be successful, right? That means putting yourself out there. I left some at home for the delivery boxes too, but I snagged some for today."

"Okay." She visibly deflates, her confidence slumping at the task. I turn my attention on the sidewalk to pick out a target before she loses all of it.

"There's Mrs. Libman." I point across the street to where she is browsing the curbside selection at the antique shop.

"Go give her your business card and talk yourself up," I encourage Naomi.

She blows out a breath and takes a business card from the pile. I bite back a laugh when she does a few lip buzzes without me even prompting her to.

"Are you loose enough?"

There's a small hint of annoyance detectable in her expression, but she still shimmies her arms out at her sides, loosening her limbs.

"Don't pretend like these warmups don't help," I chide.

"I feel like a child," she retorts. After stretching her neck to both sides, she walks off, straightening her shoulders.

I lean against the lamp post as I keep my eyes trained on her.

The confidence in Naomi's stance slightly wavers as she approaches Mrs. Libman, her fingers visibly twitching with nerves, enough for me to see all the way over here. But once the card is handed off and a smile grows on both of their faces, Naomi stands a little bit taller. My chest blooms with pride. I had no idea being a direct cause of someone else's inner strength would be this rewarding, but I'm absolutely finding it to be, especially when it's with someone I care so much about.

After a couple minutes, and a wave goodbye to Mrs. Libman, she comes rushing back to my side. The beam radiating on her face seems to do something to my breathing, the air getting stalled in my throat as I take her excitement in.

"How did it go?" I ask with a matching grin.

"So good!" She claps her hands together, then playfully pinches my arm. "I even bragged about my lemon custard. You would be so proud."

"Right on." I chuckle, giving her a high five.

"She said she's planning to place an order soon."

"That's great! Let's keep the momentum up and move along." I jerk my head, signaling for her to follow as we leisurely stroll down the sidewalk. We pass by the bank and grocery store before stopping in front of the flower shop.

"Why don't you head in there and talk to Gina?" I suggest, pointing inside the building.

"Yes, sir." She grabs another card and bounds inside, not a hint of hesitation this time.

While she's inside, I relax a shoulder against the brick building and then my eyes snag on a group of bicyclists on the other side of the crosswalk—more specifically, one male rider who the sight of makes my stomach instantly drop and the hairs on my arms stand straight up.

My dad.

I hastily duck out of sight, nestling into the corner of the entrance of the flower shop. I hold my breath the entire time it takes for them to cross the street and continue onto the sidewalk, headed in the opposite direction.

Nausea hits me in full force, a blunt reminder of why it's so uncomfortable for me to be back in Pine Falls that hits me straight in the gut. I mentally kick myself for being too focused on Naomi to do my usual scan of the crowds when we got here.

"Hey, are you okay?" Naomi places a hand on my arm. I jump, having not heard the door open.

"Yeah." I mentally shake off the negativity as best I can.

I can do this. Focus on her. She's right in front of you.

"How did it go?" I manage to ask.

"Great," she beams. "Gina wants to place a weekly order for cookies that she'll leave on a tray for her customers. Can you believe that?"

"Wow, that's awesome, Naomi." I welcome the hug as she enthusiastically wraps her arms around my neck. I grip her back tightly, allowing the warmth of her touch to further ease my nerves.

"Are you ready for the next one?" I ask, ready to move on, albeit with more of an awareness this time.

"Yup. Just tell me where to go."

I chuckle, checking the streets thoroughly before continuing down the sidewalk. As we walk, we pass by a few out-of-towners before spotting Sylvia waiting patiently out-side of the bait store.

"You know what to do." I hand Naomi a card, and she heads off, leaving me alone to flick my gaze up and down the street, checking yet again for signs of bicyclists, even though they are likely long gone by now.

"I think this is my favorite exercise we've done," she announces happily when she returns. "Everyone is so friendly. Why are they all so nice and welcoming about this?"

"Because they want to support you." I throw an arm over her shoulder. "How about a couple more and then we'll call it a day?"

I'm more than ready to get out of town and back to the quiet sanctuary that is her house.

"Sounds good." She grabs a stack of cards and heads off without me needing to tell her where to go.

"Are you sure you don't want any more help in there?" I call to Naomi in the kitchen, where she's putting the last dirty measuring cup into the sink.

"Just say the word..." I slowly lower onto the couch with an exaggerated groan. "And I'll run right over."

"Relax, you're off the hook," she calls back. "I kicked you out for a reason. I'm sorry, I know you're trying to help, but I just can't stand the way you load the dishwasher."

"Shots fired." I clutch my chest as I fully drop onto the couch. Finally able to relax now that I'm out of the public eye in town, I rest my head on the armrest, clasping my hands comfortably over my chest. My feet extend all the way to the other end, and I point my toes to stretch my calves.

"No offense." She walks out of the kitchen and lingers in the space between the kitchen and living room, as if she's unsure of her next steps. I fight the urge to beg her to stay awake with me for a little while longer, as I'm equally unsure of my own. I'm hesitant to push anything out of fear of ruining our friendship, so I'm more than content to follow her lead on this.

"Well, I'm going to call it a night," she says, sending a rush of disappointment through me when she turns toward her room. "Goodnight, Robbie."

For a split second I consider taking my chances and rolling off the couch to close the gap between us, but I stop myself.

"Goodnight," I say quietly. "Great job today, slugger. A-plus."

She throws me a bashful smile over her shoulder before disappearing into her bedroom. I keep my eyes hovering on her open door, again debating how I can manage to squeeze even one more second of time with her before the day is over.

Thunder rumbles softly outside, breaking me from my trance. As I'm reaching for the blanket I left neatly folded on the back of the couch, my eye catches on movement across the room. Naomi cautiously inches out of her doorway, wearing a charcoal-gray cotton pajama set. The sight of her alone fills me with anticipation, and I freeze, waiting for her next move.

"Actually," she says quietly but with a forced strength, "is there room for two on that couch?"

An exhilarated relief rushes out along with my exhale, and somehow, the breath sends adrenaline all the way to my toes.

"Get over here." I shift onto my side, patting the leather cushion in front of me. She crosses the room slowly, cautiously even, as if the weight of every step is being carefully considered. Each step seems to melt any hesitation within her, and by the time she reaches the couch, there's nothing but a steady resolve in her eyes. Her movement has the opposite effect on me. I'm a slow-coiled ball of nerves by the time she lowers in front of me.

I push myself further into the couch as she settles her back comfortably against my chest. I bring my arm instinctively around her torso, letting my knuckles graze against the leather fabric in front of her, careful not to push my luck by resting my hand on her just yet. Her hair brushes against my nose, and the proximity of her sends a rush of warmth through me, along with an electric buzz of anticipation.

Neither of us says anything—or focuses on the TV for that matter. I couldn't even say what's on the screen right now. The only thing capturing my attention is the way her whole torso expands with each breath, filling my arms in the most soothing way.

She shifts her shoulders, and a strand of hair falls away from her neck. I can't for the life of me think of anything except for how tempted I am to bend down and find out how soft that spot is right where her neck meets her shoulder, if it tastes the same as when I kissed the spot above it on the boat.

Gone are the worries of seeing my dad earlier, along with my hesitation about the line that I won't be able to uncross if I move an inch. Everything else seems so inconsequential when she's in my arms like this. The temptation becomes unbearable, and I lower my head.

"Is this okay?" I whisper against her neck, my bottom lip snagging on her skin. Thunder rumbles outside, rivaling the way my heart is pounding in my chest.

"Mm-hmm," she breathes, exposing more of her neck.

When I place my mouth, again, on her skin, I feel the gentle thumping of her pulse underneath me. She slowly threads her fingers through mine, tucking our hands against her body.

I sigh against her, pulling away to nuzzle my chin on top of her shoulder, then I grip her hand tightly, savoring the way she feels tucked into me like this.

I'm starkly aware that nobody is watching us. We're not putting on an act for anyone else. It's just the two of us—alone—letting ourselves simmer in the undeniable chemistry between us. I sneak my top leg through hers as she molds her whole body even flatter against me.

And there we lie, glued to each other for the rest of the night, pretending to watch the TV while faint thunder rumbles in the sky.

CHAPTER TWENTY-ONE

Naomi

"Ouch," I mumble to myself, dropping the hot baking sheet onto the stovetop with a thud. Using the oven mitt, I move the tray back while I suck on the tip of my freshly burnt thumb that somehow managed to graze the pan.

Then I can finally step back to admire the spread of three dozen assorted cookies that need to be cooled and boxed up for an order. They look as delicious as they smell, if I do say so myself.

As I work to clean the kitchen island of my baking mess, I watch Robbie out on Mrs. P.'s dock, fixing her boat canopy that came loose in the storm last night. I bite the corner of my lip and smile as I think back to our moment on the couch last night. I've tried—and failed—to keep the butterflies at bay all day. His effect on me is unavoidable at this point. The chemistry is there—no doubt about it. The only question now is what do we do about it?

My mind wanders to a far-off reality where this is our day-to-day life. Robbie is not a touring musician but instead a successful mortgage banker. He works in town, helping Pine Falls residents as well as out-of-towners who need financing options to purchase their dream cabin on the lake. We live a simple life, one that's slow and steady, filled with an obnoxious amount of the sweetest unconditional love.

I huff, noting how my daydreams have become much less grandiose and more realistic lately. Less outlandish and more attainable. Ones that are simple. Soothing. Practical.

But...this isn't a dream. My life is a far cry from a fairy tale, and we have real-life roadblocks in the way of whatever this is—big ones too. The man can't leave this town fast enough, for one.

He starts crossing the yard toward my house and I dip my head, busying myself with the rest of the cleaning.

"Hey," he says as he comes in through the deck door.

"Hi. Did you get the canopy fixed?"

"All done." I don't miss the look of pride on his face as he says it. Seeing it now makes me realize just how rare it is for him to look like that.

"Who knew you were such a run-of-the-mill handyman?" I tease, leaning a hip against the island as I fold the towel.

"Definitely not me." He smirks, grabbing my laptop as he slides onto a stool.

"Do you have a second to look at your website?" he asks. "I can show you what I did."

"Sure." I put the towel down and slide onto the stool next to him, feeling every single inch of where my shoulder slides against his. "You do know that I'm in IT, right? I'm fully capable of building my own website."

"Yup," he says simply.

"Alright, show me what you got."

"We can change up the colors if you want, but I just ran with the ones you chose for your logo." He uses the pad of his thumb to scroll down, revealing a stunning pink-and-orange-cream-themed website, complete with a candid picture at the top that he must have taken of me at some point, mid-dough roll, complete with flour streaked across my hair.

"You have an 'About Me' section and a tab where I list your menu here. Right here is where they can place an order. Oh, check this out—I even got a few glowing reviews from some previous customers."

"When did you do that?" I gape at the screen, amazed at what he created.

"I called a few of them from the road last week."

"Seriously?"

"Oh, don't give me those sappy doe eyes. You have no idea how embarrassing it was to admit to myself that I have Iris's and Opal's phone numbers memorized."

I giggle. "We're coming back to that...I need to know who else's numbers you have memorized."

He continues, "I have order inquiries set up to go to both you and me. I hope you don't mind. I can add them to the calendar if I see them come in before you do. I want to be able to help out if I can, even from the road."

"Robbie, this is incredible," I say under my breath, shaking my head. "I can't believe you did all this."

"I'm not done," he croons. "Over here is where the calendar is. All your orders and their due dates will be entered here so you can look ahead and see what's coming up. Like the Pine Falls Flea Market this weekend, see?"

"Oh, you mean the market that you signed me up for without asking?" I chide.

"That's the one." His cheery tone tells me he doesn't feel bad in the slightest. "Do you know how many favors I now owe Fred for convincing him to squeeze another booth in?"

"I don't think I want to know."

"I thought it would be great exposure," he explains, growing serious.

"No, you're right. It definitely is," I agree with him. "I'm just nervous. I've never done anything like this before. You know, I'm not great at the whole 'putting myself out there' thing."

"Are you kidding?" He twists in his seat so he's now facing me, his outer thigh pressing against my own, caging me in. "You're going to kill it. Think of it as another exercise. I'll be there to help."

"You don't have to leave?"

"Not until the day after."

"Okay." I smile. Knowing he'll be there with me does put me at ease.

"I bet you'll get a ton of new inquiries. Plus, all the out-of-towners will be up here for the weekend so we'll see plenty of new faces who could, of course, turn into new clients."

"That would be amazing. Did I tell you how many orders I've done in the past week? A lot, Robbie. I never expected this many so soon. I'm actually staying consistently busy," I say incredulously. I'm still in awe and feeling overwhelmingly grateful that this is my reality right now.

"That's the beauty of word-of-mouth in a small town, right? Especially when you deliver a killer product like you do." He beams back at me.

"I kind of feel like I'm jinxing it if I say this out loud, but...if my orders stay this steady, I might even be able to cut back at the dealership in a few months, at least to part-time. My dad will love that."

"That's your goal, right?"

"It is." I nod. "It's all I've ever wanted."

We both fall silent naturally, my words left hanging in the air, as if referencing the word 'want' somehow touches on a broader meaning for both of us.

He stares intently at me. "I'm really proud of you, Naomi."

My chest warms at the words I don't hear often—if ever.

"Really?" I ask quietly as he slowly leans in, a gradual pull from an invisible magnetic force that hums between us. I let the same force pull me closer too.

"I am." He hovers closer to my mouth, making my heart beat wildly in my chest. Before he fully closes the gap, once again, the logical part of my brain takes over, cutting the romance of the moment.

"What are we doing, Robbie?" I whisper.

"What do you mean?" He pulls back but still hovers close, intently probing me for answers.

"You know. You. Me. This kissing that seems to keep happening—with or without anyone else around."

"I'm not sure," he admits with a subtle shake of his head. Except, now there's a softness to his gaze as he tucks a strand of my hair behind my ear. "But I know that things have changed for me."

"How?" Nerves dance on the top of my skin, and I'm suddenly terrified of what he'll say next.

"I definitely have feelings for you," he admits with a slight crack in his voice. The implications of what that means and the challenges we face play behind his tentative smile.

My throat constricts at his words, but my chest balloons, nonetheless...as if I don't have a choice in the matter but to feel the same exact way.

"Me too," I say quietly.

"I don't know exactly when it happened or what it means, but there's no denying it, Naomi. There's something here."

"I know," I whisper, hoping that something in my stare will convey that I feel the same way he does. "Do you think it could work?"

"You and me?"

I nod, feeling terrified again.

"I don't know. There's a lot to figure out, I guess. You know how I feel about Pine Falls. I can't stay here. I won't," he says adamantly, regret playing deep in his eyes. "I know that complicates things."

"I know." I nod. The last thing I would want to do is force him to stay if it wouldn't make him happy. "Let's just see what happens, yeah?"

His gaze skates across my face slowly, as if taking all of me in.

"See what happens," he repeats with a nod.

"Although, I'm fully aware of what happens in here." He taps a finger against my temple. "Are you sure you can take it slow? Or have you already married us off in your mind?"

"Oh, don't worry, I've already envisioned several different ways you permanently sweep me off my feet."

He chuckles, closing the gap to give me a quick yet firm kiss.

"And how do I do?" he murmurs against my lips, not pulling away.

"Grade A. Top-tier boyfriend material," I say through a grin.

"Good." Only then does he pull away slowly, still much too quickly for my liking.

"I'll print out the invoice for those cookies." He winks at me before keying my laptop.

"I guess I'd better finish baking—now that I have to bake for an entire flea market." I playfully roll my eyes, pretending to be complaining as I slide off the stool.

"Hey, is that how you should talk to your business manager?"

"Is that what you are now?" I laugh.

He shrugs, a boyish smile on his face. "I think I missed my calling. I'm pretty good at this if I do say so myself."

"You are, and thank you," I say sincerely from across the island. "I've seen the work you've put in, and I appreciate it, Robbie. I really do."

"Yeah, yeah." He waves me off as he focuses on the computer. "Enough sappy stuff. You better get moving. I promised them you would fill a whole table with goodies—including a few pies."

I get to work but not before playfully tossing a handful of flour in his direction.

Chapter Twenty-Two

Robbie

"What if I didn't make enough brownies?" Naomi asks, a wild, panicky look in her eyes as she scans the table of goods.

"You did," I reassure her for the fifth time while I adjust the tray of individually wrapped cookies to sit at a better angle.

"What if my credit card scanner doesn't work?"

"It does. We checked it three times," I say calmly.

"What if I fumble over my words when someone asks me about the exact ingredients in the mini cakes?"

"Then I promise to hide my laugh."

"Ugh, I should have made another dozen cream puffs," she says, making it clear that she's ignoring my responses. She bites repeatedly at her lower lip, and her breathing starts to become erratic.

"Okay. Hey." I lightly grip her forearm, making eye contact. Sliding my hand down to grab hers, I gently lead her behind the tent, out of view of the other vendors that are setting up.

"Take some deep breaths," I say calmly.

She inhales sharply then dramatically puffs her cheeks out with her exhale, the panic still evident in her eyes.

"That's one way to do it," I remark, holding back a laugh. "Try another one."

She repeats the same deep breath, allowing her shoulders to sink with her exhale this time.

"Come here." I pull her gently into a hug, wrapping my arms around her shoulders. She wraps herself around my torso and squeezes me tight. We stand like that for a while, until I'm convinced at least some of her nerves have disappeared.

Eventually, I unwrap myself just enough to bring both hands to cradle her face, making sure her own arms are still locked around me. I tilt her face up, ensuring I have her full attention.

"Repeat after me," I say. "I, Naomi Tillman..."

"I, Naomi Tillman..." she says, her cheeks moving against my palms.

"Am a confident business owner..."

She starts to protest with a shake of her head.

"Uh-uh," I interrupt. "You should know this by now, but you've been a business owner for a while, sweetheart. Keep going."

I wait for her to repeat the affirmation.

"Who knows my own worth and is not going to diminish the space I take up just by existing," I continue.

She repeats, keeping her eyes locked on mine.

"I deserve to be here. I'm offering quality goods that meet my own personal standards—and Robbie's—and what anyone else thinks of them is none of my business."

She repeats, a slow smile forming.

"Do you feel better?" I remove my hands, tucking her hair behind her shoulders, before sliding all the way down the length of her arms.

"Yeah." She sighs, rotating her shoulders, looking noticeably more relaxed. "I do. Thank you."

"That's what I'm here for. Now can we go sell some stuff?"

"Yes," she says confidently. "Let's do it."

I follow, ducking under the tent back to the table where her first customer, Mrs. Solis, is browsing the two-tiered tray of macaroons.

"Hi there, would you like a sample of those?" Naomi asks without a hint of hesitation in her tone.

"Oh, hello, dear. I tell you what, I could smell your delicious table from all the way over at Minnie's crochet stand. I couldn't resist coming straight over after I bought a new pair of gloves from her," she gushes.

"Oh, well, thank you." Naomi smiles, a hint of a blush appearing on her cheeks.

"You have made quite the name for yourself around town, honey," Mrs. Solis says with a smile as she peruses the macaroons.

"Aw, little old me?" Naomi asks humbly, and I watch the whole interaction with a stupid smile on my face. Pride blooms in my chest. I love seeing her get the attention she deserves.

"Absolutely. Now, tell me more about these."

While they drone on about the inner makeup of macaroons, I zone out, watching the once-empty field of grass filling with more and more people. They are mostly Pine Falls residents from what I can see, but inevitably, some unfamiliar faces pass by too. Thankfully, I've never known any of my family members to come to this flea market, so my apprehension about being in town isn't too terribly high.

Four long rows of vendor tables fill the field, each one more unique than the last. The faint smell of mini donuts and hot apple cider threaten to overpower the sweet aroma of Naomi's desserts, wafting over from the booth next to Ed's agate and glass figurine table.

"Hello, Robbie," Opal sings as she sneaks up on my left.

"Hi, Opal." I nod a greeting at her sidekick as well. "Hi, Iris."

"I was so excited when I spotted your table, Naomi," Opal says to Naomi, who averts her attention to us now that Mrs. Solis has successfully checked out. "I simply must bring a few of these muffins home with me."

"I recommend the banana chocolate chip muffins. They're to die for," I tell her.

"How sweet to see the two of you together again," Iris gushes while Opal makes her selection.

"Yeah, I've been trying to get rid of him, but he keeps coming back," Naomi teases, winking at the women.

"I'll say," Opal chimes in. "Hey, do either of you enjoy playing bridge?"

"Not really," Naomi says at the same time I say, "Sure."

Naomi whips her head to me, looking at me quizzically.

"What?" I chuckle. "We have long hours on the road."

"Oh, perfect!" Iris says. "We have an opening on the Pine Falls Area Ladies Bridge Team, and I think you'd be just perfect for it, Robbie."

"Oh, um…" I stammer, immediately regretting my admission.

"Wouldn't he be a great addition, Opal?" Iris nudges her with an elbow.

"But I'm not a lady," I point out in a feeble attempt to backtrack.

"Minor detail." Opal waves her hand, dismissing me. I don't miss that Naomi has stayed quiet next to me, hiding a smirk behind her sleeve.

"I'll have to check my schedule before I commit," I tell them.

"No worries. We know where to find you."

I give Iris my best smile, but I'm fairly certain it falls flat.

"You know, I saw your mother yesterday, Robbie, and she just cannot believe how often you've been spotted around town. This must be a new record for you," Opal says nonchalantly, as if those words don't completely wreck me as soon as they come out of her mouth.

The half-smile immediately falls from my face at the mention of my mom, my stomach souring and twisting at the same time. I nod politely but turn to grab a to-go bag, needing a distraction to remove myself from the conversation.

Just like that, my good mood vanishes as I'm confronted yet again with another reminder of why I can't stand being here. I can't escape them—nor the long-buried feelings that always seem to surface here—no matter where I go.

Frustration billows in my gut at the inconvenient reminder, but I convince myself to take a steadying breath before it gets too out of hand. The last thing I want to do is ruin Naomi's day. I push the turmoil down as far as it will go then silently slide the muffins into the bag while Naomi takes the payment.

"Well, we better mosey on along and see what other gems we can find today. See you two lovebirds later!" Iris says.

I can feel Naomi's eyes on me as we wave the ladies off. Then, with a break in customers, we settle down onto the two card table chairs.

Giving her a reassuring smirk, I grip the leg of her chair and slide it bumpily over the grass closer to mine until the outside of her legging-clad leg brushes against mine. It's a purely selfish move to get her closer to me in an attempt to drown out the thought of my family, but she doesn't seem to mind.

"So, you leave tomorrow?" she asks cautiously, testing my mood. I immediately feel guilty for making her worry about me.

"Tomorrow afternoon, yeah." To say I have conflicting emotions about leaving would be an understatement. I desperately need to get out of here and away from the painful reminders that I clearly can't escape...but the thought of leaving her makes my chest physically ache.

"Where are you playing this time?"

"I think we're playing at an outdoor music festival near Lake Powell. That's what Dane mentioned this morning, anyway."

"That sounds like fun." Her eyes dance with delight, and I'm convinced that she's already envisioning everything that my travels will entail.

"Why don't you come with me?" I blurt out, suddenly desperate for her to have the chance to experience it for herself—not to mention the selfish urge I feel to have her all to myself outside of Pine Falls.

"Go with you?" she asks, her brows flying up in surprise.

"Yeah. Seriously, it would be fun."

"Oh, I don't know... I have to work. My dad has a very strict advance notice policy for vacation time."

"Why does that not surprise me? When was the last time you took a vacation day?"

"Well, I had to leave early on a Friday last month for the baking trade show, but I only missed an hour and a half, and I put in the request two whole months prior, per his rules."

I contemplate how we might be able to convince her dad to let her go, but just then a gentleman saunters over to check out the cookie selection at the same time a family stops to peruse Naomi's business flyer.

"Alright. Think about it, anyway," I tell her as we both stand up, ready to give our full attention to the customers.

CHAPTER TWENTY-THREE

Naomi

"How did it go?" Robbie asks through the phone as I press it to my ear.

"Hold on." I hastily shuffle across the showroom floor, tugging on the bottom of my skirt as I walk quickly. Once back in my office, I promptly shut the door behind me.

"Do you want the positive or the negative first?" I say with a cringe.

"Oh boy...give me the positive, I guess."

"Well, I was approved to take the next two days off, miraculously, but the bad news is...I wasn't exactly the one to convince my dad, so I can't get credit for acing this test," I say sheepishly while stuffing my laptop in my carrying case.

"I'm going to need you to explain that one."

"Okay, so my dad was at the welcome desk with a bunch of my colleagues. You know, drinking coffee, talking about the inner workings of car engines or whatever it is they talk about. Anyway, I tried to ask him if we could speak in private, but of course he insisted I spit whatever I needed out right there on the spot."

"Uh-oh."

"When I asked for the time off, he started giving me a lecture on the importance of company policy and giving adequate advance notice. But then Austin, my department boss, cut in and offered to cover for me while I'm gone."

"I knew I always liked him."

"You've actually never met him," I point out.

"That's irrelevant."

"Anyway, my dad agreed...reluctantly. And now I need to book it out of here before anyone has a chance to change their minds."

"No, you do not need to rush out of there. Have I taught you nothing? You walk out with your chin held high, like the confident woman you are who knows her own worth and lawful right to vacation time."

"You know what? You're totally right." I pause my packing. There's no need to race out of here. I *am* a confident woman...although the affirmation loses strength each time I replay it in my mind.

"I know I am," he says matter-of-factly.

"I am a confident woman," I say aloud, telling myself more than I am him.

"Atta girl. Keep saying it until you believe it."

"I am a confident woman," I mumble repeatedly into the phone as I shut and lock my office door, glancing around to see if my dad is lurking anywhere nearby. Seemingly in the clear, I make a beeline toward the door.

"I am a powerhouse professional who deserves a day off." The confidence is strong in my voice, enough that I start to feel a bit of it simmer on the inside. But what Robbie can't see is me skittering across the showroom floor as fast as I can in these heels. I don't slow down, even when I make it out of the building, until I've rounded the corner of the parking lot and reached my car.

"Made it," I breathe into the phone once I slam the door shut.

"Nice job. I finished delivering the rest of your orders this morning, so I just need to finish packing, and then we're good to go. I have a ride picking us up in an hour. Will that still work?"

"Yes, that's perfect. I'll be home in ten."

When we disconnect, I drive through the familiar, tree-laced streets of town, musing on what sort of adventures the next couple of days are bound to hold. Anticipation flutters in my chest, and I can't help but grin to myself. The possibilities are endless, and I'm positively brimming with delight.

By the time I reach home, I've crafted about one hundred different scenarios of the people we'll meet, the things we'll do, the interactions we'll have, and the new friends I'll inevitably make.

Fueled with excitement, I rush inside to Robbie.

The backstage dressing room at the venue has more of a grungy vibe than anything close to glamorous like I was expecting. The burnt-orange couch looks worn and weathered, patches of wallpaper are peeling off the wall, and the chairs are barely hanging on by wobbly legs.

But there's a steady stream of adrenaline running through me all the same. I could be in a small hole in the dirt for all I care.

Because I'm here.

Out of Pine Falls.

Out of my normal routine. It feels awakening to be living each moment in the present, actually experiencing an adventure instead of mentally fabricating an alternate universe to live in.

"So nice of you to join us," a man I recognize from Robbie's pictures as Dane says as Robbie shrugs his jacket off, rushing to his guitar case in the corner of the room.

"I told you, our plane was delayed," Robbie says breathlessly. Not only did we deal with a two-hour departure delay, but we got stuck in traffic on the way to the venue. It's now just minutes before showtime, which adds a layer of rushed exhilaration to the already palpable adrenaline hanging in the air.

I step out of the way with a flinch to avoid being stepped on by another band member, but I'm not bothered by it. In fact, there's a permanent whisper of a smile on my face as I watch with eager eyes as everyone chaotically rushes around doing last-minute pre-show things.

"Guys, this is Naomi," Robbie says, taking a moment in the rushed chaos to pause, wrapping an arm around me with a clear look of pride beaming on his face. The way he says my name, as if he's showcasing a prize, sends a rush of butterflies fluttering in my stomach. I settle against his side, deepening my perma-smile.

"So, you're the longtime 'friend' Robbie keeps sneaking home for, huh?" Dane asks mischievously, stopping to address me with a wink.

I wonder what Robbie has told all of them about us and our situation. Regardless, there's a relieving sense of freedom being here with him. There's no false pretense of a fake relationship, no made-up story to remember. It's just the two of us, enjoying life while figuring out what we are to each other.

"Hi, it's so nice to meet you guys." I wave as everyone else's attention falls on me.

"Please don't pay any attention to the stories these guys have to say about me," Robbie says, releasing me to pull his guitar strap around his shoulder.

"Ah, you mean like the time you desperately needed to use the bathroom during the set and forced us to pause the entire show while you ran off stage," Dane says with a grin.

"There's no truth to any of it." Robbie winks at me, unaffected.

"Or what about the time—"

"Showtime, gentlemen," someone announces, popping their head in the room.

"Saved by the bell." Dane smirks, playfully shoving Robbie. "Stick around long enough, Naomi, and you'll hear it all."

"Oh, I'm looking forward to it," I say. "I could probably think of a few doozies about him from high school as well."

"Yes! We want all the details." The boys scramble out the door, leaving Robbie and me to take up the tail-end of the group.

"Go easy on me, please," Robbie jokes against my neck, where he places a quick kiss before turning to the gentleman with an earpiece. "Javier, can you escort Naomi to the VIP tent, please?"

"My pleasure," he replies.

"Have fun!" I grin as Robbie rushes down the hall after his bandmates.

"This way," Javier says, leading me through the winding back hallways of the building and eventually through a door that leads us outside. The noise of a buzzing crowd instantly fills the air, further amping up my excitement. After maneuvering through a few gates, he leads me directly into the crowd. I marvel at the number of people that fill the outdoor stadium, and a rush of pride and adrenaline runs through me.

As I look around, I take in the mix of eclectically dressed people, each one with more accessories and flair to their outfit than the last. I absolutely love being right in the midst of such a vibrant crowd, and a part of me feels completely at home being surrounded by this much commotion.

Javier leads me into the VIP tent where I'm greeted with warm smiles of other friends and family of the band members.

"Hi, I'm Naomi," I say to the group and smile as each one introduces themselves to me.

I find a spot to stand, right next to a cousin of the lead singer, then take a long look around the stadium, intent on soaking it all in. There's hardly an empty chair left open now, and the two large neon screens that hang next to the stage buzz loudly with a countdown, the numbers displaying brightly with a loud horn as each second passes.

Adrenaline continues to surge through me, pulsing right along with the blaring horn that I can feel beating inside my chest. The crowd goes wild, filling my ears and my body with a rush I've only ever daydreamed about, as the countdown reaches two seconds.

I didn't think it would be possible, but my smile grows even wilder when Robbie and the band run out onto the stage.

CHAPTER TWENTY-FOUR
Naomi

"Hold on tight," Robbie says, squeezing my hand as he cradles it carefully behind him. I grip tightly as he leads me up the narrow rocky path.

"Where are we going?" I'm not sure why I'm whispering, but for some reason, it feels necessary out here in the elements. As if the rustling wind and faint croaking of distant frogs feels somehow too sacred to interrupt. As if I'm not meant to be encroaching on their space.

"You'll see," is all he says, continuing down the path.

The sun is just high enough on the horizon to make the vast burnt-orange canyons of Lake Powell still visible in the daylight, and the lake water slowly glistens below us.

I tighten my grip on his hand when we walk carefully over some uneven rocks, my shoes slipping on a particularly loose one. Eventually, the path levels out into a flat surface, and he comes to a stop in the middle of nowhere.

"This'll do," he announces. My hand falls abruptly to my side as he releases it to spread the thick wool blanket he was carrying across the ground.

"So...are we sleeping out here?" I ask, still not clear on what we're doing, and truthfully, feeling hesitant about the prospect of spending the night out here.

"No." He laughs then lowers down to lie on his side. "There's too much wildlife in this area. It wouldn't be safe."

"You know it's about to get pitch dark out, right?" I ask as I accept his outstretched hand to settle next to him. I lie on my back with my elbows propped up behind me, shifting to get comfortable, and then bite my lip to hide a smile when he scoots closer to my side once I'm situated. Like a moth to a flame.

"That's the point," he says.

"Are we safe here?" I look around, keeping a watchful eye out for snakes.

"To be determined."

"I still don't understand what we're doing, but I'm along for the ride. I'd do anything to hang out with the famed bass guitarist of Copper Snake, after all," I tease.

He smirks, lazily roaming his gaze over my face. "Did you have fun at the show?"

"Ugh, Robbie. It was..." I struggle to find the right words for what I felt while watching him and his band play. "Absolutely incredible."

"Ah." He waves his hand, shrugging me off.

"I mean it." I nudge him with my elbow. "You should be proud of yourself, Robbie."

The night sky is almost completely dark now, but I don't miss how his expression changes. It goes neutral somehow. He shrugs and looks off in the distance, as if he doesn't put a lot of weight in my words. I wonder how often he's been told that he makes anyone proud.

I open my mouth to ask him about it, but he moves, shifting to lie flat on his back. The moment passes by before I can figure out how to approach the subject again.

"This is it." He taps my leg with his hand then leaves it to rest just above my knee. "Look up."

"What?" I ask in confusion.

"Look up," he repeats, pointing to the sky.

I tip my head and suck in a sharp inhale at what I see. An obscene number of stars blanket the sky from one end to the other. Grayish-white tiny beams of light illuminate the darkness as far as I can see in every direction. It's magnificent and breathtaking all at once, and its beauty brings a rush of emotion that tingles my nose.

"Wow," I breathe, settling all the way onto my back, my arm now pressed firmly against his.

"Isn't it cool?" I can hear the grin in Robbie's voice without even turning my head to see it.

"It's incredible. How do you know about this spot?"

"Dane drew me a map."

I snort a laugh. "Seriously?"

"Yup. Apparently, he stumbled on this perfect stargazing spot the last time we played a show here."

"It's truly stunning," I whisper while rotating my head, wanting to see the entire sky.

Sure, we can see stars in Minnesota, but being here on top of this canyon makes me feel like I'm literally immersed in them. Close enough that if I reached my hand out, I just might be able to touch one.

"Absolutely incredible," I murmur. "All of it. The concert. This evening with you. This is the kind of stuff I'm always dreaming about, Robbie. This kind of adventure. I want it so badly."

He falls silent for a moment next to me in the dark while I taper down the sudden ache in my chest...the yearning for a life like this.

"You can have it, you know," he says quietly. "What's tying you to Pine Falls?"

It's a question I've asked myself countless times over the past few years. One that always ends up confusing me more than anything as it points out the mixed opinions I clearly have.

"You mean other than my family and friends? My job? This new business endeavor? Everything I've ever known?" I point out gently. "That's what's holding me back from leaving. Those aren't just small things to me, you know? I enjoy living in Pine Falls."

"So, you don't think you'd ever leave?" His voice is small and quiet.

I know what he's implying, and it makes my next words catch in my throat.

"Never say never, I guess. But what would be the point of building this baking business if I ended up leaving it all behind?"

"Yeah," is all he says.

"It's weird," I admit. "I have this strong urge to leave Pine Falls and explore the world, to have adventures exactly like this, but I stall when I think of actually making such a drastic change like that. I honestly don't know if it's lack of courage, or if it's knowing, deep down, that my heart wants to stay. Either way, it's a strong enough feeling to make me hesitate."

He doesn't say anything back, so I silently watch the stars, ruminating on my own words and what they mean for us.

"What about you?" I ask him. "Is there any realm of possibility where you would stay in Pine Falls?"

I hold my breath for his answer, knowing this conversation has a direct impact on what our future looks like.

"No," he says emphatically almost instantly, causing my heart to sink. I already knew that would be his answer, but to hear him verbalize it again makes it feel like my heart is being ripped out.

"Is it that terrible being there?" I whisper.

"I just...can't, okay?" He squeezes my hand in what I know is an effort to smooth the roughness of the conversation.

I breathe out a slow and steady sigh, wishing he would open up to me. Tell me why it's so hard for him. Is there even any point of pursuing something with him if there's no chance he'll stay? How would this ever work between us?

The questions run through my mind repeatedly, but I respect the finality of his tone and fall quiet, keeping them for another day.

"Hey," he says, rolling onto his side, letting his head fall against his fist that he props up on an elbow. I tilt my head toward him, staying flat on my back. The starlight makes the outline of his face just visible enough that I can see the warmth behind his eyes, and I note the way it soothes something inside me. Calms me in a way.

"Thank you for coming with me. To the show. Up here tonight. All of it." The sincerity in his voice is almost palpable.

I smile as he scooches even closer, pressing his torso to my side and snaking an arm across me to tuck under my hip.

"Thank you for bringing me." I bring my free hand up to run it through his thick hair, watching as the waves fall back into place as I go. Being affectionate with Robbie has always been a part of our friendship, but lately, every time I touch him, it's like I'm discovering a new part of him that I've never known before. Each touch feels brand new and sparked with an electricity that's never been there—or perhaps it has, and I just never looked closely enough.

He squeezes my side, clutching my waist as he brings his head forward, softly connecting his lips to mine.

My heart races, and my eyes flutter closed as I press myself against him, relishing the heat from his hand as it slides up the center of my back.

He kisses me with a softness that somehow soothes the uncertainties of our situation. A promise that, while he doesn't know the right answer or the direction we should be taking, he's right here with me, feeling this connection and cautiously exploring it just like I am.

When he pulls back, we lock eyes, exchanging more with this shared gaze than words ever could. He pulls me to him as he lies on his back, and I curl onto my side, melding myself to him. When I rest my open palm against his chest, I zero in on the way it rises and falls with each breath he takes. The movement comforts me in a way I can't explain. I do know one thing is crystal clear. Regardless of the future, I would like nothing more than to fully enjoy the present with him, to soak up every minute I can, starting with this quiet night under the stars.

Chapter Twenty-Five

Robbie

"Are you ready for your next assignment?" I ask Naomi, raising my voice to be heard over the loud patrons enjoying live music at The Squirrely Bear.

"Here? Now?" She whips her head to me. Our friends are well out of earshot, playing pool in the opposite corner of the bar, but I lean closer to her anyway. I'll take any excuse to be near her these days. Our fake relationship may have melded into very real feelings, but I still feel a different sort of spark when we're out in public like this, as if we're putting on a show. Like I'm allowed to be more open and candid with my affection without needing to be cautious about our future at the same time.

"Operation Make Naomi a Boss is an ongoing project, sweetheart," I say against the shell of her ear, relishing the goosebumps that spark against my lips in response.

"I don't remember setting any timelines." She smirks. "But okay, I'm game. What do you have for me?"

"Not so fast," I chide, raising my eyebrows expectantly.

"Oh! Something I want out of life. Hmm." She scratches her chin with her finger, looking incredibly adorable as she looks up at the ceiling while she ponders. I watch each neon strobe from the jukebox as they dance across her face in this dimly lit bar, memorizing this version of her. This carefree, relaxed, alive version I've come to crave.

"I want to run a marathon someday," she says decisively, her answer surprising me.

"Do you run?"

"Not a day in my life," she deadpans then points a finger at me. "But that doesn't mean I can't train."

"Alright." I chuckle. "I'll keep my skepticism to myself and not point out your two left feet, then."

"Saying it out loud isn't keeping it to yourself, you know," she chides with a smile.

"I'm aware." I give her an open-mouth smile before rubbing my hands together. "Alright. I'd like you to practice setting a boundary today—like, actually set one...face to face with someone."

"Okay," she says slowly, unsure of my request. "With who?"

"Stick with me. I have someone in mind, and they just so happen to be here tonight...but if you don't like it, you can go another direction if you prefer."

"How convenient." She gives me a side-eye, pursing her lips together. "Who is it?

"Let's have a look, shall we?" I gesture out into the crowd. "Can you see anyone here who might, say, overstep at times?"

I watch as she scans the bar, perusing the Pine Falls residents, many of whom would realistically fall into that category.

"Perhaps someone who...brings their laundry over without asking? Has a rude way of asking for what she wants?" I hint.

Her eyes go wide with understanding.

"Gabby," she mouths, even though, again, we're still out of earshot.

"Bingo."

"But...what am I supposed to say?" A look of uneasiness spreads on her face.

"Let's practice first." I shift in my seat so I'm facing her side, blocking her in between my legs. She twists in her own seat to face me with an air of confidence that only has a slight layer of hesitation underneath this time.

"So, you're Gabby, I'm assuming?" she asks.

"Correct. How's my confidence? Is it conceited enough?"

I chuckle when she uses her fist to slap me on the shoulder.

"I'm kidding. Okay, hit me with it."

She clears her throat, leaning forward. "Hi, Gabby."

"Naomi." I dip my head curtly then wait patiently.

"So...I just wanted to let you know that I'm enforcing a new house rule." She poses it like a question and statement in one.

"What would that be?" I fold my arms across my chest, attempting to exude the specific attitude that makes Gabby, Gabby.

"I'm no longer keeping my laundry room open for use." She pauses to build momentum. "It's just getting to the point where monthly laundry essentials are extremely expensive, and I'd like to keep the space to myself. And this isn't just a rule for you, by the way. Robbie uses it without asking too."

"Fair enough." I nod, ignoring the jab she threw in there.

"I hope you can understand," she says gently.

"Okay, there was a little bit too much guilt at the end there, but overall, good delivery. Really good." I reach a hand up for a high five, which she returns.

"Now, do you think you can say exactly what you said to me to her face?"

"I think so?" she says, a bit of uncertainty playing on her face.

"Is it something you want to do? I don't want to force you to confront her, so I can come up with a plan B assignment if you want," I offer.

"No, you're right. I think I've let her have too much free rein for too long. I don't want to be mean, though." She cringes.

"You don't have to be. But it's your house, Naomi. Your life. Take control of it if you want to," I remind her gently.

"Okay." She smiles at me, holding my stare, and for a second, I get lost in her eyes, forgetting what we're supposed to be doing. A loud beat from the music refocuses me a moment later.

"Jumping jacks?" I offer with raised brows.

"We're in a bar, Robbie." She laughs.

"So? You know the whole place would join in, flash-mob style, if we started jumping right now."

"That's true." She giggles and then grows serious, running her palms along her thighs. "No, I can do this. I'm ready."

"Yeah?"

She nods. "Yup. But do you promise to come follow me if I run out crying?"

"I promise. I'll even pull the getaway car around back."

"Fine." She rises to stand. "And then we're stopping for ice cream."

"Deal. You've got this." I don't even attempt to cover my grin when I catch her buzzing her lips as she walks off.

She weaves between the people on the dance floor to where our friends are playing pool. I watch, sipping my beer, while she starts a conversation with Charlie, biding her time for the right opportunity with Gabby, who's talking with Luke.

Even with my eyes trained on her, not having Naomi right next to me as a distraction makes my mood sour quickly. The same dark, unsettling cloud that's been following me around ever since we boarded a plane back to Pine Falls creeps over me with a vengeance—a flight I would have happily never taken in the first place if I had my way.

To say I didn't want to come back would be an understatement. Everything about life was absolutely perfect when she was with me at the show. I got to have the two most important things to me in one place—my band and Naomi. If I could be completely selfish and keep her out on the road with me all the time, I would do so in a heartbeat. Wouldn't that be the easiest solution to this roadblock standing in our way?

An email notification pulls my attention down to the phone in my pocket. At first glance, I see a message coming through from Naomi's website with the words 'cancellation notice' in the subject line.

Hmm. That's odd. This makes two canceled orders this week alone. I open the email and peruse it for any hint of an explanation, but there's nothing there, just a quick apology and a request to refund the order.

I make a mental note to ask Naomi about it later, but a text message comes through, stealing my attention.

> **Steven:** I heard you're back in town again. Can we talk, please?

The sight of his name causes a surge of anger to run through me, causing the pit in my stomach to grow insanely heavy. I delete the message immediately, having absolutely no desire to text my brother back.

I slide my phone back into my pocket just as Toby and Rachel come to the table.

"Any idea what they're talking about?" Rachel asks, gesturing a thumb toward where Naomi and Gabby are now talking.

"We hightailed it out of there as soon as I heard Naomi say, 'Gabby, can we talk?' That never leads to anything good," Toby says, sliding into the chair next to Rachel.

"Something that should have been done a long time ago," is all I say, settling against the chair back with my arms crossed, keeping my eyes trained on the other side of the room.

I watch their interaction, noting Gabby's clear defensiveness and Naomi's assertion, even with a few twinges of uncertainty sprinkled in. Watching Naomi this intently provides a little bit of a calming effect, and I push the thoughts of my brother completely out of my mind.

"Oh no, here it comes," Rachel murmurs, nervously peering over her hand as Gabby throws her hands up in frustration, turning sharply on her heel before booking it out the side door of The Squirrely Bear.

I hold my breath, awaiting Naomi's reaction. I was not expecting Gabby to make a scene, let alone leave the bar altogether like that. If I did, I wouldn't have put Naomi in this situation in the first place.

When Naomi spins slowly toward our direction, her guilt-ridden eyes meet mine. Nothing could stop me as I push away from the table, rising instantly. I give her my best encouraging smile as I cross the dance floor as quickly as I can, feeling anxious to make sure she's okay.

As soon as she's within reach, I slide my arm around her shoulders, squeezing as I place a kiss on her temple.

"She'll come around," I whisper against her hair as it tickles my lips.

"I know." She smiles sadly, turning into me, wrapping an arm around my waist, her hand gripping my shirt.

She tilts her head up. "Want to know something?"

"Desperately," I say gruffly, getting caught up in the breathless way I feel when she's in my arms like this.

"That felt really good," she admits.

"I'm glad." I squeeze her closer, running my hand up and down the soft skin of her arm.

"Yo, Robbie, are you sticking around until next week?" Luke asks. "There's a big boat parade on Gull."

Naomi tilts her head up with excitement, looking at me expectantly.

"No, I'll be leaving before then. I wish I could stay, but we've got a couple shows in Atlanta."

I watch as my words slice through both of us, the reaction on Naomi's face matching the way I feel on the inside—disappointed at the reality that keeps us from being together as much as we both want to be.

"No worries. We'll take care of Naomi." He winks, tossing me a pool stick.

"Your turn to rack up," he tells Charlie.

Before I let Naomi go, I lean in. "I'll be back before you know it."

"I know." She looks up, resting her chin on my chest. "I'll survive."

"Barely, though, right? You can't breathe without me?" I force some sarcasm into my tone, wanting to lighten the mood.

"Obviously." She rolls her eyes playfully.

Determined to enjoy the rest of the night, I give her one last squeeze before releasing her to play pool with our friends.

CHAPTER TWENTY-SIX

Naomi

"Robbie? I'm home!" I call out, tossing my car keys on the entryway table.

"In my office," he replies back. "If you can't find it, that's because it's also known as the kitchen."

I snicker, smiling to myself. "I'll be right there. I'm going to change out of this darn work uniform first."

"Take your time. How was your day?" he asks loudly enough for me to hear as I walk into my room.

"Eh, the usual," I say from inside my closet where I strip off my clothes to change. "Hey, I made a decision today."

"Just one?"

"One important one. Are you ready for this? I'm planning to have a meeting with my dad in two weeks to talk about going down to part-time at the dealership. I want to wait until after the opening to talk to him about it, but I put in the meeting request today."

"Oh yeah?"

"Yup." I pull on a tank top and a pair of loose joggers. "I've been running the numbers, and I'm at a point where it finally makes sense now. I'm limited with how many orders I can do outside of dealership hours—thanks to the life rules we wrote down—so the only way I can grow Naomi's Nummy Bakery is if I prioritize more time toward it during the workday."

"I think that sounds like a great plan," he says enthusiastically.

"Plus, I think I'm finally ready for that conversation." The thought of having a sit-down with my dad is intimidating, and I'm wary of what his reaction will be, but I feel optimistic about it. I'm ready to at least try.

"I know you are," he answers back.

"Anyway, how was your day?" I cross the room to find some Chapstick, wanting to get as comfortable as possible before settling into the baking marathon I have planned for the rest of the evening.

"Great. I went through your cupboards and organized your shelves. You know, for as much grief as you give me for being messy, you have a surprisingly chaotic organizational system," he rambles just loud enough for me to hear. "Anyway, everything has a place now. I'll show you later. There also may have been an incident with Mrs. Pelinski while you were gone."

"Did she not remember you again?" I shut off my bedroom lights and round the corner to the kitchen.

"No, she did remember me, which was nice. But we had a bit of a tangle out on her dock. I noticed her out there watering her flowers, so I went over to help her. But by the time I got there, she had dropped the watering can into the lake, which, of course, prompted me to reach for...and subsequently fall into the lake."

"Oh no." I start to laugh, but the sound gets caught in my throat when I see what's laid out on the kitchen counter. All my most used baking utensils are set out neatly, placed right next to the where canisters of flour, cane sugar, and eggs have been placed. Parchment paper, baking sheets, and three delivery boxes are open, arranged in a row on the counter, ready to be packed up with logo stickers applied and customer names already written on top. Everything I need to bake for the evening is there, all prepped and laid out for me.

"Did you do all this?" I ask with wonder, my heart swelling at the sweet gesture.

"I also color-coded your ingredient spreadsheet," he says flatly.

"Were you bored today?" I snicker, running my fingers along the countertop, taking it all in.

"No, not bored." His shoulder lifts in a shrug. "I like helping with the operational side of things."

He pushes his lips together, a hint of a smile forming. "Okay, maybe there was a little boredom. You weren't home, and I didn't want to go into town by myself."

I sink onto my elbows so I can lean forward against the island.

"Thank you," I say, hoping the sincerity in my eyes conveys how much I appreciate him.

"My pleasure." He smirks, his eyes boring into mine. A chill runs up my spine at the way his expression changes, darkening with intensity. For a moment, I get lost in the way it makes me feel.

Alive.

Exhilarated.

Dangerously close to abandoning all responsibilities for the evening in favor of spending it doing anything at all that requires me to be closer to him.

"You better get moving," he says, his voice gravelly, a clear giveaway that he's having thoughts similar to mine.

"Right." I give my head a shake, mentally clearing my thoughts of any distractions, and get started on my first order.

"Do you need any help?" he asks, tapping his hands on the counter.

"I don't think so. It should be a pretty easy evening. Two dozen white chocolate macadamia nut cookies, some macaroons, and an assortment of muffins."

"Really?" His eyes light up at the mention of what I'm realizing is his favorite thing I make.

"I'll make you an extra muffin, don't worry." I snicker under my breath.

As I measure out the flour, he leans back, getting comfortable on the stool while he continues to watch me.

"Have you talked to Gabby at all?" he asks.

"No," I say, pursing my lips in disappointment. I was hoping she'd come around by now, but I haven't heard from her since our conversation at the bar the other night, nor has she been participating in our friend group chat. At the same time, I keep reminding myself to not feel bad about it—that was a conversation that needed to happen.

A sudden tapping on the sliding screen door by the deck causes both of us to jump.

"Knock, knock," Mrs. Pelinski says, gently sliding the door open, carrying a wide assortment of stemmed flowers in her hand. I hadn't even noticed her crossing the backyard.

"Come on in, Mrs. P." I offer her a genuine smile.

"Hi, dear. Oh good, you're here too, Robbie," she says, noticing him. I'm impressed that she not only remembers him but also his name. "I feel just terrible for the ruckus I caused earlier out on the dock. That darn watering can slipped right out of my hands. Please tell me you dried off quickly?"

"I sure did, Rose," he says. I smile at him calling her by her first name. "You might not believe it, but it wasn't the first time something like that has happened. I've fallen off more docks than I should have in my day."

"Well, I wanted to bring you flowers anyway. Nobody is falling into the lake on my watch without getting taken care of afterward." She hands the flowers to him.

"That's sweet, thank you," he says sincerely. My heart warms at their interaction and what seems to be a growing friendship.

"Naomi, honey." She turns to me. "I told all the ladies in my water aerobics class about your fledging baking business, so expect some orders coming in."

"You're the best, Mrs. P. Truly."

She waves me off, retreating to the door. "Ah, nonsense. I'll leave you two be. Have a good evening."

"Bye! I'll swing some donuts over tomorrow morning," I call out before she leaves. My eyes trail her as she crosses the backyard, ducking under a tree branch while the lake softly laps onto shore behind her.

"She's the sweetest, isn't she?" I gush.

"She is—once she gets past the interrogation stage." He smirks, coming to a stand. "I better put these in a vase."

"There's one in that cupboard there." I use my foot to gesture to the one next to the fridge.

He fills the vase with water while I melt some butter and crack a couple eggs into my wet ingredient bowl.

As he moves around my kitchen, I'm hyperaware of every small move he makes, noticing instantly when he places the vase in the center of the island in front of me and doesn't attempt to move back to his chair.

His closeness leaves me breathless, a buzzing force in my chest that only intensifies as he slowly inches even closer to my side. He stands there with his arms folded, his gaze ever so slowly scanning me.

"Fine. You can help," I say just above a whisper, my voice coming out more strangled than it should. "Do you want to pour the white chocolate chips in?"

"Sure." He moves directly behind me, gently pressing himself against my back. He presses a kiss to the side of my neck before snaking an arm underneath mine to grab the measuring cup.

"Like this?" He settles his chin on the crook of my left shoulder, peering over me as he pours them into the bowl.

"Uh-huh," is all I can say, unable to think of actual words at a time like this. He crowds me in the best possible way, his woodsy scent engulfing me from every angle, and the weight of him at my back feels deliciously heavy.

"Okay, next, add in the salted macadamia nuts," I say softly, smiling when he struggles to reach the cup but refuses to untangle from me.

"Now mix."

He places his hand on top of mine, pressing the stand mixer into place, then moving with me to flick the machine on.

While it mixes, he nuzzles his face deeper into the crook of my neck. His warm breath sends waves of goosebumps across the top of my skin, and I automatically tilt my head to expose more of my neck while I bite at the corner of my smile.

My mind races, flashing with images of the million different daydreams I've had of baking in my kitchen this exact way with someone I like. Of getting lost in the overwhelming chemistry with another person the same way I can get lost in the rhythmic trance of baking. As everything with Robbie seems to be, reality proves to be so much better than my imagination, and I relish the way my heart feels exhilarated and oddly settled all at once.

"Alright, alright," I laugh huskily, turning the mixer off before he gets too carried away. "Now use this scooper to place the cookie dough in even circles on the tray."

I hand him the scooper while moving the bowl within reach.

"Is there a technique to this I should know about?" he says close to my ear while he scoops a clump onto the tray. "This doesn't look as pretty as when you do it."

"It looks just fine."

"Just fine," he repeats. "The mantra I live by."

I smirk, watching him fill the trays. "Alright, now you can pop these in the oven."

He pushes away from the counter, taking the warmth of his body with him, leaving me feeling breathless and slightly jittery. While he slides the trays into the oven, I put the dirty dishes in the sink and grab some clean mixing bowls. In the process, I accidentally spill some flour onto the counter, which I rarely ever do. I chalk it up to being an outward sign of the unsettled energy still buzzing through my veins.

When I turn to open the fridge, I yelp as Robbie meets me right there, grabbing my waist with a devilish grin.

"Hey," I squeal as he tickles, lifting me easily into his arms before twisting and setting me on top of the freshly spilled flour.

"You did not just do that," I say with a gasp as my body slips against the surface. "I'm literally sitting in flour."

He slides between my legs, coming face to face, sporting his typical unbothered grin. His warmth is back too, searing my thighs as he gets as close as he possibly can to me.

"Yeah, well, maybe this batch should be just for us," he whispers as he dips his head.

I can't help the budding smile on my face or the rush of adrenaline that surges through my veins. I don't even think twice about the fact that my hands are dusted with flour when I bring them to lightly touch his jawline.

His lips meet mine at the same moment his hands find my hips. He squeezes gently as he deepens the kiss with urgency, sending me reeling. As he slides a hand up the center of my back, an overwhelming emotion threatens to consume me. At his touch. At the delicate way he kisses me. At the way my heart feels like it's about to combust. How is it that my once strictly platonic friend has now become someone who has the ability to make me feel like this?

When he pulls back, our eyes lock, and I hold them with near desperation...to acknowledge whatever this is between us. To name it. To know that he feels the depth of this too.

"This is real, isn't it?" I whisper, sliding my floured finger against his cheek, watching it leave a powdered white streak across his skin. "This thing between us?"

His stare somehow softens and ignites at the same time. He dips his head in a curt nod while rolling his lips.

"Yeah," he says gruffly.

Nothing more. Nothing less.

I blink at him, letting my hands slide down the outside of his arms as he loosens his grip on me. The buzz ruminates steadily in the center of my chest, reluctant to cease even as he backs away, putting space between us.

"You're terrible for productivity. Do you know that?" I murmur.

He chuckles, helping me off the counter. "I'm sorry. I can't seem to help it when you're around."

"Why don't you go sit on the dock while I finish the last two orders?" I suggest, still attempting to catch my breath. "Then I'll join you."

"Deal. I don't think I have a future in baking, anyway, do I?"

"Hey, you could surprise us all." I wash my hands as Robbie cleans the flour off the counter first and then his cheek.

"I need to change again," I say, making my way out of the kitchen. "Try not to fall in the lake this time, okay?"

"Ha-ha." He salutes me as I disappear into my room.

When I re-emerge from my room with a fresh pair of pants on, I catch sight of Robbie outside, sitting with an arm outstretched along the top of the bench out on the dock. The image calls to me with a fervor—a subtle pull for me to go sit under that arm.

I heave a deep breath, refocusing myself so I can get to baking as fast as I can and join him.

CHAPTER TWENTY-SEVEN

Robbie

"Now this is how a Saturday morning should be," I muse, carrying a plate in each hand while Naomi slides the deck door open for us. She throws me a smile that nearly knocks the breath right out of me as I pass her.

"It is a nice morning, isn't it?" She takes one of the plates from my hand and lowers onto the first wooden step of her deck, resting the plate on top of her bent knees. I lower next to her, doing the same with mine.

"Not as beautiful as this steak and eggs. Thank you for making breakfast," I say as I slide a forkful into my mouth. The sky has a bit of pink left over from the sunrise, a tiny strip of it reflecting across the water, and a flock of ducks swims out in the distance, lazily drifting between two docks on the other side of the lake. It's a perfectly serene setting to start the day that I've now grown accustomed to.

We fall into a comfortable silence as we eat, listening to frogs croak their morning song. Eventually, she clears her throat.

"So...I was thinking," she starts, setting her empty plate next to her.

"Uh-oh. That's never good." I huff.

"I mean it." She laughs softly. "I was thinking about our conversation after your show—when you asked me if I would ever bake from anywhere else? If I would ever leave Pine Falls?"

"Yeah." I nod, a low simmer of something like dread starting to ruminate in my gut. I wasn't exactly expecting to have this conversation so early in the day, so I scramble to brace myself.

"And I want to be upfront and honest with you." She tucks a strand of hair behind her ear and shifts toward me, the tension in her shoulders giving away how difficult the coming words are for her to say.

"I feel like I need to stay here," she admits with a sheepish cringe. "For sure. At least for a while, to get this business off the ground. This is my dream, Robbie. It's all I've ever wanted, and it's actually coming true. I don't like the idea of having to start all over somewhere new where nobody knows me, you know?"

Guilt flashes across her face, and I instinctively reach a hand out to grab hers, ignoring the intense gnawing in the pit of my stomach. At this moment, I want nothing more than to comfort her, to make sure she's okay.

"Please don't feel bad about that, Naomi," I tell her earnestly. "I completely understand. And truthfully, it's what makes the most sense for you. I would be doing you a disservice if I asked you to leave Pine Falls."

"Are you sure? I just... I don't want to go forward with this"—she waves a hand between us—"without being straightforward about that first. I want to lay everything on the table so we both have clear expectations."

"I totally get it," I insist, the corner of my mouth tipping into a smile. Even being on the disappointing end of her pointed conversation, I'm proud of her assertiveness. "I'm still on board, by the way. With this. With us. We'll figure this out together, okay?"

She nods, dipping her head down as I pull her in for a side hug.

"I'm on board too," she whispers.

I hold her to me as I squeeze her arm, hoping that we'll be able to find some way to make this work.

While I think through what the reality of us being together might look like, she tilts her head up. There's a soft probing there in her gaze—a vulnerability.

"Do you think you could tell me why it's so hard for you to be in Pine Falls?" she asks gently. "I'd really like to understand why being here is so terrible for you. Maybe I could help."

My stomach clenches, and nausea grips me at the mere mention of it. I haven't talked about any of this out loud in a long time—maybe even ever. Avoidance and deflection are my knee-jerk reactions to this topic, and this time is no different.

But looking at Naomi, who has always been upfront and honest with me, I feel the smallest urge to at least try to do the same. For the sake of building something real with her. Something honest and transparent.

If I'm sure of anything, it's that she deserves that.

"Okay," I agree, setting my plate down beside me. I run my now sweaty palms down the front of my jeans, my next breath coming out slow as I wonder if I'll be able to pull it all to the surface to explain. At the same time, I wonder if there's any point. "Where do I start?"

"Wherever you want to," she encourages me gently.

I run through my memories, considering which of them I should pull from—which painful details I should share out loud.

"Okay." I clear my throat, mustering the courage to continue despite the lump in my throat that protests. "I guess it started as far back as I can remember—my parents' obvious favoritism for Steven. He was always the smarter one. The 4.0 GPA. The valedictorian. Med student. Everyone around town constantly raved about how amazing he was, which my parents relished. Meanwhile, I was scraping by with my mediocre grades and below-average accomplishments. I don't remember a time when I didn't feel inferior to him, honestly."

She places a gentle hand on my forearm.

"He ate it up too," I continue, gaining momentum now, "always boasted about his accomplishments and rubbed Mom and Dad's affection in my face, especially in front of his friends. Being a typical older brother, of course, but he knew how much it bothered me. That's what hurt the most."

"That wasn't very nice of him," she says weakly.

"Anyway, my parents were never shy about showing their favoritism loud and clear. Out in public. At the grocery store. Anywhere and everywhere they shouted his praises, making me feel about as small as an ant. They're both doctors too, you know. So, the fact that only one of their sons followed in their footsteps was apparently crushing for them. I know for a fact that they planned out a doctorate path for me too before I was even born."

I pause, running my palm across my jaw. "But no matter how hard I worked in school, I couldn't ever reach the bar they set for me. They saw my insecurities—I know they did. Not only did they do nothing to appease them, but, to me, it felt like they put them on display to pick apart and ridicule in front of the whole town."

"I'm so sorry," she whispers.

"I overheard them, on several occasions, telling their friends or people they ran into how much my inability to measure up to Steven disappointed them. They hardly tried to hide it."

I inhale deeply and clear my throat, grounding myself before continuing. "The times when they weren't tearing me down, they flat-out ignored me. It wasn't neglect, necessarily. My basic needs were taken care of, but they didn't show any interest in me or my hobbies at all by the time high school rolled around."

My chest tightens as I push my fist into my hand, needing to push some energy out in a physical way.

"It was heartbreaking," I whisper, my voice cracking under the pressure of the words. "These were supposed to be the people who loved me unconditionally and supported me no matter what—at least that's what I knew parents were supposed to do. But eventually, once my underachieving tendencies didn't change, they sort of just...gave up on me."

"The last straw for me was at my graduation party when they were openly criticizing my choice to pursue music instead of applying to med school—in front of a whole group of people that were supposed to be there for me. They were all laughing about it, talking about what a waste of a party—and money—it was."

"I don't remember that," she says quietly.

I shake my head. "It was after you guys left."

She rubs her thumb along the skin of my arm. I appreciate her comforting touch, but I don't dare look over at her just yet. I might not have the courage to keep going if I do.

"So, I left," I continue. "And I literally haven't heard from anyone in my family since. Not my mom, my dad, or my brother. They never reached out to me, and I certainly didn't want to be the one to call them—at least until I saw Steven at the hospital, that is."

"I'm so sorry. I had no idea." The pity in her voice is loud and clear, which I both loathe and find comfort in at the same time. "That's why you didn't come home for such a long stretch after graduation."

I nod. "I just couldn't. And then when I did, the stares and whispers around town were too much to handle. I have no idea who all knew about my parents' ridicule, but I'm assuming a lot of them did. The embarrassment and shame were so overwhelming that I had to turn right around and leave."

"I had no idea," she whispers as she slides closer to me, wrapping her arms around my elbow. Her touch seems to soften some of the tension in my muscles, and I lean into her.

"Anyway, to answer your question, that's why I don't like it here. Not only because of the risk of running into them and what that conversation might be like, but also because of the stares from everyone else, the judgment from my parents' friends. Everyone I run into—Iris and Opal, for example—always brings up my family and I just don't want to constantly be reminded, you know?"

"I get that," she says quietly.

"I'm fine. I really am, Naomi. I've moved past a lot of it, and my trauma could absolutely be way worse. But I can't help but feel uncomfortable when I'm here, which is why I don't come home that often."

"Until you offered to be my fake boyfriend and help me with these silly exercises." Her face pinches together in a cringe. "I'm so sorry, Robbie. I shouldn't have let you do all this for me."

"Hey, no. Absolutely not." I turn toward her, squeezing the spot above her elbow. "We're not doing that. It was my idea, remember?"

She nods wearily, unconvinced, resting her head on my arm.

"Besides, I'm happy I did. I don't regret it for a second. Because it led me to this. To us. This means a lot to me." I blow out a slow, steadying breath. With each passing second of her head resting on my shoulder, some of the discomfort of reliving it seems to quell, although the weight of it all still feels heavy. I'm not sure there will ever be a time that it won't.

"For what it's worth, I would choose a musician over a doctor any day," she whispers, causing the corner of my mouth to curve up.

"Thank you." I force out a low chuckle, struggling to push everything back down where it belongs so we can move on with our day. "Anyway, enough about that."

I clear my throat again, mustering enough stability to do what I originally planned for this morning.

"Can we start our day with a mini exercise?" I ask.

She rolls her head off my arm, rolling it backward dramatically.

"Sure," she eventually says, sitting up straight.

"That's the spirit." I rub my hands together, breathing through the lingering pressure in my chest. "Let's do a little mantra building to start our day."

"Aren't you forgetting something?" she asks.

"That's right." I lightly bump her nose with my finger. "Look at the perfect little student you've grown into."

She playfully rolls her eyes. "Okay, one thing I want out of life is...to have multiple storefronts of my bakery in different locations. Have I mentioned that yet?"

"You haven't, but that's a great one." I brush aside the mental reminder that if she leases a brick-and-mortar building here, the chances of her ever leaving Pine Falls would be even slimmer. But I can't focus on that right now on top of everything else.

"Back to our mantras. Super simple. Just repeat after me," I say. "I am a confident woman."

She repeats.

"I am worthy of respect."

She repeats.

"My wants and needs are valid and worth fighting for."

She repeats.

"I am deserving of good things."

She repeats.

"I am allowed to set boundaries when needed in order to preserve my well-being."

She repeats.

I continue on, helping boost her confidence for the day. All the while, mine seems to be slowly deflating under the still-present heaviness from our conversation. As much as I try to focus my attention on building her up, my mind reels, and the tension ends up lingering for far longer than I'd hoped it would.

CHAPTER TWENTY-EIGHT

Naomi

"What exactly constitutes a perfect strawberry?" Robbie asks, bending over to pluck a lush piece of fruit off the plant.

I crouch down in the next row over to lift a leaf from the bush. "Well, obviously they need to be the perfect color. I like mine to be a deep, almost blood-red color. If they're still pink, then they're too tart for me."

"That is oddly specific," he says in a distracted voice.

"You asked." I smile, gently tossing a strawberry into a cardboard crate with *Emerson's Berry Farm* printed on the side.

"Just so we're clear, I have no idea if any of the ones I'm picking are actually good. I'm more of a 'throw anything in there' kind of a picker," he says.

"That's alright, we'll sort through and save those ones for you to eat."

"You know, I've lived in Pine Falls my whole life and have never been here," he comments, moving on to the next plant.

"Do you like strawberries?"

"I suppose. I don't *not* like them."

A perfectly ripe one is hidden behind a branch, and I can't resist sinking my teeth into it for a taste. "Mm. These are so good."

I move on to inspect the next strawberry plant as Robbie does the same to a nearby one. My eye catches on the subtle way his face clouds over, the same way it has all day.

My heart cracks as I watch him with such a pained expression. It's a far cry from the jovial, funny guy I've always known. I hate that he was struggling with this the entire time we were in high school—and before that even. I hate even more that I had no idea about any of it. He never clued me in on what was happening at home, but it certainly explains why he always pushed for hanging out in nearby cities or, at the very least, at one of our homes instead of his.

A pang of guilt hits me, knowing that this strawberry patch—let alone this entire town—is the last place he really wants to be.

"I think we have enough," I declare, willing to offer an end to the outing.

"Are you sure?" He straightens to stand instantly, as though he's been waiting for those specific words.

"Yup."

"What are you making again?" He takes a wide step over the row of strawberry plants and lifts the crate that's now three-quarters full.

"A strawberry glaze for angel food cake." I fall into step next to him as we make our way out of the berry patch.

"Was that on the calendar? I don't remember seeing it."

"This is just for us."

He shifts the crate under one arm and reaches for my hand with the other. I weave my fingers through his, holding on tight. Hoping that being with me lessens the burden he's feeling, even if it's only a small amount.

In an attempt to focus on anything other than the heaviness that practically radiates off him, I make note of how the farm looks absolutely picturesque on this sunny, summer day. Long rows of strawberry plants span the length of the field with tall blueberry plants skirting the perimeter of the farm. Lush green trees surround the main building where canned jams and homemade pies are available for purchase.

As we pass by the vegetable stand on our way inside, I eye the assortment of fresh veggies that are laid out in heaping piles. Robbie stops first, as if he already knows I want to look. He waits patiently for me to peruse the selection, and I quickly grab two zucchinis from the top of the pile.

"Could you grab a couple carrots over there, please?" I ask, pointing to the other side of the stand.

"Have you learned nothing from my strawberry picking?" His effort to lighten the mood sends a brief surge of relief through me. Any little glimpse of a normal interaction makes me cling to the hope that he's okay. That we can somehow make this work.

"It's kind of hard to mess up carrots—any will do." I smirk.

"Whatever you say."

We pick a few tomatoes to add to our selection and then head inside the building to pay. My phone pings with an incoming text message as we're waiting to be rung up.

"Charlie wants to know who's in for going to the turtle races tonight," I say mindlessly, then immediately regret saying it out loud. Pine Falls's annual turtle races are a spectacle in and of themselves. Patrons go wild cheering to see whose turtle crosses the finish line first, and it just so happens to be one of the most popular events around here. It draws crowds of people from neighboring cities, let alone almost the entirety of Pine Falls—which would include the exact people he's trying to avoid.

One look at his face confirms my regret for asking. His expression is hard and distant. The internal conflict he's wrestling with is clear, settling deep in the crease between his brows.

"I don't know," he spits out, his tone now holding a bite of frustration.

"It's okay," I say quickly. "We don't have to go."

"No, it's just... Do you want to go?"

The fact that he pushes past his discomfort enough to ask that question makes my heart both soar and break into a million pieces at the very same time. I'm struggling, at a complete loss for how I'm supposed to navigate this with him.

"No. The turtle I choose never ends up winning at those things anyway." I wave it off, scrambling to come up with a quick segue conversation that will lessen the heaviness.

"Should we bring one of these blackberry pies home?" The display case next to the register has several freshly baked pies boxed up and ready to go.

"Sure," he says with a forced smile. It's apparent how fast his mind is racing, how much he's struggling. He doesn't offer anything else, not even murmuring in my ear that the pie wouldn't compare to mine—a comment he would, without a doubt, normally make in a situation like this.

Nevertheless, I add the pie to the counter where it gets added to my order. I wait patiently for the young girl to ring me up. When I hand her my credit card, I hear Robbie curse under his breath, his body twisting sharply. He grips the counter with one hand and twists his neck the opposite direction, as if he's trying to conceal himself from something.

"What is it?" I watch with dread as he fidgets nervously, feeling even more helpless than I already was.

"One of Steven's friends is here." His voice comes out gruff and laced with pain. My heart drops, struggling to know what to do.

"Oh," I say meekly.

I watch as his gaze tracks the movement of someone out the window. Then he shifts back to face me, a cloud of anxiety following him as he does.

"Are you ready?" He bites his lip, assessing the speed of the girl checking us out.

"Yes, let's go. Thank you so much." I smile timidly to the girl, offering a quick wave before following Robbie out the door.

The walk through the parking lot is silent with me practically jogging to keep up with his racing pace. I don't push to have a conversation, knowing he's not even close to being in a great headspace right now.

"I think a quiet night in sounds nice," I offer once we climb into my car.

"That sounds good to me too." He grips my hand tightly, as if he needs something to hold onto. I squeeze back, finding that I need the same. He drives us home, my hand in his, while I desperately try to give him whatever it is that he needs.

I dip my toes lazily in the lake water below, gripping the edge of the dock with both hands as I lean over. Robbie sits close by my side, his own legs dangling into the water. I take comfort in his closeness, even if our interactions have been stilted ever since our heart-to-heart talk and trip to the berry farm yesterday.

"It's a beautiful night, huh?" I straighten my arms, leaning even farther forward while I twist my neck to look at him.

It's yet another attempt to start a conversation with him, to lighten the mood. None of them have been successful so far.

"Yeah." The slightest glimpse of the boy I know comes through in his crooked smile, but the heaviness that's been clouding him wins out, pushing his expression right back into a stony, cold resting state.

We both jump a little as the sound of his phone cuts through the otherwise quiet evening air. I watch my reflection as it bobs in the lake below while he checks his message. When he slides the phone back in his pocket, his heavy sigh makes me bite my lip with apprehension. This can't be good.

"Who is it?" I dare to ask.

"Steven." He pushes the name out as if it takes a great deal of effort.

"Really?" I ask in surprise. "What did he want?"

"His friend told him that he saw me at the berry farm yesterday. He knows I'm in town and asked if we could talk. Again."

I nod silently, unsure of what to say, or of what might rock the boat even more.

"I don't know why, though." The muscles on his forearms flex as he pushes his fist against his thigh. Then he rolls his lips together quickly with clear agitation.

A few moments pass silently as we watch a pontoon boat glide along the far shoreline, the last boat left out on the lake at this hour.

"Do you want to come with me to my gig this week?" His question cuts through the silence, his tone suggesting a subtle desperation. A quiet plea.

"Oh, I wish I could, but I can't," I say with intense regret. "There's no way I'd be able to get time off at the dealership again. Plus, I have a full schedule of baking orders to fulfil."

He pushes his lips together while nodding, then he hangs his head down. I can see the way he's getting himself worked up in his head, which fills me with a desperation of my own. To figure out what will make this all better. To turn it all around and rewind to how we were just a few short days ago.

"I wish it was easier for me to leave at the drop of a hat, but it just isn't," I whisper, bringing my hand to rest on his thigh. It's probably foolish of me to think it might bring him some small comfort, but I do it anyway.

He runs both palms down his face gruffly before pinning me with a look. One with clear yearning and a touch of a wild anguish to it. "I need to know something, Naomi. Believe me, I hate myself for putting this kind of pressure on you right now, but I have to ask...is there even the smallest chance in the world that you'd ever be okay with moving away from here someday? Even one day down the road?"

I blanch, taken aback. "I..." My voice trails off as I struggle to think of the right answer.

"Because this is eating me up inside," he continues before I can say a word, rising to his feet in a jolt as if he suddenly can't stand being still. I stand too, before freezing in place as he paces on the dock in front of me.

"I'm falling for you, Naomi. I really am." He runs his fingers messily through his hair while my entire world stops. My heart pounds rapidly in my chest at his admission, and I wait with bated breath for him to inevitably take it all back. "In an overwhelming kind of way. And it's beautiful. And consuming. And awakening. In more ways than one. But it's also tearing me apart inside because I. Can't. Stay. Here. I can't escape them here, Naomi. Please...I need to know if there's a chance."

The only thing worse than the feeling of my heart ripping in two is seeing the look of complete torment on his face. Of course I want to jump and shout yes! Yes, of course I would move away with you. Isn't that what I've always wanted? A future filled with more adventure than this small-town life can offer? With a wild, uncontained love that it feels like we could be on the cusp of? I had the time of my life with him on the road. I would love more of that life.

But at the same time, my heart is refusing to let go of my bakery business that's just barely off the ground. It's mine. And I'm proud of it. And isn't that what all this practice has been for anyway? To be bold and assertive? To know and stick up for what's important to me?

After a few seconds of me hopelessly trying to reach for the right words to say, he beats me to it and nods somberly.

"That's what I thought," he says quietly.

"I didn't give you an answer," I scramble a protest, feeling my control of the situation slipping away rapidly.

"I get it. I really do. Your life is here."

"Yours is too?" I whisper meekly, both a statement and a desperate question.

He holds my gaze, his eyes saturated with emotion-laced exhaustion. He walks slowly toward me, each step making my heart pound even faster. I feel the soft grip of his hand around my wrist seconds before he presses a kiss to the very center of my forehead. I squeeze my eyes shut, breathing in the scent of him, the feeling of having him so close...as if a part of me fears I may need to memorize it.

"I'm gonna go," he says quietly against my forehead.

"Go where?" My eyes fly open to find him already backing away.

"To Vegas. I'll bump up my flight. I just... I need to get out of here." The way he says it has a hint of finality to it. My heart completely shatters as he lets go of my wrist and turns to walk off the dock.

A voice inside my head screams to fight for him. To fight for us. But how do I beg him to stay when I know that very thing is causing him so much pain?

"Will you be back for the grand opening?" I manage to ask before he reaches the end of it. He pauses in place and twists to lock eyes with mine. The sky is almost completely dark now, but I can still see the distinct shade of blue in them that I've come to know so well.

"I'll be back." Something in his tone leaves me questioning if he really will. I watch helplessly as he walks briskly past the swing and into my house to pack his things.

CHAPTER TWENTY-NINE

Robbie

The blinding white stage light strobes across my face, cutting through the dark sky. I squint, casting my gaze down to focus on the way my fingers pick at the strings of my guitar. For the millionth time tonight, I need to force myself to focus on the set of songs we're playing for over two thousand screaming people in the audience.

One more song left. I can do this.

If I'm honest, this whole show has been a blur. I'm trying to be acccuntable for my bandmates and not let my personal life affect my performance, but it's been nearly impossible to focus on anything other than Naomi.

I miss her so much it feels like my lungs are being tightly squeezed—I haven't taken a full deep breath in days. Performing for a crowd? Yeah right. Not at my highest level anyway. What's the point when my heart is breaking into a million pieces?

With a shake of my head, I force myself to move to the outer corner of the stage, looking out at the faces in the crowd, desperately hoping some of their adrenaline might rub off me and cover some of this heartbreak.

Finally, I strum the last chord, faintly hearing Rylie and Dane saying goodbye to the crowd. I numbly follow them to the stage exit while the crowd's cheers sound like something in the distance.

"Good show, man." One of the sound guys gives me a pat on the shoulder as we jog down the stairs. I'm sure he's just being polite—there's no way my performance tonight was anything other than subpar, but I nod a thanks anyway, wiping the sweat from my forehead.

Dane jumps on my back, hanging on with one arm, the other fist pumping the air.

"Not bad for a lowly bass guitarist," he drawls in my ear, fueled by excitement.

I know he's teasing, but given my current mental state, I'm immediately transported back to the time I walked by my dad's study and overheard him entertaining his fellow cardiologist buddies.

A bass guitarist. Can you believe it? A nice hobby, sure. But a career? No chance. When I was his age, I was already earning college credits. It's pathetic, honestly.

Nausea swirls in my gut as I fight to push the thought out of my mind. The memories from my childhood have been sitting closer to the surface ever since opening up to Naomi a few days ago, popping up to blindside me out of nowhere. And that pretty much sums up my last few days since I left

Pine Falls: alternating thoughts of missing Naomi and then cutting sharply to memories from my past.

"Vegas is a breed of its own, huh? That crowd was electric." He jumps off me, barreling into our dressing room. I follow behind and head straight for the food table in search of something to bury in my now sour stomach.

"Where's everybody heading tonight?" Rylie asks the room as he grabs a slice of pizza.

I barely listen as everyone shouts out their vote for which Vegas club would be best to hit up. We've racked up enough experiences here over the years to give them plenty of ideas, and they argue over which one they want to try and relive.

As for me, I can't for the life of me seem to tear my attention away from the chocolate chip cookie in my hand that isn't nearly half as good as Naomi's. Another pang of guilt hits me as I stare at it.

Even with these overwhelming feelings, there has been one silver lining. It's been much easier to breathe now that I'm out of Pine Falls—and I feel terrible for that. At what that means for a future with Naomi. I feel even worse that I wasn't able to shake the tension before I left. She didn't deserve the funk I ended up lost in.

She still doesn't.

"You guys go ahead. I'll catch up," Dane's voice breaks me out of my thoughts. He waves to the rest of the band who are already halfway out the door and I throw up a sorry attempt at a wave, having not even noticed they were leaving already.

Then Dane pins me with a knowing look as he sinks down into a chair.

"Alright, spill, bro," he says, pulling an empty chair next to him.

"What do you mean?" I take a big bite of the mediocre cookie to get it out of my sight.

"How long have we been friends now? Do you think I can't tell when you're in a mood?" He gestures again to the chair and this time I take the hint, sliding into it.

"I know. I'm sorry. I was really hoping this wouldn't affect my performance," I say apologetically.

"Screw the show," he huffs. "I just want to know that you're good. Because to be honest, you don't look good."

I blow out a breath, contemplating how exactly I'm supposed to explain this confusing mess I've found myself in.

"Is it Naomi?" his voice softens.

"Yes...among other things," I admit, letting my head drop down to the floor.

"I'm listening," he prompts me to go on.

"I...I guess I'm realizing that I don't know how a future with her would truly work. I've told you that I don't get along with my family—I absolutely despise being back in Pine Falls."

"And that's where she lives," he cuts in.

"Yup. And she doesn't want to leave there anytime soon. Which she shouldn't have to, but...it's tearing me up inside, Dane. I've never felt the way I do for her with anyone else.

I'm falling in love with her for sure. But what toll would it take on us if I don't want to be in the city where she lives? How could we ever last? Long distance rarely works as it is."

He nods his head, quietly allowing me to go on.

"I guess I'm torn," I say simply with a heaving exhale.

He leans forward, hands clasped. "Do you want to know what I think?"

"Please. Clearly, I'm desperate," I say, leaning back against the chair.

He adjusts himself, angling toward me.

"All I know is that real, true love isn't as easy to find as everyone makes it seem." A shadow passes over his face as he continues. "It's even harder to hold onto. I'm not saying it would be easy, or that it's even the right decision. Only you can decide how much she means to you, but I say if you're lucky enough to think you might have found it...I don't know, man...I sure as heck wouldn't let it go."

I nod slowly, absorbing his words.

"Let me ask you this. What is the stronger feeling? Anger and resentment toward your family? Or the way you feel about Naomi?"

"Naomi," I answer immediately. "I wouldn't even have been there as much as I have if she wasn't pulling me there."

"Well...then maybe your answer is clearer than you think."

I lift a defeated shoulder, the discord I feel toward my family holding me back from fully agreeing with him. Why can't I just let it all go? What's holding me back?

"Are you planning on avoiding your past for the rest of your life?" He huffs. "'Cause I'll tell you what…that stuff will follow you around wherever you go regardless."

"When'd you get so philosophical?" I ask with a smirk.

He tips his mouth in a grin. "I've seen a lot of things. Been a lot of places."

"I don't know." I grow serious, sighing again. "I guess I have some thinking to do. I'm done waffling, though. It's not fair to her. I need to choose a path and commit to it. In or out with Naomi."

"Do you want to meet up with the boys? You know they're bound to get into all kinds of trouble—the distracting kind."

"Nah, I think I'm going to head back to the bus. But you should go out. One of us might as well have some fun." I rise, sliding the chair back where it was.

"I've seen Vegas enough. I'll come with you."

I pat him on the back, grateful for his support, then grab a cookie for the road—because, apparently, I'm also feeling like a glutton for punishment tonight.

The walk through the now-empty hallways of the venue is quiet. Every step has me pondering Dane's words, deciding what I can and can't live without. He walks beside me, a silent, steady support, until we get back to the bus.

"I'll be right here for the night," he declares, grabbing a beer from the mini fridge before sinking onto the couch. I grab one for myself and slump down next to him.

I contemplate calling Naomi just to hear her voice.. and maybe apologize for leaving the way I did. Ultimately, I resist reaching for my phone—what else would I say? I shouldn't call her until I have a solid plan figured out.

As I mindlessly watch whatever show Dane selected, I contemplate the question I've asked Naomi over and over again. but have never stopped to consider for myself.

What do I want out of life?

Regardless of my aversion to Pine Falls, am I even ready to settle down in general? I don't exactly live a stable lifestyle. Am I destined to be a drifter for the rest of my life? Or is the pull to be with Naomi strong enough to convince me to keep coming back to a city I despise?

With another swig of my beer, I sink even farther into the couch, spending the rest of evening pondering these life-altering questions, and what my findings mean for the direction of my life.

CHAPTER THIRTY

Naomi

The knock on my front door catches me by surprise, making me drop my mascara tube in the sink.

"Shoot," I mutter to myself. Careful not to smear the black liquid, I set it upright and head toward the door. For a brief second I foolishly let myself hope it might be Robbie, but the thought vanishes when I remind myself that he wouldn't knock. He would walk right in after already letting me know he was on the way.

When I pull the door open, I'm caught off guard by who I see.

"Gabby," I say in surprise. She's standing on my front step with her arms crossed and a hesitant smile on her face.

"Hi, um. I was hoping we could talk?" The softness in her voice has me immediately opening the door wider to invite her in.

"Of course. Come in."

She slides past me, hesitantly lingering in the entryway as if she hasn't been here a million times before, as if she's waiting for me to show her that I want her here.

"Would you like a slice of banana cream pie?" I offer, leading her to the kitchen. "I just made it this morning."

"No, thank you. I can't stay long. I know you have the grand opening tonight, but I wanted to catch you before you go."

I lean against the kitchen island, readying myself to talk about our conversation at The Squirrely Bear.

"So, what's up?" I ask.

"Well...first I want to apologize." She offers a shy smile, followed by a cringe. "I know I haven't been the most supportive friend in general—or the nicest. I, uh...admit that I can be a bit abrasive, and it's something I'm going to work on. I've been doing some reflecting since our talk. I just wanted you to know that."

"Gabby," I sigh through a smile, feeling a rush of both relief and pride for her at the same time. This was all I ever wanted. "I appreciate it, but there's no need to apologize. We're all a work in progress, right? I certainly am...we can do it together."

"Deal." She nods as I pull her in for a hug. I'm not one to hold a grudge, especially when she's actively making changes to better herself. Feeling relieved that she made the effort to come over here tonight, I am hopeful for a different kind of friendship between us moving forward.

When we separate, I notice instantly how her expression darkens. "And there's something else you should know…you might want to sit down for this."

"Uh-oh." I take her advice, sliding into a chair as I study her apprehensively. "What is it?"

"Edith canceled her cupcake order for next week, right?" she asks with a cringe.

"Yeah…how do you know about that?" My neighbor's order cancellation just came through this morning.

"Well, my mom was walking with Edith this afternoon, and somehow your baking business came up. She, uh…spilled the beans."

"What do you mean? What beans?"

"Apparently, Edith ran into your dad at the grocery store yesterday, and she was gushing about how proud she was of you and your new business—as the whole town is, by the way. And get this, your dad told her that he would offer her a discount at the dealership if she canceled her order with you."

"Wait, what?" My stomach drops, and the hair on the back of my neck instantly stands up.

"Yeah. I'm sorry," she says regretfully.

"That was the fourth cancellation I've had recently," I process out loud, my mind reeling with this information. "Has he been doing the same thing with them?"

She shrugs. "I wouldn't put it past him, honestly."

"Wow." I shake my head in disbelief, feeling a range of emotions. "Thank you for telling me, Gabby."

"Of course. I thought you should know." She dips her gaze down at the floor. "I'm planning to get out of town for a little while...do some traveling. Get some space."

"You don't have to do that, Gabby," I say, feeling guilty that she feels the need to leave Pine Falls.

"No, I want to." She nods. "It won't be for very long. I just need to...I don't know...think about some things. Figure out my life. Who I want to be."

"Okay." I taper my frustration with my dad long enough to give her a genuine smile. "Well, let me know as soon as you come back. Maybe we can do a movie night or something."

"I will. I'll get out of your hair." She heads toward the door. "Have fun at the opening tonight."

"Thanks. I'll try." I walk her out and give her one last hug goodbye. When I shut the door, I linger in place, staring at the floor while anger comes racing back with a vengeance. My dad's been going around telling people to cancel their orders with me? So that I won't succeed?

I can't believe it.

Or, actually, I can. Which makes it even worse.

I instinctively pick up my phone to call Robbie, wanting to fill him in, before remembering the current state of our relationship. We haven't spoken since he left three days ago for his gig, and I keep talking myself out of being the first one to reach out to him.

He did say he'd be back for the grand opening tonight, but I have yet to hear from him, so at this point, I doubt he's coming. My heart twists painfully at the mere thought of him and the mess we're in, which adds to my already jumbled emotions.

I'll have to deal with my dad another night—maybe at the meeting we have coming up. For now, I attempt to shake off my anger and finish getting myself ready so I won't be late.

"Hi, Naomi," Fran says cheerfully, placing her glass of wine next to mine on the linen-draped high-top table.

"Hey, Fran. Congratulations, again. You did an amazing job planning this event," I tell her warmly.

"Oh, thank you. If I'm honest, I'll be happy to have it over with after tonight. This was a feat."

"I bet," I chuckle, looking around the shiny new dealership. There's a space left open for a makeshift dance floor off to the left in front of a live band that's performing on a removable stage. Their soft music fills the air while crowds of people mingle between cars on the grand showroom floor.

As I scan the room, low-key looking for any sign of Robbie, I see familiar faces of people I've known my entire life—residents of Pine Falls, Brainerd, and other neighboring cities. Opal and Iris are over by the temporary bar, huddled together, and Mrs. Fitzpatrick is peering inside the windows of a brand-new Jeep.

My mind drifts, and I can't help but wonder what kept each of these people here in Pine Falls. What drew them to a small town in central Minnesota? Or, if they were born here, what made them stay and not move away to a bigger city with more opportunities? How many of them moved here on a whim, and alternatively, who has never stepped foot outside of the tri-city area? Did any of them also have to choose between chasing love and the comfort of home? Am I foolish for wanting to stay?

I don't find Robbie, but I do catch my breath when I spot his brother, Steven, in a suit and tie, mingling over by the tray of mostaccioli that was catered in by The Italian Place. Thankfully, I don't see their parents in sight. I'm not sure what I would say if I came face to face with them, given everything I now know. Steven is hard enough to see from across the room. I'm half-tempted to march over there and give him a piece of my mind about not sticking up for Robbie when they were kids and being a sorry excuse for a brother.

"Hi, dear," my mom says softly, sneaking up on my left. "Hi, Fran."

"Hi, Mom." Seeing her brings me back into focus. It's also like a balm to my soul, soothing a rough edge inside of me that's been sharp ever since Robbie left, enough that I instinctively throw my arms around her in a much-needed hug. A brief flash of surprise crosses her face before she returns the hug with a tight embrace.

"You look beautiful," she says into my ear before pulling away to admire my black dress. "Do you think they have this in my size?"

"I'm sure they do." I grin, feeling a hint of emotion tugging at the corner of my eyes. Something about seeing her makes me realize how much I've needed her comfort lately. How much I wish we could be closer.

"Yeah, yeah, you're both gorgeous. We get it." Fran waves a hand in the air. "Marion, I need to show you something."

I see the hesitation on my mom's face, as I'm sure it matches mine. We hardly ever get to be around each other without my dad, and we're both aware of that fact enough to want to soak it up while we can.

"Go ahead," I urge her. "We can catch up later. I'll come find you."

As soon as they leave, I return to my people-watching, still pondering whether or not Robbie could still show up, hoping desperately that he'll prove the doubt in my mind wrong.

"Is this thing on?" my dad's voice bellows out from the stage. The sound of it alone makes my toes curl with anger. I've successfully managed to avoid him so far this evening as I don't think it would be possible to put on a fake happy act in front of him after hearing about what he's done. I take a sip of my champagne and reluctantly turn to watch his speech.

"Thank you all for celebrating with us tonight. This second dealership has been a dream in the making for some time now, and I'm thrilled to finally be opening the doors here in Brainerd."

The sound of clapping fills the space, complete with a few cheers from somewhere in the back. I keep my hands still at my sides as I watch with a straight face.

"We're excited to have the opportunity to serve this community and become family with its residents, as we have over in Pine Falls."

Again, more clapping.

"This second opening brings a few exciting promotion opportunities for my staff," he boasts. "I'd like to announce some of them right now, if you don't mind helping me congratulate them."

He clears his throat before continuing. "The first is Zander, who'll be making the trek over here to lead the sales department. Come on up here, Zander."

A round of applause breaks out as he makes his way onstage to shake my dad's hand. Huh, so that's what those extra meetings between those two have been about. There hasn't been a company-wide memo or even rumors of any of my coworkers relocating, but I suppose I shouldn't be surprised. I'm not exactly privy to staffing meetings.

"Next up we have Luna, who has graciously accepted the role of office manager. Come on up here, Luna."

I join in clapping, watching with a faint smile as she takes the stage.

"Last, but certainly not least, joining Zander and Luna to head up the IT department is...drumroll, please." I look around, wondering which of my colleagues he's chosen from my department.

"None other than my daughter, Naomi Tillman."

CHAPTER THIRTY-ONE

Naomi

"Naomi likes to dabble a bit with different hobbies, as I'm sure some of you know. She's got a touch of a silly dreamer's spirit in her. But luckily, dear old dad knows what's best. Nothing solidifies your commitment to the dealership quite like leading a department, am I right, dear?"

My cheeks heat with embarrassment, and I struggle to keep my composure and my jaw from dropping open. The nerve of this man. Not once did he ask me if I wanted the position, and to call me out in front of basically the entire town is absolutely uncalled for. How could he make a decision like this without talking to me? There is zero part of me that wants to head up an entire department, and he should know that—he would if he had bothered to ask.

"Come on up here, Naomi. Don't be shy," he chides from the stage.

I feel about as small as an ant as he points in my direction, drawing attention toward me. My first instinct is to cower and hide. Slip away and disappear into the crowd. But a powerful frustration and hint of courage bubbles in my gut. I feel emboldened with each second that passes as I watch him continue to gesture for me to join him. The smug glint in his eye is the last straw, further maddening me.

This is it. The culmination of everything I've been working toward with Robbie.

I can do this.

I can do this without him here.

If I don't stand up for myself with my dad right now, I have a feeling I never will. I summon every last scrap of assertion I can find and push my shoulders together while clearing my throat.

"Actually, Dad...I respectfully decline the position." My strong voice does not sound like my own. I hardly recognize the unwavering confidence behind it, but it immediately fills me with even more.

A silent gasp rumbles through the crowd as Dad's jaw clamps shut, his eyes narrowing at me. Both things would have certainly deflated the old me, but I refuse to focus on either of them.

"Pardon?" My dad huffs a haughty laugh in an attempt to cover his admonishing tone. "Surely, I heard you wrong. Now, don't be difficult, and come on up here, Naomi."

"No," I say loud enough so there is no mistaking it this time. His eyes burn into mine, and his face grows red with anger. My confidence wavers under his glare, and I swallow, trying desperately to maintain my posture.

"Thank you for the opportunity, but I can't accept the position." My voice is quieter this time, but still assertive enough to garner my dad's continued glare.

After a moment, he clears his throat and turns to address the crowd. "Well, clearly that minor issue still needs to be sorted out. Moving on..."

He continues with his speech, boasting about trivial things such as the shiny floors and fancy new inventory. All the while, I keep my feet stuck to the ground, intent on holding my position. My entire body flushes with adrenaline, but I don't dare move. I can feel eyes on me from every different angle, and I refuse to slink away into the crowd.

To my relief, he wraps things up quickly and exits the stage to the right, immediately getting lost in the sea of people. Feeling like I can finally release a breath, I make a half-turn toward the bar—and that's when I see him.

Robbie.

He's here.

More specifically, in the corner of the dealership, wedged behind a brand-new silver pickup truck and the coat rack. He's wearing a black suit and tie, and his gaze is firmly set on me. My chest warms instantly, a rush of relief mixing with a brand new surge of adrenaline. He immediately starts a slow saunter toward me, and I find my feet absentmindedly doing the same. Eventually, we're close enough for him to reach for my hand.

The slow gesture comes with a probing look in his eyes.

A question.

An apology all in one.

"You're here," I whisper, running my free hand down the front of his coat pocket, admiring how handsome he looks dressed up.

Gosh, I missed him.

"I'm sorry I'm late," he says gruffly.

"It's okay," I say meekly with a shake of my head.

"No, it's not," he says firmly. "I planned to be back to take you here tonight, but my plane was delayed."

"Oh," is all I can say. A million questions run through my mind, but none seem pressing enough to ask in this moment. He's here. And that's all that matters right now.

"Dance with me," he says. It comes out as a desperate plea rather than a request. He should know it would be an easy yes.

"Alright," I whisper.

He leads me to the middle of the dance floor, where I'm keenly aware of the prying eyes in the crowd that are still following me. I tuck myself into him as he places a strong hand on the small of my back. I breathe him in, and the relief of having him so close quiets my still-pounding heart. Being in his arms feels soothing. Like returning to something familiar. Like the comfort of home.

"Are we okay?" he asks quietly.

I nod my head, keeping my eyes locked with his. "We can talk tomorrow. But for now, I'm just glad you're here."

"I wouldn't want to be anywhere else." He says it pointedly, as if to emphasize the truth behind his words. It's the first time he's ever mentioned even remotely wanting to be here, and I store every little bit of that detail in the back of my head for later.

"I'm guessing by the look of pride in your eyes that you saw what happened with my dad." My mouth curls up in a bashful smirk.

"This is just the way I look at you," he murmurs. "But yes, I did. And it was incredible. I was this close to starting a slow clap for you from back there in the corner."

"I embarrassed him in front of his entire company." I cringe. "Do you know how mad he is right now?"

"Let him be mad. That's not your responsibility, remember? You stood up for yourself like the confident woman you are."

"Does this mean I'm no longer a pushover?" My head dips to his chest to hide a grin.

"I would say you aced the final." He laughs. Then he tilts my chin up and presses his forehead to mine. "But can I still be your boyfriend?"

My heart soars, threatening to jump out of my chest. "Yes, please," I whisper.

"That easily? I was prepared to do some groveling."

"I mean, groveling never hurts."

He chuckles, pulling me even closer.

"Oh...you should know that your brother is here," I say cautiously, bracing myself for his reaction.

"I know," he says calmly. "I saw him across the room when I walked in."

"And you're okay with that?" My eyes narrow.

He nods, his eyes skating across my face. "I'm sick of letting my family dictate what I do and what I want. I'm done with all that. I'm here because you're here. End of story. I'll figure out the rest as I go."

My teeth bite into my bottom lip through a grin as I wrap my arms tighter around his neck. Words don't come to my mind, only a rush of overwhelming relief.

He came back.

For me.

I absentmindedly graze my fingers along the scruff at the base of his neck as I soak in the reality of his words and roam the crowd that has, thankfully, shifted their focus off me.

I freeze when I notice my dad on the other side of the dance floor and I hold my breath, waiting to see if he'll storm over here. But Mom is the one who catches sight of me first. To my relief, she loops her arm in his and turns, distracting him with something in the opposite direction.

When she looks back at me, I give her a small, grateful smile. I know I'll have to face my dad soon enough, but I'd be more than happy if it doesn't happen tonight.

I tuck my head into Robbie's neck, soaking up the warmth of him, not wanting to let go now that he's actually here. We stay on the dance floor for the next hour, my arms locked firmly around him, wishing with all my might that I won't ever need to let go.

CHAPTER THIRTY-TWO

Robbie

"Good morning." I yawn, pulling myself up to rest my back against Naomi's headboard. My eyes feel heavy, tempting me to fall back into the comfort of sleep, but the reality of where I'm waking up this morning leaves me with a surge of excitement that springs me all the way awake.

"Morning," she replies sleepily from where she lies next to me, stretching her arms above her head. A beam of sunlight from her lakeside window spreads slowly across her face, and she squints, shifting her head out of its path. Her blonde hair cascades over her pillow in a messy, wild way that causes my heart to physically ache.

She brings her arms back down to her sides and tilts her head to look up at me. Her still-puffy eyelids and sleep-wrinkled cheek are raw and imperfect, yet she's still the most gorgeous sight I've ever seen. If this was my view every morning for the rest of my life I would die a happy man.

Our first night together was everything I could have imagined it would be...and so much more. It was intimate, passionate, and awakening. The level of comfort we've always had with each other further fueled our connection, making it feel powerful in the most beautiful way. The mere memory brings a flush to my skin and a subtle desperation to do it all over again.

"How are you feeling after last night?" I ask, referencing the night as a whole—not only what transpired between us but how she stood up to her dad at the grand opening. Her defiance caused a ripple of chatter to spread through the entire showroom and I feel nothing but pride at the courage it took for her to do that. I can only imagine it will continue to make its way through the town gossip fodder for a while to come.

While I wait for her to answer, I glide my fingers through her hair, lightly pushing the strands away from her face, unable to ignore the urge to touch her in any way I can.

She gives me a lazy smile, her eyelids fluttering closed at my touch. "Really good," she admits.

"I'm so proud of you." I reach down to squeeze her forearm to emphasize the statement, although I already know there's no way it can convey the magnitude of what I feel. She looks up to meet my gaze, then abruptly shifts out of the covers to climb effortlessly onto my lap in one swift, excited movement. Her bent legs fall to either side of me, her bare thighs a stark tan amidst the sea of white bed sheets and her oversized white T-shirt.

"Did you see me?" she whispers, grinning slyly as she asks the same question for the millionth time. I don't mind, though. Seeing her filled with this much confidence makes me wildly happy.

Her hands come to either side of my face, and she slowly scooches her body up even farther until she's flush with my hips, pinning me to the mattress. Her body smothers mine in the best possible way, and her perfume from last night lingers around her. I'm consumed, completely drowning in her, and reminded of exactly why I came back.

"I did." My smirk hitches against her mouth as she squeals with delight, pressing her lips to mine. Joy practically radiates off her in an almost palpable way and I let it flow off of her to cover me too.

I run my hands lazily along her thighs, relishing the feel of her soft skin before tucking a strand of hair behind her ear. My gaze stays pinned on hers as we both grow quiet, settling into a comfortable silence.

"So, can we talk about what happened? About why you left?" she asks quietly, letting her hands fall softly to my chest. "And more importantly, why you came back?"

I nod, feeling more than ready to take accountability for my actions and finish our conversation from last night. I clear my throat, feeling the weight of my words to come, knowing I have one chance to get this right.

"First, I'm very sorry for the way I left," I tell her intently, holding her stare. "That wasn't okay. I let my emotions get the best of me, and I just...needed to get out of here."

She nods, dropping her gaze, but I tilt her chin up with my finger. It's absolutely crucial that she hears what I'm about to say.

"But what I realized while I was gone is that I'm always doing that...leaving. Drifting. Avoiding." I shake my head "I don't want to do that anymore."

"You don't?" Her hands find my face again, her thumbs ever so slightly sweeping against the skin of my cheeks as she looks at me with hopeful eyes.

"Nope. You're it for me, Naomi. And I'll follow you any-where...even if you want to stay in this tiny town," I say as firmly as I can.

She grins. "What changed your mind?"

"Dane," I say.

"I wasn't expecting that." She laughs, her brows flying up in amusement.

"It's true." I chuckle. "He helped me realize I don't want to live without you."

I run my hands up her arms, relishing the way that or my words create a slew of goosebumps that cascade across the surface.

"Even with your family here?"

I nod, my face going somber. "I don't want to lose you over some baggage from my past—I can't. You're my home base. No matter what happens with my family, I'm meant to be wherever you are. I'm certain of that."

"Well...thank you, Dane," she says against my lips as she presses them to mine.

"This is where I want to be," I murmur again through the kiss.

"You and me, huh?" She whispers, resting her forehead against mine.

"You and me," I confirm, feeling the weight of the promise deep in my bones.

She settles back against her thighs, pushing her lips together in a small, knowing smile. Her soft gaze tells me that she's hearing me, that she's accepting what I'm saying—without a trace of guilt on her part, no less.

"Come on. I'll make breakfast," she says as she rolls off me and pads out to the kitchen. I follow quickly behind, scrambling off the bed to block her path.

"I have another idea." I'm able to reach her just before she gets to the kitchen. I gently avert her shoulders toward the deck door.

"You're always in the kitchen. It's my turn to cook this morning. Go have a seat outside and I'll bring you an omelet and coffee. How does that sound?"

"Amazing. But who's going to make it for me?" she asks cheekily.

"Get outta here." I swat her out the door and get to work pulling ingredients out of the fridge. Out of the corner of my eye, I watch as she walks slowly across the grass to the dock. A soft-pink-and-orange sunrise serves as the perfect backdrop to an already beautiful sight. It's not until she lowers onto the bench that I can fully peel my eyes away from her and get to work.

I get lost in the satisfied bliss that runs through me while I pull the carton of eggs out of the fridge and grab a frying pan from the drawer. After a few minutes I hear the faint text message notification on my phone from her bedroom. Once I successfully flip one side of the omelet over, I jog to her room to retrieve it.

Steven: I saw you last night. I know you're in town again. Can we talk? Please?

His message gives me a pang of anxiety as I re-read his words more than a few times, but it's nothing I can't taper down quickly. I'll deal with him another day. I refuse to let him hinder my happiness right now. Today is all about Naomi and me and the start of something new. I slide my phone into my pocket, leaving the message unanswered. I know my issue with my family is something I'll need to address in the future, but today is not that day.

As I plate omelets for both of us, my gaze drifts again to Naomi out on the bench, waiting for me. A feeling of being right where I'm supposed to be—of feeling at home—settles over me, and I savor the comfort it brings. It's a feeling I haven't felt in...maybe ever. And I make a silent vow to do everything in my power not to lose it.

Grabbing both plates, I head outside, eager to get back to her. As I walk across the grass, I remember her bravery from last night and the monumental effort she made with her own family dynamic.

Maybe someday soon, I can do the same.

CHAPTER THIRTY-THREE

Naomi

The car comes to a stop as I shift the gear into park. Without Robbie's presence, nerves threaten to bubble below the surface of my skin as I take a minute to collect myself. I'm fully aware that I'm not nearly as confident as I would be if he were here with me.

But I asked him not to come. This is something I need to do alone. I know I can do this.

I replay a few mantras in my head to hold tight to the conviction I've been feeling ever since opening night. To say I'm proud of myself would be an understatement. Despite my long pattern of doing the exact opposite, I finally stood up for myself and what's best for me and my dreams—and I did it all by myself. Now I just need to get through this next hurdle of facing my dad and figuring out what direction we go from here.

Grabbing my phone off the center console, I make note of two new baking orders that came through on the drive over here and the red check mark that means Robbie has already marked them as entered into the calendar. Then I open the new message from him.

> **Robbie:** I would say good luck, but you don't need it.

The faintest of smiles tugs at my lips as his words succeed at further putting me at ease. I slip the phone into my purse and climb out of the car, ready to get this over with. Each step I take toward the front door brings a new flutter of nerves that threatens to take over, but I manage to put force behind each movement and maintain a confident posture.

Mom answers the door shortly after I knock, and the sight of her proves to be a welcome sight.

"Hi, sweetheart." She smiles, exuding a warmth that comforts me in the way only a mother can.

"Hi, Mom." I smile back but brace myself as I step inside. No other words are spoken between us, but she squeezes my arm in a silent show of support as I pass by. I follow her to the living room where Dad is sitting on the edge of the couch, his reading glasses sitting on the tip of his nose.

"Hey, Dad," I say, keeping my voice light. I might as well try for the sweetness angle to see how he'll respond. In one fell swoop, he rips the glasses off his face and hits me with a menacing glare.

"Mind explaining what in the world that was?" he asks, his voice rising with each word.

Okay, we're jumping right in, then. I heave a sigh, sinking down onto the couch across from him, bracing myself.

"You didn't ask me if I wanted the position, Dad," I say softly.

"That's irrelevant," he huffs, tossing his glasses onto the coffee table.

"Actually, it *is* relevant, Dad. Very much so. This is my life. Don't you think I should have a say in my own career?" My voice wobbles slightly at the edges, matching how uneasy my stomach feels, but somehow it still holds firm.

"You're not going to make me feel bad about offering you a promotion, Naomi," he admonishes.

That's all he thinks this is. In his mind he sees it as giving me a reward—a career advancement—instead of seeing it for exactly what it is...a manipulation tactic to keep me under his thumb.

"What about bribing my customers to cancel their baking orders? Do you feel bad about that?" I bark out the accusation, anger starting its slow simmer in my stomach.

"Curt!" Mom blanches, clearly not aware of his recent antics.

He huffs defensively, yet clearly not denying it. "Trust me, it's for your own good—just like this new position is."

He holds strong, erasing my hope that he might see my side of things. Fighting with him is absolutely useless—not to mention something I have no desire to do.

I lower my voice to a near whisper, not defeated but resigned, "No, it's not, Dad."

My calm response seems to fuel his irritation, and he slams a fist on the coffee table. "You can't tell me making desserts for people is a lucrative business."

"Well, I'm sorry you feel that way, Dad, but this is my passion."

"What am I supposed to tell your colleagues on Monday, huh? Do you know how irresponsible this makes you look?"

"You don't have to worry about that...because I quit," I say decisively, as if I didn't just make the decision mere seconds ago. It feels right—quitting my IT job. Not because I'm worried about what my coworkers will say, but because I'm ready to take complete charge of my life, to say goodbye to a job that no longer serves me.

He and Mom both flinch at my declaration, and I see the flash of fear in Mom's eyes, no doubt worrying about what this means for us as a family.

I stand, crossing the room confidently before sitting on the edge of the coffee table in front of him.

"I love you, Dad. But I need to live my own life. I know you're upset, and I'm sorry about that. I'm not mad at you...but I do need some space right now."

He doesn't say a word, just stares at me with the look of a man who's desperate to regain some semblance of control. Outrage and disbelief linger right behind that.

I give him a kiss on the forehead and walk directly out of the house without another word, feeling oddly okay about everything that transpired.

As soon as I pull the door shut, it opens behind me.

"Naomi, wait," Mom calls, coming to a halt on the top step when I turn around. I hold my breath, not sure if she's here to console or admonish me. Neither of us are used to standing up to him.

"I'm so sorry." Her face twists together with clear anguish. "I had no idea he was doing that."

"It's not your fault, Mom," I say with a soft smile...I don't hold her responsible for any of this.

"He just... He doesn't mean to be so harsh. You know he loves you." I see the struggle in her eyes, of agreeing with my stance but not quite knowing how to support me. After all, having my back in front of him would mean fighting years of complacency of her own, creating cracks in their dynamic that she might not be ready for.

"You don't have to make excuses for him," I say softly "I love you both. I just need a little bit of space right now from him. It's time I live on my own terms."

"I'm sorry," she whispers again with a nod, struggling to find words. "I wish it was different."

After a moment, I say, "It can be. For you too, you know."

At that, I return her somber smile and walk away.

"Happy unemployment," Robbie says, extending a bouquet of flowers to me as I roll dough out onto my counter.

"Aw, how sweet." I grin at him before pointing out the obvious. "Although, I'm technically not unemployed."

"Yeah, you're right." He grimaces. "You're basically running your own business, which is the exact opposite. Never mind. That sounded better in my head."

I laugh, leaning over to give him a kiss, my floured hands still on the rolling pin in front of me. "Thank you anyway. They're beautiful."

When I pull back, I notice the shirt he has on.

"What in the world are you wearing?" I immediately clamp my mouth shut to stifle a laugh that threatens to burst out. He looks down at his chest and grins back.

"Do you like it?"

He's wearing a forest-green *Welcome to Pine Falls* T-shirt that has a row of six smiling cows across the front of it—the kind of design we usually only see on tourists or children around here. Not on locals, and certainly not on rockstars like him.

"I really do," I say with heavy sarcasm. He sets the bouquet on the counter while he goes in search of a vase. "Care to explain?"

"So, I wanted to try going into town while you were at your parents'—you know, getting myself comfortable being out in the open by myself. Anyway, I was at the flower stand,

and Opal came running out of the gift shop with this shirt in hand. She insisted I needed to have it, that it suited me."

"Is that right?" I don't even try to hold back the perma-grin on my face.

"She told me I would look ten times more handsome—and who am I to argue with that?"

"You do look very handsome." I set the dough aside to start making the cinnamon mixture for the cinnamon rolls.

"Hey, I'm proud of you for going into town," I tell him quietly. He starts clipping flower stems but flicks his gaze over to meet mine.

"I'm trying." He pulls the corner of his mouth up in a meek smile. "How's baking going?"

"Great." I immediately dove into orders as soon as I got back from my parents' house. It turns out that word got around about what happened at the dealership, and orders have been flooding in with people wanting to support me It's a tangible showing of support for me from the town, and I'm so grateful for each and every one of these nosy people.

"Oh, and look what Gabby dropped off on her way out of town." I point to a piece of paper next to my purse.

"What is it?" He picks it up.

"It's a flyer about the space for lease on Main Street—where the old bakery was. And guess what? They lowered the price," I say giddily.

"No way," he breathes, his eyes going wide.

"I mean, things would definitely be tight for me—especially given I'm losing an entire salary now—but I'm close to being able to make it work, Robbie. Really close."

"Should I call to set up a time when we can go look at the space?"

"Sure! Or I can do it too," I offer.

"Hey, I'm basically your office manager anyway. Let me help." He sets the flyer down and comes behind me.

"If you insist."

"I do. I'll call tomorrow." He leans in to kiss the space where my neck meets my shoulder, and a soft hum comes from my throat in response. It feels good to have him back in my kitchen with me...it feels natural. "I know what else I can help with."

"No, sir." I lightly shrug him off, laughing, despite my flushed body clearly begging me to indulge him. "I know what happens when you try to help. Go sit across the room, please, so I can get this done. Then I'm all yours."

He laughs, reluctantly trudging to a chair. "Fine. But I call being your official taste-tester."

He grabs a magazine to flip through while I focus on the cinnamon rolls.

"Deal."

CHAPTER THIRTY-FOUR

Robbie

"Thanks," Charlie says with a grunt. He's standing in waist-high water, reaching up for the beer I'm leaning over the side of the boat.

"Don't forget your sunblock," I say, saluting him as he wades in the water toward shore where he, Luke, and Rachel are starting a game of sand volleyball.

The sun is sticky hot and the sky is clear, which means Gull Lake is buzzing with boats today, along with plenty of jet skis that are whipping around on the water.

I look up to the front platform of the boat where Naomi is lying, shielding her face from the sun as she sunbathes. We made the obvious decision to forgo the volleyball match in favor of some quiet alone time on the boat.

"Lemonade?" I yell to be heard above the roaring motor of a ski boat that passes by a little too close to shore.

"Yes, please!" she shouts back. With two of them in hand, I turn the radio on and step over a pile of beach towels to get to her.

"Thank you." She smiles widely as I approach.

"At your service," I say, setting our drinks in the nearby cup holders. Then I lower flat on my back with my entire right side pressed to her left. Even on this hot, humid day, I can't bear to not be touching her.

"So, when's your next gig again?" she asks.

"Not until next week. We had two shows slated for this week, but there was an issue with the venue, so they bumped those shows out to next month."

"Oh, really?" She perks up.

"Yeah. Remind me to start writing my schedule into your calendar, okay? So I can keep you in the loop...unless you've been lying to me this whole time and really don't care about me or my whereabouts," I ramble.

"Wow...that spiraled." She snorts.

"I'm just kidding." I nudge her leg with the base of my palm. "I know you care."

"Well, I'm glad I get you all to myself for a little while." She rotates her head to smile at me, and I can't resist leaning in to steal a sweaty kiss. When I pull back, I run my thumb down the swell of her cheek, soaking it all in, soaking *her* in, and feeling incredibly grateful that I made the step to come back.

We lie quietly for a while as I tuck my hand behind my head, the burn of the sun scorching directly onto my forehead. The boat rocks gently as waves crash against it, lulling us into a comfortable lazy summer trance. My gaze snags on an eagle that flies overhead, dipping and swerving before ending its flight on the perch of a tree in one of the more remote stretches of shoreline.

"Do you ever wonder what it would be like to live on a boat?" she asks out of nowhere. As I do often, I marvel at her imagination, wondering how her thought process brought her there.

"Like on a cruise ship?"

"Sure. Or any kind of boat. A cruise ship. A houseboat. Crab-fishing boat. Do you think you'd get sick of it?"

"Are you telling me you want to live on a boat?"

"Not even in the slightest. I'm just thinking out loud. I love that some people do that."

A lazy smile plays on my lips as we fall quiet again. I imagine her mind wanders to the next random topic, but mine goes directly to thinking about the effort I made today and am still coming to terms with.

"I sent Steven a message today," I mutter quietly, noticing how saying the words out loud makes my voice feel foreign and unnatural.

She whips her head to me. "What? You did?"

I nod while rolling my lips. "I did. This morning. You inspired me to do it, actually. After all the strides you've made, fighting for yourself and your dreams, I figured I could at least make a baby step."

"I'd say that's more than a baby step." She shifts onto her side, squeezing closer to me while her hand finds the one

I have resting on my stomach. She intertwines her fingers through mine, and I squeeze back.

"What did it say? Did he say anything back?"

I blow out a steadying breath. "I told him I'd be willing to talk to him. He's going to let me know when he's free." She looks about as surprised as I feel. I still can't believe I offered to see him face to face. I've spent the last eight years avoiding that exact situation, and here I am initiating it.

"That's a really big deal, Robbie," she gushes.

I nod silently, letting the reality of the situation sink in, all while trying my best to not regret it.

"We'll see what happens, I guess." I don't have high hopes about it, but I'm willing to try. For the sake of my relationship with Naomi, I have to.

I release the hand that's wedged behind my head and reach across to slide it through her hair, resting my palm against her cheek. It's a move with no intention or purpose behind it. No end goal or attempt to get anything from her in return. It's a simple automatic response to her being next to me. A need to feel her again under my fingertips.

I'm not sure what will happen with my family, but I'm getting to the point now where I'm finding that it doesn't affect me like it did before. Once I made the decision to come back to Naomi, I set myself free from a large chunk of the weight of my past. A lot of it is still there, obviously, but she's more important to me than any possible outcome with my family.

Period.

I lazily admire the subtle smile on her lips as she closes her eyes to soak in the sun. My thumb softly traces the skin of her temple, watching as goosebumps spark in its wake. An aching grip clutches my heart, and I try my best to breathe through it, to not be completely knocked over with the force of feeling like the luckiest man on this planet.

Naomi's phone buzzes from inside her boat bag that's on the other side of me. She slides up onto her elbows while I retrieve it.

"Huh," she says, examining the screen with raised brows.

"What's up?"

"It's from my mom. She wanted to let me know that she finally signed up for a flower-arranging class on Wednesday nights. It's a class she's been wanting to take for years now. She says I inspired her to do something for herself." I watch as her smile slides into a full-grown one. "And she didn't even ask my dad's permission first."

"Good for her."

"It's a small win"—she smiles to herself—"but a monumental one too."

"Look at you, inspiring people left and right." I jab her with my elbow.

"Stop." She waves me off with a playful eye roll.

Rachel calls out from the beach, "Hey, you two lovebirds want to join us?"

We twist our bodies up onto our elbows to get a view of where they're gathered on the sandy beach court. A haphazard gathering of flip-flops is piled off to the right and a few beach towels lie crumpled on top of a picnic table. With no other beach dwellers on this stretch of sand, the three of them are spread out wide.

"I'm dying over here." Luke waves, stretching his arms out to showcase his lack of teammates.

Naomi smirks. "Should we go help him?"

"It's up to you."

"Let's go show them how it's done, huh?" She stands first and offers her hands to help me up. I follow behind, maneuvering to the back of the boat where I help her climb onto the edge.

She jumps with a squeal off the side of the boat, her legs splashing as they land in the water. I follow her immediately, not regretting for a single second my broader decision to do just that.

CHAPTER THIRTY-FIVE

Naomi

"Ah! Look how adorable it is!" I gush, grabbing Robbie's forearm. My mouth gapes open, and my head feels fuzzy as I spin in a slow circle, examining every square inch of the retail space. My mind races with possibilities and ways I could make this my own.

Although I did frequent this space often when the last owner was running her bakery here, the inside looks vastly different with everything cleared out. I've also never looked at it with fresh, hopeful eyes before—as if it could actually, potentially be mine.

"The lease amount does include the existing appliances, sales counter, and display case," Joan, our local realtor, explains, pointing the tip of her pen toward each area.

"So, I would need to furnish the interior," I process out loud, noting the empty space reserved for indoor dining. Not to mention it needs a fresh coat of paint and a few pieces of commercial baking equipment that weren't on the listing. We could maybe even remove the far wall completely to make the space more open if I got really ambitious.

"That's correct," she answers before leading us through double doors into the kitchen area. The perimeter of the room is lined with multiple ovens, a large sink, and floor-to-ceiling cooling racks. A large rectangular stainless-steel island sits in the middle of the room, absolutely ideal for prepping scones, rolling dough, and decorating cakes. It's perfect—anything I could possibly dream up to bake can be done within these four walls.

I imagine an alternate reality where the racks are filled with baking sheets of freshly baked goods ready to be boxed, and the smell of dough and sugar hangs heavily in the air. It's calm and quiet back here, but the bustle from the front of the store can still be heard in spurts through the swinging double doors.

"I can see it, Robbie," I whisper as I keep close behind him, gripping the back of his T-shirt with my fists as we follow Joan back to the front of the store. "I can envision it all."

The smile on his face is only half-visible as he reaches a hand behind him to squeeze my side with a firm grip. I stifle my squeal, burying my face in his back. The excitement is almost too much. What if this could actually be mine someday? Do I dare dream this big?

"That's the gist of it. Do you have any questions for me?" Joan asks, pausing when we reach the front door.

"Yes, how much interest have you had in this space?" Robbie has the business sense to ask. Good thing, because all I can think about is what I would bake first in that kitchen—a cinnamon-streusel coffee cake. Or maybe a chocolate drip cake.

"Well, it's been sitting vacant for a few months, as I'm sure you know. But with full disclosure, you're not the only people I've shown the space to this week," Joan says.

"Oh, really?" My stomach drops, the fate of having a store-front bakery hanging in the balance. I've never been so close to this particular part of my dream before. One where I get to bake for the familiar faces of Pine Falls that will come and go through that door every single day. For the people who stop in on a whim just to say hi and grab a donut to enjoy while they run the rest of their Main Street errands. Or the ones who have turned into regular clientele, placing orders in advance and stopping in at their convenience to pick it up. Who believe in me and support me as one of their own, because I've always supported them. I feel it just within grasp, yet it could so easily slip away in an instant.

"I won't disclose personal information, but yes, there's another potentially interested party—an out-of-towner who wants to turn the space into an ax-throwing bar."

"No way." Robbie chuckles, giving me a sidelong glance. "That's actually pretty cool."

I give him a sad but agreeable smile before shaking Joan's hand. "Okay, thank you. Keep me posted if anything happens with that. I'll crunch some numbers and be in touch."

"You bet. Enjoy your day." She waves and stays back to lock up as Robbie and I step outside onto the sidewalk.

"What do you think?" Robbie asks once we're out of earshot. He intertwines his fingers with mine as I fall into step with him. We stroll leisurely along the sidewalk, waving to Mrs. Fitzpatrick from the other side of the street when she pokes her head out of the antique store.

"I think I'm scared to love it," I reply truthfully.

"What do you mean?" He smirks.

"I love everything about that space—I really do. And I would absolutely love to make it my own. I can perfectly envision what it would be like to operate my business from there. But I'm nervous to take the plunge, especially so soon after quitting my full-time job. The financial risk scares me a little bit," I admit.

"It is a big step," he agrees.

"But oh my gosh, did you see the floor?" I gush, tugging on his arm. "There's something about diagonal pastel-pink tile...it just speaks to me."

"I can help," he offers quietly, coming to a stop in front of the ice cream parlor.

"What?" I twist, halting in front of him. Surely I didn't hear him correctly.

"I would love to contribute to the rent," he says again. "If you'll let me and are okay with it, that is."

"You have money?"

"Firstly, that's offensive." He smirks.

"You know what I mean."

"Second. Yes, I would love to. I mean, I do get paid for shows, you know. I don't pay a mortgage or rent...so I've got quite a bit saved up."

"And you'd do that?" Emotion prickles at the corners of my eyes as I stare blankly back at him, my brain not quite able to accept the depth of what he's offering.

"Of course. To be honest, I've really enjoyed the whole business side of your operation, and I already feel invested." He shrugs. "I've been looking for more direction in my life. I think this is it...the path I want to take. *You* are my path, Naomi. So are your dreams."

Although my mind is racing a million miles per minute, it takes absolutely no amount of thought to grin wildly at him. I shake my head in amazement, feeling adrenaline rush through me.

"You're amazing. Do you know that?" I gush.

"I've been told a few times." He shrugs me off.

Would signing a lease together be risky? Probably. Would any decent business advisor condemn going into business with a new romantic partner? I can imagine. But do I trust him? With my life.

And that's always been good enough for me.

"Okay," I agree with a quick nod.

"Yeah?" He extends his arms out, which I immediately—and eagerly—jump into. I wrap my legs around his waist and squeeze his neck tightly with a grin plastered on my face so big that my cheeks actually hurt. His hands grip my thighs, holding me up and securely to him.

"Yeah," I whisper against his ear.

A squeal flies out of my mouth when he twirls me around suddenly—without a care in the world that we're in the middle of town, vulnerable to prying eyes.

"You don't think you'll regret going into business together?" I ask just to be sure.

"Nope," he says firmly, giving me nothing else.

"Okay," I say again, searching his face for any sign of doubt.

"Let's do it, then." He places a quick kiss to my lips, grinning back at me. I can't help but squeeze his neck tighter, planting another kiss to his lips and then one to the center of his forehead.

Then he nonchalantly starts walking—with me still in his arms—down the sidewalk. I laugh out loud at how we must look to onlookers. Heaven knows this kind of PDA sparks a lot of chatter on these streets. The worried thought leaves as quickly as it came, and I hang on tightly, relishing the possibilities that were just opened up for my life.

And for our life together.

CHAPTER THIRTY-SIX

Robbie

"Are you sure you don't want me to come with?" Naomi asks as we walk to her front door.

I shake my head. "No. Thank you, but I'm good. Besides, I don't plan on this taking too long."

The worry crease between her brows deepens as her gaze roams over my face. "How are you feeling about seeing your parents too? He kind of sprung that on you, didn't he?"

"He did." Nausea churns deep in my stomach at the reminder. When Steven invited me over to his house to talk, he casually informed me that Mom and Dad would like to be there as well. I compromised and agreed to talk to all of them as long as we met somewhere that was neutral ground. The last thing I want to do is feel ambushed on his own turf.

"It's alright, though. Honestly, seeing all three of them is the same as seeing only one at this point—I might as well get it all over with in one shot."

She inches closer to step into my arms. Her chin rests against my chest with her head tilted up, and her arms wrap tightly around my waist.

"Are you nervous?" she asks quietly.

"A little," I admit. The truth is, I've been nauseated and worked up about this meeting all day. There's an annoying cloud of dread that's been following me around relentlessly—not nearly as overwhelming as the last time I was in a funk, but I'm definitely ready to have this conversation and be done with it.

"I've heard lip buzzes are really helpful," she mutters, eyeing me playfully.

I snicker, cradling her head with both my hands while I bring my lips to hers. Her gentle kiss sends a soothing wave of comfort through my bones, easing some of the tension. When I pull back, I can't resist placing a quick peck against her temple too.

"I'll keep that in mind." I wink at her, twisting the door open behind me.

"Good luck," she calls out as I make my way to the car.

The entire ride to the diner, I hold tight to the way I just felt when Naomi was in my arms, reminding myself why she's worth going through with this in the first place. Why this conversation is necessary.

If I'm going to make a life with Naomi here, I don't want to have this shadow hanging over me. I owe it to her and our relationship to at least hear them out.

Shifting the car into park, I roll my shoulders, do a few lip buzzes through a timid smile, and head inside the diner.

I find them already at a booth in the back corner as soon as I walk in. They're early, just like I am. My legs feel like bricks and my shirt starts sticking to my body with an anxiety-induced sweat, but I push through, each step bringing me closer to them.

Mom and Dad are sitting on one side of the booth, and Steven sits on the other with an open space next to him, clearly for me. Instead, I opt for grabbing a nearby chair from an empty table and settle it on the end of the booth. Far enough away to put some distance between us yet still be a part of the group.

With a curt nod I make eye contact with all three of them, quickly studying faces I haven't seen this close in many years. The expressions that peer back at me are laced with emotion, trepidation, and uneasiness, as I imagine mine looks as well.

"Hey, Robbie," Steven says first. I give him my best smile with Naomi's image in the back of my mind giving me strength. I can feel my parents' stares like laser beams on me while I keep my gaze set on Steven.

"You wanted to talk?" I ask as nicely as I can muster.

"Yes. I'll go first," he says, folding his hands on top of the table. "But I'd like you to know, first and foremost, that this isn't an interrogation. Or an ambush. It's simply a conversation. A door cracking open, okay?"

"Alright," is all I can say, my chest feeling tight with anticipation and something similar to dread.

"I want to apologize for my part in this rift." His words—ones I never expected to hear—have me freezing in place. "I know I wasn't the best older brother to you, and I have some major regrets about that."

"Not that I think you were a perfect gentleman your whole life—"

"Steven," Mom cuts him off, and the sound of her voice, although not directed at me, feels like a balm to my soul. I flick my gaze to her for only a moment before settling back on my brother.

"That's irrelevant," he admits with his palms up. "Again, I'm sorry."

"Um, thank you," I mumble, not entirely sure what to make of it all.

"I'll go next, if that's okay," Mom cuts in. I inhale a few breaths before locking eyes with her, and I immediately notice the sheen of emotion watering them, which makes my own sting in return. I've wondered what this conversation would look like for so long now. What she would say. How it would feel to hear her say it. It's surreal to finally be in it and it feels starkly more intense than I imagined it would.

"Robbie, I don't blame you if you don't want to speak to us for the rest of your life." She wipes a tear that outlines her distorted face that struggles to hide the emotion she's feeling. "But I need to say my piece, okay?"

I nod, prompting her to go on while I hold my breath—breathing normally is not an option.

"I didn't realize until you left home how fractured our relationship was," she admits. "Call me naive, call me blind...I was all of it. Stupid more than anything, I admit that. I was self-absorbed and a terrible mother."

I swallow hard around the lump in my throat.

"All these years of no contact with you have opened our eyes to our parenting failures," Dad cuts in. One quick glance at his expression makes it clear he's regretful too.

"After you left...I didn't know how to connect with you," Mom continues. "I was terrified that I'd screwed up enough that you wouldn't want to hear from me. So, I was never brave enough to call. And then, every time I heard you were back in town, it just...ripped me apart."

"It's true," Steven cuts in. "It emotionally devastated her each time. Dad and I would try for days to get her to come out of bed, but by the time she did, you were always gone again."

So that explains why I'd never run into her around town when I came home. I clear my throat, processing everything I'm hearing. It turns out they do know what the reason for my absence all these years has been. Not only that, but they're acknowledging and apologizing for it.

Not exactly what I expected out of today.

Still...the wound runs deep, and I have a hard time digging up enough empathy to brush everything under the rug so quickly. I'm not capable of doing that.

"We never meant to make you feel like an outsider or not good enough," Dad says. "But we're aware now that's exactly what we did."

"And we're sorry," Mom squeaks out, wiping her face again with a sniffle.

Watching the tears that fall down her face makes my chest ache, and I'm grateful for everything they've said. But agreeing to talk to them is one thing. Forgiving them is another thing entirely—and not one I take lightly. I need to follow Naomi's lead and put myself first. Healing takes time. I remind myself of the words I spoke to her not too long ago.

Their emotions are not my responsibility.

I can appreciate them and their efforts—forgive them, even—without feeling like I owe them something in return.

"I, uh...I heard what you've had to say. And I appreciate it," I choke out through my own voice that's become thick with emotion.

"I know you're a grown man," Mom says. "And you have every right to do what's best for you...but maybe we could see you again?"

"I'd be open to it...but I need some time. This can't be repaired fast. It has to be slow."

She vehemently nods, seemingly willing to take whatever I'll give. Fatigue presses heavily on my bones and I suddenly feel like I've had more than enough conversation for today.

"I'll reach out when I'm ready to, okay?" I stand, sliding my chair back where it belongs. I hover by the booth, lingering there, not quite sure how to end a conversation like this.

"Take care, Robbie," Dad says sincerely. I look all three of them square in the face one last time, memorizing everything about them and this entire conversation to process later.

"See you around." I turn, walking out of the diner, feeling simultaneously heavy with exhaustion, yet also as if the largest weight has just been lifted off my chest.

CHAPTER THIRTY-SEVEN

Naomi

The veil between my dream-like state and consciousness slowly lifts as I feel the weight of the mattress dipping behind me. Lying on my side, I stir, inhaling deeply to rouse myself to wake up and be present enough to hold a conversation. Robbie curls his body against my back, his arm snaking around my stomach, scooping me closer to him until I'm fully surrounded by his warmth.

"How did it go?" I murmur, forcing my eyes to slowly blink open. I have no idea what time it is, but given the pitch darkness, it has to be late.

My room, and everything in it, is only slightly illuminated by the moon's glow through my window. The stillness of the night sets a somber ambiance that makes the quiet room seem intimate—almost charged in a way.

The soft movement of his leg against the sheets and the way his chest heaves rhythmically with each breath against my back further stirs my senses, until I'm wide awake, waiting with a bated breath to hear how it went.

"It went okay," he says softly against the crook of my neck. I try to analyze his tone for any hints of how it went, but there isn't much to go on.

"Was it hard to see them?" I slide my fingers between each of his knuckles, tucking his arm as tightly around me as possible, as if the closeness might provide an extra comfort.

"Yeah, it was definitely weird," he admits through another heaving sigh.

I wait for him to give me more, but nothing comes. He stays silent. I imagine he's still processing it all.

"Were they mean?" I can't help but ask. My stomach clenches at the thought, desperately hoping they were gentle with his heart.

"Surprisingly, no. They apologized...for everything," he says with a soft wonder in his voice, as if he can't quite believe it himself.

"Really?" My heart lurches, a glimmer of hope growing that he might be okay here, that he might actually find some healing.

"Yeah, they took full responsibility. I just...I don't know." I pick up on the struggle in his voice.

"What is it?" I squeeze his hand gently.

"I don't know if I'm capable of forgiving them," he admits, his voice thick. "I don't think I know how to."

The pain in his voice draws me onto my back, needing to feel closer to him. I twist all the way against him until I'm on my side, my face centered at the base of his neck. I tuck my arms into myself, the backs of my hands resting softly against his bare chest, as his arm stays draped around me.

"There's so much history there," he continues. "So many years of feeling cast aside during such vulnerable years for me...I...it's just a hard wall to tear down, you know?"

I nod, contemplating what kind of response he needs from me in this moment, how I can be the best support to him, as he's been to me for so long now.

"Do you want to know what I think?" I whisper.

He runs his fingertips along my spine, causing a cascading rush of goosebumps to come alive in its wake.

"More than anything," he mutters against the top of my head, his breath tickling my hair.

"I don't think you have to rush mending a relationship with them," I say softly, treading carefully. "It's okay if you need to do it slowly."

Even in the dark, I can make out the way his head dips above me in a nod.

"And I think there's healing in the simple acknowledgment of it," I say. "In exposing it all. The raw. The ugly. The mistakes. The regrets. On both sides. Laying it all out there and then carrying those with you as you move forward. That counts as something, you know?"

After a few quiet seconds, I keep going. "Healing isn't linear. It isn't cut and dry. And knowing what you can handle, going at your own pace, is not only smart but necessary."

"Yeah," he agrees gruffly.

"I'm proud of you," I whisper, untucking one arm to slink over his torso.

He huffs a breath that puffs against my hair. "I feel like we've been telling each other that a lot lately."

"We have." I smile to myself in the darkness. "Isn't that great?"

"It is." The sound of his laugh makes my soul hum as he brings his hand up to run through my hair.

"Well...if you need help deciphering your needs and setting boundaries, I happen to know a guy."

"Oh yeah?" I can hear the smile in his voice.

"Yeah. He kind of changed my life."

"Sounds like a great guy," he mutters.

"He is a little relentless and kind of bossy sometimes, but I wouldn't change him for anything." I smile against the skin of his chest before growing serious. "You'll get there, Robbie...even if it takes time."

"I think so too. I'm not ruling out mending our relationship by any means, but I'm good with moving slowly."

"Sometimes the best things in life take time." I yawn, feeling the comfort of sleep pulling on my edges.

He huffs. "Kind of like realizing you're falling for your best friend of ten-ish odd years? That kind of time?" There's a twinge of mischief in his voice, the change of topic giving him a little spark back.

"Exactly. Although, that seems like an obnoxiously long time to all of a sudden see me as the prize that I am," I tease.

"More like a rock in my boot I didn't know was there, affecting my gait and posture without me even realizing it," he rambles sleepily.

I blink, processing his statement. "I truly can't tell if that's a compliment or an insult."

"Yeah...keeps things fun, doesn't it?" The playfulness in his tone brings a smile to my lips. I bite my lip, poking him with my finger.

"Ouch," he chuckles. "No, you're right. You were worth every second of the wait."

I press a kiss to the center of his chest as we both fall quiet, savoring the feeling of being wrapped up in each other's arms.

"I left a chocolate walnut muffin on the counter for you for the morning," I tell him, my eyes drifting closed.

He slides his fingers across my back lazily. "I can't wait. Should I make omelets again?"

"Oh, no, that's okay."

"Were they that bad?" He chuckles sleepily.

I bite my lip to contain a grin. "Let's just say your talent lies in other areas."

He sighs, accepting defeat. "That doesn't even hurt my feelings."

I squeeze him tighter as if in consolation. I couldn't care less about his lack of culinary abilities. All that matters to me is the fact that he keeps showing up for me. Over and over again, in any way he can.

After a few quiet moments, when I'm just seconds away from falling asleep, his voice softly jolts me awake.

"Do you know what's actually insane?" he murmurs, fighting sleep of his own. "How much more comfortable this bed is than the couch."

I chuckle against the warmth of his skin, falling right back into the soft trance of sleep. "Goodnight, Robbie."

"Goodnight, Naomi."

Chapter Thirty-Eight

Robbie

"So, I know this isn't anybody's favorite part, but we need to look at the schedule six months out," Aiden says, kicking off our monthly virtual band meeting. "I need to make sure we're all on the same page."

"Shoot, boss," Dane says, his voice coming from the small square on the bottom left of my phone screen. The reflection of the lake takes up my peripheral vision, eclipsing my sight, so I have to squint and shield my eyes in order to see all of them.

"We've got Atlanta the first week of February for a three-night show, followed by a two-night stint in Alabama," he says.

"Wait, let me flip my calendar," Dane says. He's the only twenty-six-year-old I know who keeps a physical calendar, but it fits his personality. He's been running both of our lives with that thing for years now.

After a minute, Aiden continues. "We've been invited to participate in a new music festival in St. Petersburg the week after that if you guys are interested."

"Hold on. I need to double-check that one," I cut in, jotting the dates down on a notepad. I know there's an annual winter fest in Pine Falls around that time, and if things pan out with the bakery storefront, I would absolutely want to be here to help Naomi run it during that busy time.

"Seriously?" Aiden asks in surprise, proving my point for how little I've cared about the schedule in the past.

"Yeah. I want to make sure nothing interferes with bakery stuff," I say.

"That's right. Our little Robbie-poo has become a run-of-the-mill bread maker up there in small-town Minnesota," Rylie teases.

I smirk, not at all affected by the relentless jabs that have come my way ever since I told the guys my plan to potentially invest in a bakery and settle down here.

"You'll be singing a different tune once you visit. I'm telling you, Naomi's blueberry pie will change your life," I boast

"Do you wear a chef's hat too? Because I'm there in a heartbeat if you do," Dane chimes in.

Aiden clears his throat. "Alright, alright. Back to business, fellas. Robbie, get back to me by the end of the week about those dates."

"You got it."

"The only other show I have on the schedule is a mini East Coast tour the following week," he says. "We'll hit Maine, Rhode Island, and Pennsylvania in one fell swoop."

I smile to myself while I jot down the dates, knowing I have to figure out a way to get Naomi to come with me on that stretch. I know she's never been, and she would absolutely love the vibe of the East Coast.

"That's all I have for today's meeting, so unless anyone else has anything to add, I'll see you all in a few days for the next show."

"I'm good here," Dane says, and we all nod in agreement.

"See you," I say. When we disconnect, the sound of their voices is instantly replaced by the soft waves of the lake lapping onto shore and a distant loon call on the other side of the lake. The sweet smell of sugar and dough wafts from inside the house behind me, where Naomi is finishing up her orders for the day.

Yet again, I'm surprised—and relieved—at my general mood while being in Pine Falls. The heaviness from the conversation with my family the other day hasn't lingered like I anticipated it would. Instead, I feel more hopeful than anything—content and more than happy to be here with Naomi.

I'm not rushing to fix my broken relationships, but I'm not feeling threatened and blocked off because of the fractures of them either. I'm very much in the place of 'let's take it one day at a time' at this point.

The allure of whatever she's baking inside the house pulls on me hard enough that I hop off the bench and make my way off the dock.

"What in the name of Indiana Jones are you making in here?" I ask, sliding the deck door shut behind me. In the kitchen, Naomi looks up with a smile.

"It's going to be a sprinkle-wrapped raspberry buttercream cake," she says proudly, showcasing her cake creation. "Isn't it cute so far?"

"Cute is the exact word that comes to my mind."

"It needs to cool before I can apply the frosting and sprinkles." She places her hands on her hips to study the cake.

"Do you have anything else to bake today?" I ask.

"Nope."

"Perfect timing, because there's something I'd like to do."

"Oh, really?" A gleam in her eye flares as excitement shines through.

"Yup."

"Wait, I should probably shower first." She cringes. "I have flour everywhere."

"That's not necessary." I dismiss her with a wave. "You'll probably get sweaty."

"Oh. Well, on second thought, maybe I *am* busy." She pauses in place, cringing again.

"Ah, suck it up. It won't be that bad. I promise." I motion for her to follow me out the front door, which she does. When we round the front corner of the house, I step off to the side so she can see the two bicycles I have resting against the garage door.

She gasps, bringing a hand to cover her mouth. "Oh! Where did these come from?"

"I asked Toby to drop them off." I smile smugly, feeling proud of my efforts. "He said we could borrow them for the afternoon."

"How fun! I don't think I've been on a bike since I was eleven or something." She lifts one bike off the garage door, testing out the handlebars.

"So, I'll go in front of you, then, not behind," I mutter.

"Hey, I could be an excellent bicyclist for all you know," she says pointedly.

"Let's find out, shall we?" I wink as we climb on our bikes. We take off down her driveway, the wheels of my bike feeling rocky against the gravel.

At the end of the driveway, we turn left, cycling side by side down the street of her neighborhood. It has a road that curves and winds for blocks on end along the shoreline, where cottages and quaint homes line the street with glimpses of the lake visible between sparse patches of oak trees. I take it all in, appreciating the rustic beauty I've often taken for granted before now.

"Not so fast," she laughs from behind me, struggling to keep up.

"Whoops." I didn't realize I was pulling ahead, so I slow to her pace.

"I'm still getting used to it."

"Sorry. You're doing great. It's kind of like riding a bike, yeah?"

Her eye roll makes me chuckle, and I lose balance, needing to steady the steering wheel so I don't fall.

"Come on, slowpoke." She surges ahead to prove a point, turning down the entrance to a local biking trail that juts off the main road.

I follow behind, soaking in the fresh air and sunshine. It feels good to be out exploring and to not feel the anxiety of a possible run-in with my family. The pressure is off, in a big way, even if the question of how things will progress remains unanswered.

When the trail splits, we veer right, following where the sea of trees creates a canopy over a narrowing path. As we bike in silence, a faint memory of biking this same trail with Steven when we were younger hits me out of nowhere. It's one of the only memories I have of us that isn't tarnished with jealousy, patronizing, or ridicule. We were too young to be anything other than playmates at that point, dare I say even friends.

We came as a family—that I know—but for some reason, only Steven and I are clear in my flashback. The way we sped ahead of Mom and Dad to get to the next checkpoint before they shouted for us to stop and wait. How Steven would wait for me before we raced down the hill that, if I remember correctly, is somewhere just ahead.

A twinge of sadness hits me at the reminder of how our early days as a family used to be. Then a punch of anger hits that they had to go and ruin our short-lived happy family dynamic, that they essentially cast me aside when I simply didn't fit into their high-achieving mold.

I mentally brush off my thoughts, focusing instead on how cute Naomi looks pedaling on the slightly-too-big-for-her bike in front of me. Life in Pine Falls with her has been nothing short of consuming this last week, and my thoughts easily turn to more pleasant things—like the way she woke me up this morning with a cup of coffee and a proposition to go for a sunrise swim to start the day, which, of course, I eagerly agreed to. It's been easy here with her. Comforting. Fulfilling.

Eventually, we reach a small clearing next to where the creek flows over large boulders, creating a small waterfall cascading down over the rocks.

"Let's take a break," she says, already hopping off her bike. I climb off my own and set it next to where she leaned hers against the wooden makeshift fence that surrounds the creek.

She leans forward, resting her forearms on the fence to catch her breath, and I come next to her as close as I can get—not crowding her, of course, but making sure my arm at least touches hers.

"So I sent our lease application to Joan," she says, albeit a little hesitantly. "But I can still take it back if you have any regrets? If you've decided it's not a good idea to be business partners after all?"

She looks at me with trepidation, a hint of the insecurity she's worked so hard to overcome sneaking through.

"Nope, I told you...I'm all in," I say confidently.

"Are you sure? Now's your last chance to back out."

"I've never been more sure of anything in my entire life. Haven't I told you that opening a bakery is my dream?" My tone comes off as playful and teasing, but the part about being sure I mean with every fiber of my being.

"Stop." She laughs, waving a hand in my direction.

"No, I'm serious." I twist so half my body is leaning on the fence, allowing me to face her. "I want this, Naomi. All of it. The responsibility. The bakery. The life here with you. You don't have to question that anymore."

I run my thumb over her cheek, then over her lips as they twist into a bashful smile.

"Okay," she whispers, nodding, accepting it all. I can't help but lean in to kiss where my thumb just traced, and then I slide my body behind her, placing one arm on each side, caging her in. She leans her head against my cheek as we watch the water flowing peacefully.

"I used to come here as a kid," I tell her quietly when another image of Steven and me at this very same spot enters my mind.

She turns her head just enough to offer me a soft smile. One that says she supports me in any way I might need in these moments. A smile I've been grateful for every single day since I made the decision to come back to Pine Falls.

She watches me, waiting to see if I'll continue, but I don't feel the need to say anything else out loud. I bring my hands up to squeeze her shoulders, then I tilt my head, motioning toward our bikes.

"Are you ready?"

"Sure," she says.

As we walk the few steps it takes to reach the bikes, I think back to the conversation with my family and their apology at the diner, the olive branch that they extended.

I act on a sudden urge by pulling my cell phone out to send a quick text to Steven. Maybe it's time I extend a branch of my own. I press send before I have a chance to change my mind.

Robbie: I'm on a bike ride on that trail we rode back in the day. The one off Pebble Road. Thought of you.

I leave it at that. Nothing more, nothing less. I'm surprised when he answers almost immediately.

Steven: That same one has always made me think of you…and how I kicked your butt racing down that hill.

I contemplate writing a response to open a dialogue between us but decide the one message is all I'm ready for today.

Baby steps.

I slide my phone back into my pocket, climb back on my bike, and steer it toward Naomi, who's waiting with that same supportive look on her face.

CHAPTER THIRTY-NINE

Naomi

"What did you do today? Tell me everything and don't leave anything out," I gush into my phone. Robbie is in Texas with the band, and my jealousy has been off the charts ever since he left yesterday morning. What I wouldn't give to be right there with him.

His soft chuckle emanates through the speaker. "Well, let's see... Aiden had breakfast sandwiches waiting for us on the bus this morning—mine was a ham, egg, and bacon on a rye bagel. It was a little on the dry side, but I added hot sauce, and that helped immensely. I washed it down with two orange juices that were a little tart for my liking." He pauses. "Are these the kind of in-depth details you're looking for?"

"Yes. Exactly like that. Keep going," I demand as nicely as I can while rummaging through my pantry.

"And then Dane and I got off the bus to do some souvenir shopping—I may or may not have bought a pair of authentic cowboy boots."

I smile to myself as I rip open and pour a bag of marshmal-lows onto the s'mores tray.

"Let's see...we stopped at a Tex-Mex restaurant for lunch—I had a chicken quesadilla and an avocado corn salad. It was delicious. Then we headed straight to sound check—oh, this venue is incredible, Naomi. I wish you were here to see it."

"What does it look like?" I open the bag of graham crackers and pour them onto the tray next to the marshmallows.

"It's got a three-hundred-sixty-degree design with the stage right in the middle. Literally, we're fully immersed in the crowd. The only access to it is through an elevator that comes up through the center."

"That sounds really cool." I layer the pieces of chocolate to finish off the tray.

"It is. And now we have about an hour before showtime, so I'm on the bus, taking advantage of the downtime to talk to you. Should I describe what I'm wearing next?"

"No, thank you." I grin. "I'm about to head back outside. The guys are currently cannon-balling off the end of the dock and I'm giving it about five minutes before Mrs. P. runs out with her broom."

He chuckles again. "They'd probably deserve it. You know, I really love the fact that you have a watch guard that lives next door. It makes me feel better about being away."

"I can take care of myself too, you know. I have for years," I point out.

"Yeah," he says in a throaty voice that makes my stomach flip. "But that's my job now—and Mrs. P.'s."

I let his words smooth over me in a comforting wave and feel the tug of another smile at the corner of my mouth.

"Did I tell you Gabby is here?" I ask, keeping my voice low, as if she might hear me from where she sits around the fire pit outside.

"She's back in town, huh? Have you talked to her?"

"Just a little. Everyone just got here a bit ago. It seems like she's in a good mood, though...less grouchy than before."

"Well, good luck. Don't take any crap from her or anyone else, okay?"

"Yes, sir," I say playfully.

"Listen, I've gotta run. Aiden is waving his arm ridiculously fast at me with a stern look on his face. I think I'm in trouble."

"Okay, have a great show. I miss you."

"I miss you more. I'll call you when I get back to the bus."

When he hangs up, I feel the same familiar twist in my gut that's been happening lately every time we disconnect. I can't quite place it, but it feels an awful lot like homesickness—even though I'm well aware that I'm standing in my own home.

I grab the finished tray and head outside to my backyard, where Mrs. Pelinski is, indeed, admonishing the boys as they bob in the lake.

"It's alright, Mrs. P. They're my friends!" I call to her with a laugh.

"Are you sure?" she shouts back, clearly not convinced as she doesn't retreat even an inch.

"I'm positive!" I smirk as she hesitantly moves back toward her deck, keeping her eyes pinned on the guys the whole time.

When I'm confident she won't charge after them, I turn to place the tray on the small bench next to the fire pit. After grabbing the roasting sticks that are leaning against the tree, I sink down into the open Adirondack chair between Gabby and Rachel.

"S'mores, ladies?" I offer them each a stick. "Might as well make yourselves one before the guys get out of the water and hog all the chocolate."

As if they can hear us talking about them, Luke yelps as Charlie dunks him, clearly the result of some sort of wrestling match I'm not invested in in the slightest.

"Sure." Gabby gives an unusually friendly smile, taking a stick and passing one to Rachel.

"Thanks for inviting me," she says genuinely as we stick our marshmallows in the fire. Things have felt different with her today. Now that I've created boundaries for us—and she's been clear about her intent to work on certain parts of her own self—there seems to be a much more authentic layer to our friendship. An 'I see your flaws and admire your efforts' kind of unspoken acknowledgment on both of our parts. It's what true friendship should look like, in my opinion.

"Of course. It wouldn't be the same without you." I smile at her.

"I like your shirt," Rachel says, pointing to the Copper Snake band T-shirt I'm wearing.

"Oh, thanks." I grip the bottom of the cotton shirt, rubbing my fingers over the fabric as if it might comfort me the same way the feel of his actual touch would. "I stole it from Robbie's backpack before he left and haven't taken it off since."

"It must be hard—him leaving all the time," she says.

"It is," I agree with a frown. It's getting harder and harder to be away from him when he's gone, but absence has definitely been making the heart grow fonder. When we finally are reunited, I swear, I've never felt anything as exhilarating as being in his arms, not even in my wildest dreams. "But he's living his dream and I'm happy for him."

"Oh my gosh, Naomi, these cookies are to die for," Gabby interrupts, taking a bite with her free hand.

"I'm glad you like them. Those are Owen's favorite too."

"Rachel, you have to try one." Gabby passes one over to her.

"Oh, wow," Rachel purrs, taking a bite of her own.

"You have to teach me how you get your cookies so soft and crisp at the same time," Gabby croons, examining the cookie in her hand.

"Yeah?" I ask, gauging whether she's actually interested or just being nice. I would love to have something to bond with her over, especially baking.

"I'm serious. I'd really like to learn," she says emphatically.

"I can show you now if you'd like?" I tilt my chin toward the house behind me.

"Really?" Her brows perk up.

"Yeah, let's do it." I nod, getting excited. "Rachel, are you in?"

"No, thanks," she says, sliding her charred marshmallow between two graham crackers. "I think I'll show the boys a thing or two about diving."

"Go easy on them." I smirk, sliding my own marshmallow onto a cracker. "Shall we, Gabby?"

I stand, dusting the graham cracker dust off my shorts. As I follow Gabby back inside, I can't help but relish the content feeling that runs through me on a night like tonight. If I have to be apart from Robbie, at least I get to enjoy this new dynamic with an old friend.

CHAPTER FORTY

Robbie

"I found them!" I yell from Naomi's office, where I grab a box of logo stickers that she has stacked on the desk.

"Great!" her muffled voice replies from the kitchen.

Box in tow under my arm, I skirt around her desk, and my eye catches on the organizational system she has hanging on her wall.

Our practice sessions are still scheduled on the whiteboard calendar from a few weeks ago, and her life goals list is pinned to the top of the board, along with several variations of mantras that both she and I have written out and pinned up. Right in the middle of the board is a sticky note that says *I am a confident businesswoman* and another one that says *I am deserving of boundaries*.

All of it makes me smile, a clear reminder of how far she's come in the last few months. Pride blooms in my chest, for both her and me. For the place we're both at in our lives and for the way we've come together, despite everything that was working against us.

With a gratified sigh, I shift the box under my arm and head out of the office.

"Ta-da!" Naomi exclaims as I cross the living room toward the kitchen. Her arms are outstretched, proudly showcasing her latest creation. "A peanut butter chocolate layer cake."

The sight of her in her element, flour dusted and smeared with chocolate icing, with a very specific glow that permeates from her only when she's baking, has my stomach doing an insanely wild flip. I truly love watching her bake and know without a doubt that it will never get old.

"That is incredible," I tell her. "I don't suppose you made an extra mini one for me, huh?"

"Not this time." She laughs, grabbing the box from under my arm. I help her slide the cake into one of her bakery boxes, and then she grabs a logo sticker to place on the top.

"That's it for the night, right?" I ask, helping set dishes into the sink.

"Yup." She runs her hands along her apron, brushing off any extra flour still left on her hands.

"Do you want to listen to the rain with me?" I ask, gesturing toward the couch. "We can leave the dishes for later."

A sudden anticipation buzzes across my skin at the mere thought of spending hours on the couch with her wrapped in my arms. It might seem miniscule or boring to some, but it's an experience I want so badly I can hardly breathe right.

"Sure," she says softly as her gaze lingers on mine, most likely seeing whatever intensity is inadvertently being projected in my stare.

Without another word, I help by placing the rest of the dishes in the sink for later, then we set the cake off to the side next to the other orders she fulfilled today.

When the kitchen is decent enough, I pour some tequila into two tumblers and follow her to the living room.

She sets our glasses on the coffee table while I grab a log to start a fire in the fireplace. Once it's roaring to life, I move to lie on the couch while she waits patiently, neither of us having said a word in quiet anticipation.

I shift onto my side, pressing my back against the cushions as far as I can to make room for her. My heart skips a beat as she lowers in front of me, comfortably adjusting herself until her back is flat against my chest, her head resting on the crook of my shoulder. I love how she molds herself easily against me, right where she belongs. I slide my arm around her, finding her hand and wrapping my fingers between hers.

The rain patters against the window behind us in a rhythmic way, lulling us into a quiet trance as we lie quietly, watching the fire. There's not a doubt in my mind that I could stay just like this for the rest of my life and still crave it.

"What are you thinking about?" she whispers, her voice cutting through the silence.

"That peanut butter chocolate cake you made," I say simply, eliciting a smile out of her. "You?"

"I'm wondering how we first determined there was a consciousness and a subconsciousness," she says quietly yet matter-of-factly, as if these sorts of thoughts are commonplace for her.

I bust out a laugh. "Are you serious?"

She nods, her hair tickling my chin as she does. "You know I have no control over this. It's just the way my brain is."

I squeeze her tighter, my stomach flipping with affection for her and her whimsical mind. We fall quiet again, my mind drifting to the life rules list hanging on the wall of her office and everything she accomplished with Operation Make Naomi a Boss.

I can't help but whisper the same question I've asked her countless times now, "Name something you want out of life, Naomi."

A charged moment passes between us before she quietly whispers, "You."

The same thing she said not too long ago out on that tree swing the moment we acknowledged the start of our genuine feelings toward each other. An ache in the center of my chest pulls tight as a low hum buzzes in my stomach. I can't think of any response that would fully convey how happy her response makes me, so I just squeeze her as tight as I can until she eventually giggles, scrambling to be freed from my grip.

Her phone notification brings us back to reality, out of the bliss-filled fog we were just lost in, and she reaches an arm over to where her phone sits on the coffee table. She gasps when she reads what's there.

"Oh! It's an email from Joan!" she squeals.

"What does it say?" I shift to sit up, allowing her to prop on her elbows as her eyes scan the screen back and forth, hastily reading the email.

"It's ours!" she shrieks. "The building is ours! The owners have agreed to our terms! Joan is writing up a lease agreement as we speak."

"No way!" I hold a palm up for a high five as she drops the phone, looking at me with doe eyes that water at the edges.

"It's really happening," she breathes, her voice cracking.

"Congratulations to you." I reach for our tequila glasses and hand her one of them so we can make a toast.

"To you as well, part-owner." She takes hers and clinks it with mine.

I take a sip, feeling the tequila burn, letting it swirl with all the ooey-gooey feelings that are already inside me.

"She says once we sign the lease, we can have the keys as soon as next week."

"You know what this means," I tell her seriously.

"What?"

"That it's time for a 'bakery goals/rules/boundaries to live by' meeting."

She grins. "I'm already looking forward to it."

"Don't think I'll go easy on you either." I smirk. "The list is going to go right on the wall in the bakery office. Maybe I'll even make it three times the normal size."

"I wouldn't have it any other way." She beams at me.

I smile lazily back at her, patting the space on the couch in front of me. She twists around and scooches back, this time in a seated position between my legs, until she's once again settled comfortably in my arms. I rest my drink against my thigh, my other arm wrapped around the top of her shoulders.

She leans her head back, sinking into me as she relaxes against my arm. I get lost in the crackling of the fire and musing over this new business adventure with her—and of everything that's yet to come for us.

My heart feels simultaneously like it could fly out of my chest at any moment or possibly explode altogether. The reality of what this feeling is sits at the tip of my tongue, and for a moment I feel ready to voice it out loud. But I hold it back, not wanting to take away from this moment for her. Not wanting to overshadow it.

However, that doesn't mean the feeling doesn't surge through me, and the reality of it has me feeling more content—and gratified—with each passing second.

Chapter Forty-One

Naomi

"This scone is delicious," I say, taking a bite of the pastry in an attempt to quell some of the awkwardness of this conversation. My parents sit across from Robbie and me at the coffee shop, both of them watching quietly as I chew. Being as this is the first time we've seen either of them since I quit the dealership, we're all still hesitantly feeling each other out and adjusting to this new family dynamic together.

"You should try it with a drizzle of honey," Mom suggests with a hint of a smile, sipping from her tea.

Dad sits beside her, stoic and firm as always. By the look on his face, he's still clearly hanging onto some animosity from my public defiance toward him. Although, I don't exactly blame him. I've been his puppet for as long as I've been his daughter, so there's bound to be some resistance on his part.

"We asked you to meet us here today so we could share some news," I say, looking excitedly at Robbie. I refuse to let the prospect of whatever my dad will think dampen my joy about this, so I forge ahead, ignoring his stern expression altogether.

"Robbie and I are officially business partners," I announce. "We signed a lease for the empty building across the road. We plan to open a storefront bakery for Naomi's Nummy Bakery together."

"Oh, Naomi, that is wonderful news," Mom says right away with pride gleaming in her eyes. "Congratulations to you both."

"Isn't it great?" I say, hardly able to contain my excitement, even though I can feel my dad scrutinizing me.

"So, he's here to stay, huh?" My dad jerks his head toward Robbie, completely ignoring the bakery part of our announcement.

"She's iffy about her feelings on that too, sir," Robbie replies flatly.

Mom bites her lips to hide a smirk. "When do you plan to open the bakery?"

For once, she seems to be the head runner of the conversation, which throws me for a loop. I'm not sure if this is a one-time situation or if she's been asserting herself more in general, but either way, it's my turn to feel pride toward her.

"Not for a few months. There are a couple things we want to do to the space before opening," I explain.

"This is so exciting." She beams, her smile wide and uncontained now.

I pause, expecting Dad to start an interrogation about our business model or whether or not we have an appropriate amount of money saved up in case of emergencies.

But it doesn't come.

Just a stare that holds neither animosity nor delight. Although, I can tell by the way he keeps rolling his lips together that words are threatening to spill out—he's simply holding them back. For a man who's never been good at keeping his opinions to himself, he's doing an impressive job.

Honestly, I'll take the silence over the public berating from him that he's always given any day.

"I was thinking of getting your input on interior design and layout, Mom. You're so good at stuff like that—if you're up for it, that is."

The flash of surprise is clear as it washes over her face, then she brings a hand over her mouth to cover the emotion.

"I would be delighted," she says, barely above a whisper, with a crack in her voice.

"Thank you," I say with an equal amount of emotion in mine.

She clears her throat, looking down to check her watch. "Well, we should be going. Your father has a meeting to get to."

"Okay." I nod with a smile.

The four of us stand, offering timid hugs and handshakes all around.

"Thank you for meeting with us," Robbie says to my parents.

"Anytime. Let me know when you'd like to get together and discuss ideas," Mom says just before they head out of the coffee shop.

I sigh, feeling content and happy as we watch them walk down the sidewalk. When they're out of sight, I turn to Robbie. "I'd say that went well."

"It could have been a lot worse," Robbie agrees. "Should we head out too?"

"Sure." I take his outstretched hand, pulling myself close to his side as we step outside. As we start down Main Street, swinging our joined hands, I feel proud at how far I've come to be at a place where I can stand my ground with my parents. And I look forward to this brand-new dynamic we get to have together.

This meeting today proved that we're fully capable of maintaining a decent relationship—one where I'm allowed to advocate for myself and my needs. It's honestly all I've ever wanted.

"How about a ride?" Robbie crouches down, his hands stretched out behind his back.

"Sure." With a giggle, I hop on his back, wrapping my legs and arms around him, feeling carefree and weightless as he hoists me up. He grips under my thighs, securing me into place.

"What service," I marvel into his ear, wrapping my arms around his neck and placing my chin on his shoulder.

"Only the best for the newest bakery owner in town." He starts to spin us in a circle, nearly skipping as he does.

In between the laughter that escapes me and the blur of being spun, I can vaguely make out Opal and Iris in the window of the flower shop across the street.

"We have an audience." I giggle, feeling wild and liberated yet safe and comfortable at the same time.

"So?" He stops spinning, although I have a hunch it's only because he's getting dizzy. He plops me down on a nearby bench between the ice cream parlor and the supermarket.

"Whoa. Apparently, I can't do that anymore," he laughs, rubbing the spot by his temple.

I grin, scooting closer to him, tucking myself under his arm. It's all I can do lately to stop myself from wanting to be glued to him. We've always been affectionate, him and I, but now it's laced with an intimacy and a sweet, constant kind of need to be attached.

He reaches out to tuck a strand of hair behind my ear, and I relish the spark his touch sends rushing over my skin.

"Thank you for this," he says quietly under his breath, as if he knows there might be prying ears.

"For what?" I tilt my head up to look at him.

"For everything." His mouth tilts up in a crooked smile. "For giving me a purpose in life. A direction. For giving me you. The bakery. Every last bit of it."

My cheeks blush at his honesty as I get lost in the vulnerability behind his eyes. My stomach swoops under his gaze, and I want nothing more than to hang onto this consuming feeling for the rest of my life.

His eyes stay glued to mine as he says, "I have a confession."

"What's that?" My voice is barely a whisper.

His throat bobs, a minor crack in his confident facade, but he remains locked on me.

"I've fallen desperately in love with you, Naomi Tillman." The way he says it makes it feel like a relief and the most comforting of promises all in one—a validation that he's feeling exactly the same way I do.

"I have one too," I say just as quietly.

"That you actually despise buttercream?" he murmurs.

I huff a laugh but hold onto the seriousness of the moment.

"I don't think I've ever loved anything as much as I love you." The words feel easy to say out loud, an outward acknowledgement of the truth coming straight from my heart.

He smiles that same boyish smile he's had for as long as I've known him. Except, now it feels monumental and wildly unbelievable that it's directed solely at me.

I marvel at how far we've come in a relatively short amount of time. For years, he was one of my best friends, my confidant, and keeper of my secrets. All too suddenly, out of nowhere, he became my fake boyfriend on a whim, and now, he's the absolute most significant person in my life.

He leans in, keeping his eyes on mine until the very last second. I bring my hand to his jawline as he presses his mouth to mine excitedly, eager to solidify the words we just spoke in a tangible way. My eyes flutter closed as I meld my mouth with his, hoping my kiss conveys all the underlying promises and truths of my own declaration.

When he pulls away, he presses his forehead to mine, a quiet way for us to soak up the moment.

"We should probably get back home, huh?" he asks.

"Yeah," I say quietly. "There's a container of flour calling my name."

He stands with a smile, again offering his hand, and for a moment, I get hit with a revelation that my own love story has been building right before my eyes—one I didn't manufacture in my head. What follows is a realization that perhaps the greatest adventure of my life is about to begin. Perhaps it already has. All those years of dreaming it would come to fruition, and it has happened right under my nose.

With a giddy grin, I take his hand, ready for wherever he's going to lead me.

Chapter Forty-Two

Naomi

"Keep your eyes closed," Robbie says somewhere close to my ear from behind me.

"Your hands are covering my entire face," I point out the obvious.

"You can never be too sure. Take a wide step forward." A bell trills above me as I take what I'm assuming is a big step through the doorway.

I already know we're at the bakery since we parked out front, but for some reason, he's insisting on leading me inside without looking.

"Can I open them now?" I'm always eager to take in every last detail of the space when we come and today is no different.

"Not yet."

I take a few more blind steps until he says, "Okay. Right here. You can open them."

My eyes fly open the second he takes his hands away. I gasp, my mouth dropping open in surprise.

"Robbie," I breathe, looking around at what he set up.

There's a blanket spread out in the middle of the empty floor with a bottle of champagne chilling in an ice bucket in the center and two flutes standing next to it. A charcuterie tray is resting on the corner patch of the blanket, filled with crackers, cheese slices, an assortment of nuts, and grapes on the vine. There are also dimly lit tealight candles spread out on the countertop by the register—dozens of them.

"When did you do all this?"

"This morning when you were in your baking zone. You didn't even hear me sneak out, did you?" He places his hands on his hips, clearly proud of his efforts.

"Nope." I shake my head. "I assumed you were in the office, updating our mantra board."

He chuckles, offering me a wink. "I did that yesterday."

I walk around the blanket, tracing my fingers along the edge of the counter where the tealights are flickering.

"Come on, let's eat. We have some celebrating to do," he says, pointing to the floor.

I lower down to sit on one corner, smiling at the effort he made with the board. The crackers look as if they've been tossed haphazardly out of the package, and the cheese squares are still firmly pressed in stacks, but it's the thought that counts...and it couldn't be more perfect to me.

"Thank you for this," I tell him.

He nods, pushing his lips together in a modest smile. "Of course."

As I reach for a cracker, Robbie's phone sings from inside his pocket.

"Uh-oh. Apparently, we're the talk of the town," he says with a chuckle, setting his phone face down on the blanket.

"That should really surprise me more than it does," I snicker. "But tell me why."

"I just got a message from Steven. He said word got out that you and I were—quote, unquote—obnoxiously twirling down Main Street and being indecent on the park bench."

I choke on my cracker, coughing at the absurdity.

"Hey, it's alright." He grins. "I'll take that reputation and wear it with pride."

I giggle, popping a slice of cheese in my mouth before growing serious. "So, Steven, huh?"

"Yeah." He looks down, brushing crumbs off his jeans. "We've been messaging here and there. Texting has been an easy first step for us. Although, we've talked about maybe meeting up again sometime soon. We'll see."

"Still nothing with your parents?"

"Not yet. Steven tells me they're respecting my space but that they are ready and eager whenever I want to reach out." He shrugs. "I'm not in a hurry. I know I'll get there eventually."

I nod, reaching over to squeeze his ankle in a show of support. I'm along for the ride as far as his relationship with his family goes, content to follow his lead. And I'm immensely proud of the steps he's already taken.

"Champagne?" he asks.

"So fancy. Yes, please."

Robbie opens the champagne bottle with a pop, then he pours us each a glass.

"Cheers to starting this new adventure together," he says, clinking his glass with mine.

"Cheers." My grin grows wide before I take a sip. "Gosh, Robbie, just imagine the possibilities of this place...think of what we can make it."

"We can make it anything you want."

I can feel his eyes burning into me as I look around the nearly empty building. I imagine it filled to the brim with townspeople on Sunday mornings, all clamoring to get donuts that are fresh from the oven. And I can envision a cake catalog with fingerprints smudged on the laminated pages from all the children choosing the perfect birthday cake. Not to mention a chalkboard sign that sits on the counter, displaying the muffin of the week selection in Robbie's honor, of course.

I can see it.

A future here filled with all the things I love the most—baked goods, the hustle of running a business, and interacting with townspeople every day. All of it with Robbie by my side, whom I love the most out of them all.

"I'm excited to do this with you," I tell him, to which he gives me a bashful smile.

"Not as excited as I am." He shakes his head.

"Did you ever get in touch with George?" I ask, referencing the contractor we hired to make a few minor changes to the space before we open to the public.

"Yes. He said he'll meet with us next week sometime to solidify a plan, and then we can move forward with getting permission from the owner and the city to do some renovations. I'll make sure to schedule it when I'm back from my gig."

"Perfect."

"Will you dance with me?" he spits out abruptly, out of nowhere, as if he's been holding the question back for some time.

I choke out a laugh. "Here?"

"Yeah." He nods.

"But there's no music," I point out.

"Oh, you have such little faith." He stands, fiddling with his phone until a slow song starts playing from it. "Easy as that."

He offers a hand to help me up. His strong arm pulls me into him, and I bring my arms around his neck, the warmth of his hands radiating on my hips through the thin fabric of my dress.

His closeness is dizzying, the smell of him all-encompassing. We sway gently with the music, his touch making me feel a myriad of things. Safe. Secure. Buzzed. Delicate.

He dips his head to tuck it into my neck and I squeeze myself closer to him, not able to get enough of how I feel when I'm in his arms like this.

I glance around the space, at the countertops where the display cases will go, and at the walls that we're planning to have painted. And then, when we sway in a circle, I take note of the office where Robbie will do his office manager duties and where our future employees will take their breaks.

A wave of gratitude hits me that not only am I living my dream, but I'm so unbelievably giddy to be doing it with the man of my dreams by my side—who, as it turns out, has been right in front of me all along.

"Tell me something, Naomi Tillman. How does it feel?" he murmurs, his voice vibrating against the skin of my shoulder.

"What's that?"

He lifts his head up, hanging it low to hover right above me. Then his mouth tilts in a mischievous smirk.

"Officially becoming a boss?"

Epilogue

Naomi

Six months later

"We just ran out of the blueberry crumble muffins," Robbie announces, his voice slightly out of breath and tinged with exhilaration as he rushes around the kitchen.

"On the cooling rack," I answer, pausing the icing I'm putting on a custom cake to point them out.

The hustle and bustle from the front of the bakery can be heard through the thin swinging doors, and I've discovered that it's one of my most favorite sounds in the entire world. My heart swells with happiness, so much so that I wonder if it's possible for it to actually burst. I consider myself beyond lucky that it's not the first time I've had that same concern recently.

"Thanks." He brushes past me, planting a quick kiss on the side of my head as he grabs the tray, exiting back through the doors at the same time Gabby breezes through them.

"Here's the sugar you asked for," she says, setting the large bag on the counter.

"Thank you," I say in a rush, flashing her a grateful smile. I'm so appreciative of her and everyone else who keeps the store up front afloat while I bake.

It only took us about a month of being open to realize we needed more hands on deck to keep up with the demand. Lucky for us, Gabby was willing and available to step right in. She helps run the front of the store, and I've been teaching her the ins and outs of baking during any down time we have.

"The place is filling up out there," she says with a genuine smile.

"It's the morning rush," I say with wonder, feeling both exhilarated and in awe, the same way I do every single day when I marvel at how busy we are. Here we are, three months since the grand opening, and there's not only a steady rush of locals who support us but plenty of out-of-towners and weekend cabin dwellers who seem to flock here on a regular basis.

It's all been incredibly humbling.

I complete the icing on the cake and slide it into a bakery box, savoring a quick inhale of frosting before closing the lid.

I use my back to push through the doors, bringing the box to the counter near where the order pickup sign is, setting it next to several other boxes that are ready to be picked up. When I look up, my eyes snag on a few people gathered near the front door.

"Hi, Opal." I match her enthusiastic wave while she chats with my mom.

Mom has become a huge blessing and an absolute staple at the bakery so far. She's not exactly on the payroll—she refuses to be—but that hasn't stopped her from showing up every single day to help in any way she can. This morning, she's been clearing tables and keeping the floors picked up and free of crumbs. In addition to the design work she helped me with before opening, it's been so nice having her around in the day-to-day duties as well.

I remind myself to set aside some cookies to send home for her and Dad. I have a strict rule to not talk about work with my dad, so he doesn't come by the shop much, but we've both made a point to check in with each other often enough on other aspects of our lives. Our relationship is mostly surface level at this point, but it seems to be growing deeper by the day, so I'm hopeful we'll be able to get to a good place.

On my way back to the kitchen, the bell dings above the door, and I instinctively swing my head in that direction, ready to wave at whoever came in. I suck in a gasp at who I see and pick up my pace, walking straight back to the kitchen.

"Robbie," I whisper, pausing as the doors swing behind me.

He looks over from where he's taking inventory on supplies and peers past me out the circular window.

"Your parents are here," I say cautiously.

"I know," he says calmly, setting the clipboard down. "I invited them."

He squeezes my wrist as he passes me, walking confidently toward them. I watch in awe through the window as he greets them, taking in this new sight.

Things with Steven and him have been good for a while now—they meet up frequently—but this is the first time he's made this step with his parents.

After a few minutes of watching how civil they all seem to be acting, I force myself to give them privacy and get to work on the next order.

As I start gathering ingredients to make apple fritters, my mind wanders once again to how incredibly grateful I am for this life I'm leading.

Robbie has given me an amazing sense of security and an incredibly fulfilling relationship in our home life. Not only that, but also the way we work together as partners to run my dream business.

Then he feeds my adventurous side by whisking me away to his gigs every so often while Gabby keeps the bakery running for us back at home. I'm so lucky to have the best of both worlds. It's been the perfect balance of having a satisfying home base and still being able to find the greatest of adventures.

It's a life I've worked hard for—one that I cherish immensely.

I get lost in the rhythm of whisking ingredients together when Robbie swings back through the doors.

"How did that go?" I ask eagerly.

"Not bad." He gives me a half-smile, a look of peace falling over him. "They didn't say anything negative about owning a bakery, so I guess that's a good start."

"I'd say so," I say with a small, supportive smile.

"We're planning to meet next week for coffee. I'd love for you to come with me if you want to?"

"Absolutely."

He keeps his gaze pinned on me and slowly inches closer, my chest getting tighter with every step he takes, as it always does.

"You know what time it is," he says matter-of-factly, as if I should know.

"Time to...get a watch?" I joke.

"Nope. Per our rules that hang in the office, it's time for a break." He stretches out a hand in invitation.

My stomach swoops, more than ready for one of my absolute favorite parts of the day—a quiet moment away from the hustle and bustle when he and I can be alone together.

"Gabby, we're taking a quick break," I say, peeking my head through the door to where she's manning the cash register.

"You got it," she replies with a wave.

I slide my apron off, set it on the hook, and take his hand. I let him lead me out the back door to the grassy area on the hill that he keeps set up just for us. Our favorite blanket—that just a few short months ago we used on the floor of the empty bakery, dreaming of the reality we live today—is spread out on the grass. A cooler and cups are set up on the nearby picnic table.

"Lemonade?" he asks while I have a seat on the blanket, sitting cross-legged.

"Sure. Thank you."

He hands me a cup and lowers next to me, stretching out to lie on his side.

"I have a surprise for you." He eyes me sneakily.

"Another one?" I laugh, remembering the news he shared with me this morning before we got out of bed.

"Well, the announcement of my induction into the Pine Falls Area Ladies Bridge Group didn't receive as much excitement as I'd hoped, so I'm here to try again."

"Okay." I snort. "Shoot."

"You know how our gig next week is in Ontario?"

"Yes."

"You and I are going to fly out a few days early. We can visit Niagara Falls, do some shopping, whatever your wild little heart desires."

"Really?" Excitement floods me as I take in what he's offering.

"Yup. I already cleared it with your mom and Gabby. Your mom is willing to help man the front of the store while Gabby bakes a limited menu while we're gone."

"Oh, that sounds wonderful," I gush, clapping my hands together. "I can't wait. Thank you."

I set my cup down, leaning forward to plant a kiss on him. It's meant to be a quick peck, a fleeting show of gratitude, but the overwhelming feeling that rushes through me when we kiss keeps me glued to him like a magnet. My thumbs brush his cheek softly, relishing the love I have for this man.

The man who has given me so much. Who strengthened me, both when he meant to and even when he didn't. He reminded me over and over of my worth until I had no choice but to believe it myself.

"I love you," he whispers when I reluctantly pull away, his eyes ever-so-slightly glistening with emotion.

"I love you too." I say those same three words multiple times a day, and yet somehow it doesn't ever seem to be enough.

"Shall we?" He stacks his empty cup with mine and helps me off the blanket.

Then I follow him back inside the bakery to live the life that's far better than any scenario I've ever dreamed up in my head.

Acknowledgments

I wrote Operation Make Naomi a Boss at a point in my life when I needed a break from the heaviness of the world. I found myself to be in a place where I wanted to pour myself into something fun and easy. Something happy that could maybe even make me feel giddy while writing. When I sat down to write, I had one goal in mind...to spread some joy and make people smile, especially if there were others out there who needed a little break from real life too. And this is what I came up with. So, that said, I hope you enjoyed Naomi and Robbie's story! I hope you were able to get lost in this fictional Minnesota town and find some joy while you were there. If nothing else, I hope Robbie's one-liners made you smile a few times. All in all, I'm forever grateful that you gave this story a chance!

A big thank you to my beta readers – Courtney, Hannah, Shelby, Brooke, Taylor, Megan, Darci, and Jessee. I appreciate you reading my story in such a vulnerable, imperfect, state and helping me to polish it to become a story I'm so dang proud of. Your excitement, encouragement, and feedback was invaluable to me!

Thank you to my editor, Jenn Lockwood, for sharing your editing expertise, and to Sarah Ward for proofreading it! I'm so grateful to have you both in my corner!

As always, a HUGE thank you to my cover designer, Lorissa Padilla, for designing another stunning cover! Your talent will never cease to amaze me, and I'm giddy at what you managed to create for this story!

Another big thank you to my husband, Nick, and my kids for supporting me while I was in the writing cave, editing cave, or pre-release stage! I love you all more than you know!

I'd also like to thank my extended family and friends for your continued support and encouragement. I quite literally would not be able to live this dream if it weren't for all of you!!

Also by Megan Reinking

Ruby Lodge Series
Say You Mean It
If You Say So

Hawaiian Getaway Series
The Ohana Cottage
The Summer Break
The Perfect Tide
The Holiday Prize

About the Author

Megan Reinking is a wife and mother who lives in Minnesota, where she spends her days reading, writing, or chauffeuring her three children around town. She enjoys writing heartfelt love stories that her readers often tell her feel like a warm hug.